All That I LOVE

All that I LOVE

RACHEL BRANTON

WHITE
STAR
PRESS

This is a work of fiction, and the views expressed herein are the sole responsibility of the author. Likewise, certain characters, places, and incidents are the product of the author's imagination, and any resemblance to actual persons, living or dead, or actual events or locales, is entirely coincidental.

All That I Love (Finding Home Book 2)

Published by White Star Press
P.O. Box 353
American Fork, Utah 84003

Copyright © 2017 by Rachel Branton
Cover design copyright © 2017 by White Star Press

Originally published by the author as *Fields of Home* under another pen name.

Printed in the United States of America
ISBN: 978-1-939203-85-4
Year of first printing: 2017

To my husband and our seven children,
who are my greatest support.
You guys are the best!

CHAPTER

1

May 2008

On the day Brandon Rhodes came back into her life, Mercedes Walker Johnson was shopping at Safeway, not expecting anything out of the ordinary and certainly not expecting to see a ghost from her past. She wandered to the aisle where the boxed cereal sat on the shelves, frowning at the contents. Her three boys loved the stuff, but she knew the cold flakes weren't as healthy as her home-cooked cereal. Still, in the past year or so, she'd taken to letting them get their own breakfast on Sundays. Everyone needed a day off—or as much of a day off as any woman on a farm could take. Even Wayne stayed away from the fields on Sundays, though the cow still had to be milked and the animals fed.

She plucked a few boxes off the shelf, the ones with the lowest sugar content. Whatever questionable nutritional value they contained would at least be boosted by whole, fresh milk from their cow.

Starting down the aisle, she wondered how Wayne and twelve-year-old Darrel were coming along on the planting. The sugar beets, of course, were already in the ground and growing. Hopefully they would have the spring wheat planted within the next week or two, so they could get in some corn to supplement their cattle's ration of hay from the alfalfa that was standing a foot tall in the fields. Wayne had been trying his hand at raising cattle these past few years because a crop of calves could be worth far more than sugar beets and wheat. The winter had been tough for the animals, though, and she and Wayne had spent many months worrying about how many they might lose to cold or disease, but spring had blessedly come on time, and most had survived well.

A man stood at the checkout as she approached, waiting for a total from the cashier. For a moment, he was any man, someone she didn't know, but then he tilted his head and chuckled at something the cashier said, and Mercedes' breath rushed from her. *Him! He's here.*

But she couldn't really believe that. No, it was only someone who looked like him. Such a recognition had happened before, and always she would stand there with elation and fear vying in her heart, until at last the man would turn and she would realize she was mistaken.

It's not him, she told herself. She pushed her cart behind a display of ketchup where she could observe him without being noticed.

"This place has changed a lot since I was here," the man said. He was handsome, she could see, with brown hair and a square jaw that bore a slight stubble. He wore dress pants and a button-down shirt, with the first button open. "Been nearly thirteen years."

Mercedes swallowed hard. Thirteen years. It could be a coincidence.

"Well, the years tend to do that to a place." The cashier was a plump Native American woman in her fifties, one Mercedes often saw here, though she didn't know her by name. "Things change. So you're a doctor, are you?"

"How did you know?"

She pointed without expression to the identification card clipped to his pocket. "Your tag. You come to work at Riverton Memorial?"

"Actually, I'm here to teach the heart procedures I developed with some universities. We're holding a seminar here."

"Well, uh, Dr. Rhodes, I hope you have a good time in Riverton. Maybe I'll see you again. Thank you for shopping at Safeway."

Mercedes' heart thundered in her chest. Dr. Rhodes. Dr. Brandon Rhodes. Once she'd hoped and prayed to see him again, thought she might die if she didn't. But that was before she'd understood the truth and begun hoping and praying never to see him again. In the past few years, she'd almost managed never to think about him at all.

A normal person would go to the counter and say hello. After all, they'd once been close. More than close. She still remembered the first day they'd met, how they'd shared lunch in the hospital cafeteria, the way the world had ceased all movement. The way her life had changed.

Mercedes closed her eyes as the familiar wave of pain crashed through her chest and spilled through her limbs and out every pore of her body. He had no right to come back. Not now. Not after all this time.

I hate you, she thought, but she knew it wasn't that simple.

The main reason, of course, that she couldn't smile and greet him was Darrel. If it could be said she had a favorite child, Darrel would be it, though her other sons were as precious, and she worked hard to treat them the same. The fact remained that Darrel *was* different. He was a part of the old life, the life that yearned for more. She knew he wouldn't belong on the farm much longer, but she wasn't ready to give him up quite yet.

You don't deserve him, she said to the man's retreating back. *I won't let you ruin his life . . . like you did mine.*

Of course, there was no indication that he was in Riverton for any reason other than the one he'd told the cashier. He might not know that she still lived an hour northeast of the city on what had once been her father's farm. Maybe he thought she'd continued her studies to be a psychologist. If so, she could be working anywhere by now.

The thoughts calmed her, and she was about to make her way to the counter when he stopped and turned back to the cashier. "Have you heard of a place called Walker Farm? Do you happen to know who owns it now?"

"Sounds familiar, but there are a lot of farms around here."

"It's about fifty miles or so out of town. Northeast."

"I don't go out that way much. Sorry."

"What about a woman named Mercedes Walker? Do you know her?"

The woman shook her head, lightly rustling the gray-streaked black hair that fell midway down her back. "We got ten thousand people living here, plus all those that come in from the other towns to shop. It ain't thirteen years ago. We don't know everybody like we did back then. Or practically."

He nodded. "Well, thanks. I figured it was a long shot."

"Maybe try the phone book."

"Good idea. I'm sure I'll be seeing you. I'm here for a couple weeks."

Mercedes' heart was pounding so loudly she almost couldn't breathe. So much for hoping he wouldn't pursue their connection. But why would he even try? Did he think she'd still be sitting here, waiting for him? And what right did he have to return after all this time, anyway? Thirteen years since he'd walked away.

He's just looking up an old friend, she told herself. Bitterness filled her mouth at the thought. Friends. She hadn't even been worth a postcard or a letter. Maybe if he'd written, it would have been different for Darrel. But it was too late now. She loved her life, her boys, and Wayne. Nothing this *stranger* could do would change that.

Unless he somehow knew about Darrel.

Mercedes closed her eyes again, fear welling up in her chest. *Dear God in heaven. Please help me.*

"Are you all right?"

Mercedes opened her eyes to see the cashier standing in front of her. "Oh, thanks. I'm fine. I was just thinking."

"You sure? You're white as a sheet."

"I'm all right. Really. I think I'm finished shopping. Could you ring me up?"

"Sure. Come on over to the register."

When the groceries were tallied, Mercedes' hand shook as she wrote out the check. The woman didn't bother to ask for ID, obviously recognizing her from other trips into town, but her eyes caught on the name. "Walker Farm? Mercedes Johnson. Hey, there was a guy in here just now asking about you. Real handsome fellow. A doctor. Been in a couple times in the past few weeks. I think he's probably still in the parking lot. You want me to catch him?"

"That's okay, I—"

"No problem, really." The cashier slammed the till shut and scooted toward the front of the store faster than her bulk should have allowed.

"Please," Mercedes called after her. "Don't—" But the woman was already out the door.

Brandon.

Panic made Mercedes wonder if there was a back door. She imagined herself vaulting over a cart of vegetables as the store manager chased her down. But the panic subsided as quickly as it came, and anger took its place. He had no right to come back into her life.

The cashier reappeared—alone, and Mercedes felt an odd piercing disappointment that made no sense at all. "He'll be right in," the woman told Mercedes. "He's putting his bags in his car."

"Thank you." Mercedes made a private note never to shop this Safeway again. Yet why should she let a man she hadn't seen for almost thirteen years chase her away? Another burst of anger gave her strength. Ignoring her cart, Mercedes hefted her plastic bags of groceries, two in each hand. They weighed nothing compared to what she had to lift at the farm.

She strode out the door, heading purposefully toward her green truck. The battered Ford had seen better days, but it was like an old friend, dependable and familiar. With any luck, she'd get in and drive away before Brandon caught up with her. Setting down the bags, she opened her door, shoved the groceries inside, and climbed into the cab. Relief was already calming the furious pounding of her heart.

"Mercedes?"

Her hand froze on the open door. Part of her wanted to slam it and drive away, but the other part was curious about the man he'd become. She turned and met his eyes. For several seconds, she said nothing. She drank in the handsome face, brown hair, and green eyes. He looked the same, and yet he didn't. There was maturity in the face and a confidence that had been lacking when she knew him before.

For a moment she felt disoriented, as though the fabric of time was somehow adjusting itself. From somewhere came the blare of a car horn and a man's distant shout. But the earth didn't stand still. Brandon Rhodes was simply a person she had once known, and if she played this moment well, she would never have to see him again.

"Excuse me?" she asked.

"It *is* you! Mercedes, don't you recognize me? It's Brandon Rhodes."

"Brandon?" She scrunched her forehead. "Oh, Brandon! My goodness, it's been so long." She gave him a polite smile he couldn't possibly know was fake. He didn't know her at all—and apparently never had. The past was proof of that.

She climbed out of the truck, leaving the door open for a quick retreat. He stepped forward tentatively, and they embraced in a loose, impersonal hug, the kind people used when they weren't close. Or perhaps the kind of hug exchanged when one of them was holding a secret. If there had been no secret, Mercedes would have been excited and pleased to see him, and the hug would have been real.

"You haven't changed a bit," Brandon said as she drew quickly away. "I mean, you have, but you haven't. Your hair is the same, and your eyes are still dark enough to be black. But I don't remember the freckles."

"They're from the sun. I didn't get much sun back in the old days. Too much bookwork."

"Life must have treated you well. You look great!"

"Thanks. You too. So what brings you to Riverton?"

"Oh, a seminar at the hospital. You know, giving back. I'm staying at the Alpine House for a few weeks. Thought I'd look up some old friends."

Old friends. She remembered her thoughts in the store. *Friends* did not begin to describe what they had been to each other. "That's nice. Is anyone you know still at the hospital?"

"Not many. Old Dustbottom is, though. He'll probably outlive us all."

Mercedes smiled. "He still in charge of the morgue?"

"Yep. And the backside of his coat is still just as speckled with dirt or ink or whatever it was. Have you ever seen him around?"

"I don't get into town much. Especially to the hospital." Only to give birth to her children. But she wasn't going there.

"So what are you doing these days? Practicing psychiatry? Psychology?"

She shook her head. "Neither. I'm married now. Raising a family. We're running my family's farm."

He blinked. "Married—of course you are. I'd heard that. I was married for four years myself. It didn't work out."

"I'm sorry."

He shrugged. "That's the way it goes."

Not in Mercedes' book. Marriage was a commitment you didn't walk out on. But then, Brandon was good at walking out on commitments.

"So you have children. I mean, you'd have to if you're raising a family." His eyes seemed intent as he spoke, and Mercedes felt a tremor of fear.

"Yeah, three boys. Good kids. In fact"—she looked at her watch—"I'd better get back to them. They're helping their dad with the planting today, since it's Saturday. But the younger ones don't have as much endurance, and sometimes they can be more of a hindrance, if you know what I mean."

"I don't have children, but I can imagine. How old are they?"

"Eight and nine. Their daddy's patient and a good teacher, but there's a limit. And believe me, they like to push it." She forced a laugh.

"And your other boy? Didn't you say you have three?"

"He's two years older." Not exactly a lie because Joseph would be ten in three months, and then he would be two years younger than Darrel's twelve. But since Joseph was still only nine, Brandon would assume Darrel was eleven. Eleven kept him safely out of reach. "He's not very tall or big, but he's got a good head."

"I'd love to meet them. I bet they look like you."

"Two of them do. The other one looks like his dad, even down to his red hair and blue eyes."

"I'll bet they're great. Oh, I wanted to tell you, I saw your brother four or five weeks ago."

This surprised her. "Where?"

"At the hospital in San Diego where I work. His company was updating some of our electronics."

"That's funny. Austin didn't mention it. He was here helping with the planting last weekend." What she wouldn't add was that the farm hadn't done well last year, and with the purchase of a new tractor, they'd had to forego hiring help until the harvest. Austin's willingness to pitch in had been a godsend.

"Well, I only saw him briefly, and to tell you the truth, I wasn't even sure he remembered me. We only met a few times when I lived here."

Mercedes let herself relax. Even if Austin had recognized Brandon, he wouldn't have betrayed her secret. He knew the stakes as much as she did. This was only one more secret in their shared past. A past where their father drank and treated his children like worthless chattel. A past where their mother had let him. "He was concentrating on college in those days. He's become quite successful, though."

"I see he left the farm."

Mercedes wasn't quite sure, but she thought she sensed a question there. Did he wonder why she was still at the farm she'd vowed never to return to after her mother's tragedy? She doubted he could ever understand. "Actually, Austin comes back quite often. We even keep a room for him. He took over my grandmother's charity when she died a few years back. Runs it part-time with his wife, Liana. He got married four months ago."

"That's good to hear."

She knew it was only something said to fill the empty space between them. Thirteen years was too long to feel comfortable.

"Do you have time for a quick drink?" he asked.

"Not really. My husband and the boys are waiting. Some other time."

"Okay."

"Okay," she echoed. There really wasn't much else to say, was there?

"Mercedes . . ."

"Yes?" She put a hand on the truck door.

"The way we left it. I didn't mean . . ." He looked up at the sky. "Time passed so fast. I didn't mean for things to work out that way. It's one of my biggest regrets."

What does he regret? she wondered. *The relationship? Leaving? Or not keeping in contact?* None of it really mattered now.

"It's okay," she said with more gentleness than she felt. "We both moved on. That's just the way it is." She thought it was particularly poetic to use his own terminology against him. In her heart, though, her fury mounted. He'd given up so much.

Worse, he'd made the choice for both of them, a choice she'd had to live with for thirteen years. He'd broken more than her heart; for a time, she'd lost even her will to live. Only Wayne had saved her. Wayne, with his quiet, unassuming love. With his constant support and refusal to judge. Though she had deserved his scorn, he'd given her back her life. In return, she'd given him that life.

And I'm happy, she thought fiercely. Turning, she climbed into the truck.

"Mercedes," Brandon said again.

She gazed at him from behind the wheel, simply waiting. "I'd like to drop by, if I may. Meet your husband, talk about old times."

"You've met Wayne before. He worked for my father."

He looked puzzled. Likely he remembered Wayne as old enough to be her father, though he was only fifty-two to her thirty-nine.

"Anyway," she continued, "you're welcome to come out, but we're still getting in the spring wheat." What she wanted to tell him was to go back to wherever he'd come from and leave her family alone. The way he pushed told her he wanted something from her. She could only pray it didn't involve Darrel. Yet what else could it be? "That means we're not at the house much." Or at least Wayne wasn't.

He nodded. "Well, it was nice to see you."

Mercedes shut her door, put the truck into gear, and drove away. She could see him in the rearview mirror watching her leave. The scene brought back memories of when he had left and she had stayed behind. Her heart felt tight.

Thirty miles outside Riverton, she pulled off the highway and leaned her head on the steering wheel. She was shaking so badly that she felt ill. "Wayne," she whispered. She needed Wayne.

Forty minutes later, she was in the barn saddling Windwalker, her white stallion. Di and Thunder, her red retrievers, watched patiently, wagging their tails with excitement. But only Thunder followed as she galloped from the barn, Di choosing to stay back with her new litter of puppies. Always the good mother, watching over her babies. That's what good mothers did.

Wind beat into her face, flattening the tears down and over her cheeks until they seemed more like a sheen of sweat than tears at all. Windwalker, a surprise present from Wayne last year, was her most prized animal. He had traded three calves to their neighbors down the road for the young horse, and Mercedes believed he was worth far more. She loved the power in his stride and the elation of moving so fast over the ground that time didn't seem to matter. Today was no exception. Hunching over his mane, she urged him onward. He flew like the wind. And for those few minutes, she was safe.

She came upon the west fields too quickly for her state of mind, but seeing Wayne and Darrel on the tractor and the younger boys, Joseph and Scott, playing in the back of the seed truck gave her a rush of belonging. These were her men, her place, and even the heartrending mound of dirt in the family cemetery past their small fruit orchard was a part of who she had become.

"Hi, Mom." Joseph and Scott waved her over.

"Can I have a ride back?" Scott added. "I'm bored."

"I'll take you both home in a minute. First I need to talk to your father."

Wayne had spotted her and opened the tractor cab, leaping down and leaving Darrel to operate the machine alone. He loped toward her in his customary gait, which was strangely graceful. Wayne was a tall man, built as strong as an old tree. At fifty-two, he had the strength of a much younger man, but his face was worn and weathered by the sun, and his red hair had gone an orangey white. His blue eyes were kind, and the wrinkles in his face were as much a part of him as the furrows were a part of the fields. Not for the first time, Mercedes understood that Wayne was the farm. He was as constant as the earth, as tender as the plants he coaxed out of the soil, as forgiving as a thirsty stalk of wheat after a spring rain.

"What's wrong?" he said as they met halfway.

She looked to the right and to the left, unwilling to meet his eyes.

"Mercedes." He spoke in almost the same way as Brandon had, but then he added, "Honey, I'm here."

She dragged in a breath and looked up into his eyes. "I was at Safeway. He's back in Riverton. He came to teach a seminar or something. At least that's what he says. But it's too much of a coincidence. I-I'm afraid."

He didn't ask her who "he" was. "He" was the only person who had stood between them all these long years, the one with the power to change their safe world.

Wayne made a noise of dismay in his throat and pulled her into his arms. Besides galloping on Windwalker's back, this was the only other place she felt completely safe, where nothing could touch her. Even as a child when he'd protected her from her father's wrath or her mother's indifference, she had felt safe with Wayne.

"I love you," he said. "It's going to be all right."

She dropped her head to his shoulder, wiping her wet

cheek against his dusty shirt. "He wants to come by. What if he knows?"

"What if he doesn't?"

She pulled back slightly to look up into his face. "Then why come? After all these years? It's not like the hospital here has anything to offer him."

"Maybe he's finally realizing what he lost." Wayne's eyes were sorrowful, and Mercedes wondered if he thought such a thing would change her life—knowing that Brandon might have come back for her.

It wouldn't, of course. Yet just for an instant, she remembered how she'd felt the day Brandon left. The certainty that he would be back for her, the belief that he couldn't live without her as she couldn't live without him.

He hadn't come back. Until now.

Mercedes swallowed hard. "He never loved me, not the way you do." She said this with a surety born of long years of knowing. Sometimes Wayne's love weighed heavily on her, as though it were a burden, because she knew everything she could give him would never begin to equal all that he gave her.

CHAPTER

2

Diary of Mercedes Walker
May 19, 1994

I'm supposed to be analyzing cases for an upcoming test, but I don't feel the least bit clinical today, though my studies are fascinating as usual. I can't believe how much better psychology is than all the other dozen things I've studied, even animal medicine. I should have tried this first. The human mind is so . . . incredible. Still, my thoughts keep wandering.

Is it possible to fall in love, really in love, in less than two weeks? It must be because I'm in love. I met this guy, Brandon Rhodes, barely two weeks ago after a lecture in the hospital. He's a resident from Boston and will be here for another year. He is perfect in every way. I know it sounds silly, but he seems to be my soul mate. I never believed in soul mates before, but I do now. Brandon knows what I'm thinking and feeling almost before I do. With him, I forget Daddy's abandonment and Momma's betrayal. I feel renewed. We are going out again tonight, as we do almost every night that he's not working at the hospital. I can't wait to see him.

randon Rhodes stared at the wall in his room at the Alpine House. Confusion filled his heart, making him doubt his purpose for being in Wyoming. Seeing Mercedes again was like returning to his own home—good and comfortable and right. Yet he also felt a great sense of loss that threatened to overcome him. This wasn't how it was supposed to be. He wanted to hate her. He wanted to condemn her for not telling him the truth, and yet at the same time he was afraid the truth he had come to find was not the same one that awaited him.

Closing his eyes, he could see Mercedes in his mind: beautiful, fierce, vulnerable. Her figure was fuller from childbirth and the passing years, but she was still an attractive woman. Perhaps more attractive than when they'd first met.

She went back to the farm. The thought baffled him. The one thing he'd known for sure about Mercedes during their time together was that she hated the farm and all it represented—her father in particular but also her mother and the way she'd been raised. It wasn't a place of good memories. Why, then, had she gone back?

The baby, of course. That was the only explanation. Yet by her own words, the child had not come until later. Or had she actually said that?

Brandon stood, purpose filling his mind. At the hospital he could find answers. He had enough influence there to get to the records he'd need. Of course, that still didn't explain the feeling in his heart.

Mercedes. So much the same and yet so different. The old longing hit him, and he fell to the bed, arms folded across his chest, holding himself, holding the pain. *I shouldn't have come,* he thought. Tears wet his face, blinded his eyes.

From the moment, he'd overheard Mercedes' brother tell the director of the hospital in San Diego about his nephew, Brandon's plan had been to come for the boy by whatever means possible. To plead, threaten, bribe. That is, *if* he turned out to be who Brandon suspected. According to Austin, the boy was twelve, and that could mean, depending on the date of his birth, that Brandon had a right to know him.

So he'd arranged to teach his procedures at Riverton Memorial, surprising the seminar organizers and his colleagues, but really he'd come to confront Mercedes. Yet he hadn't anticipated what seeing her again would do to his heart. *I didn't know I would still care for her.* He'd thought too many years had passed for him to feel anything but a mild remorse for the way things had ended. But this blinding sadness, the ache. These feelings belonged to the old days.

Gradually, the attack subsided, and Brandon wiped his face across the pillow before going to the door, his jaw clenched. He would see this through, Mercedes or no. He had no other choice, really. This was his last hope.

CHAPTER 3

Diary of Mercedes Walker
May 30, 1994

Today is Memorial Day, and I visited the farm so I could put flowers on Momma's grave. Part of me wonders if I'm so fascinated with psychology because of my mother and what she did. What was she thinking? How could she not have thought about her children before she committed such a permanent act? It's been two years. How could it have been so long? Sometimes I feel as if it happened yesterday.

If Momma had been stronger, maybe my father wouldn't have overwhelmed us all. Maybe she would have been able to survive. Not to excuse him in the least. I honestly don't believe there is much to redeem the man—and yet he is my father. My father.

*O*n Tuesday morning Mercedes strained the milk Darrel had left for her on the counter before he headed to the bus stop. One gallon she set aside for her neighbor Geraldine, to trade for remnants from her sister's fabric store in Casper. With these leftover bits, Mercedes made the quilts that gave her so much peace and joy. Something about the weave of the fabric, the design, the neat stitching helped her focus on what was important in life.

From her childhood, Mercedes had made quilts, first for her dolls and then for her own bed. It was the one thing her mother had passed on to her. Those hours working together when Daddy and Austin were away in the fields had been precious, though far too fleeting.

She'd kept a few special quilts over the years, hidden away, those that meant something no one else could share: the first quilt she'd made for her mother, the one she'd started for Brandon and never finished, the smaller one she'd made while pregnant with Darrel. Many more she'd given away or sold at shops or at the county fair. Or they were used at home with her family. Each night her three children went to sleep tucked under a quilt made with her love.

Mercedes went out to her garden. For miles there was nothing but the house, the barn, the small fruit orchard full of new leaves, and the rows of growing wheat, sugar beets, and alfalfa. After she finished here, she'd go up to the west field where Wayne was working, give him lunch, and stay to help a while before the children returned home from school. Then she'd do the washing while the boys set to their chores.

The sun was warm, not too hot, and the deep blueness of the sky took her breath away. She felt the urge to run into the fields and lie down in the alfalfa to look for marshmallow figures in the few puffy clouds overhead. But the alfalfa in the closest field wasn't quite tall enough to hide her from view—and that was part of the fun. Besides, she had work to do. Hunkering down next to her pea plants, she began to coax the weeds from the earth. The plants were tall already, signaling an early June harvest next month. The boys would be ecstatic. They loved eating them right from the garden.

Feet crunched over the grass in the yard, so quiet the sound would have been lost in the city, but she'd been expecting it since hearing the car a few seconds earlier. Everything in the country had a distinct sound, even in nature, a sound that inevitably called for a response, if only to admire the maker's industry or beauty.

Anticipating new remnants for quilts, Mercedes rubbed her hands over her jeans and stood ready to greet her visitor as she came around the house.

Brandon emerged into view.

Her smile froze on her face, and his movement ceased as they stared silently at each other. She became aware of the way she was dressed: the long-sleeved ocean blue T-shirt she wore on May mornings to stave off the chance breeze and too much sun, loose jeans falling over old white tennis shoes that were stained from the dirt, no socks, though he wouldn't be able to see that, and the wide-brimmed hat that kept the sun off her face. Her dark hair snaked in a thick braid to midway down her back, grown out during the past winter. She knew she looked exactly what she was: an aging farmwife. Not yet old but with youth somewhat behind her. She'd be forty later in the year. Too old to try for another baby. That hope had been abandoned.

"You're here," she said, experiencing a tremor of fear. Had

he picked this time because he'd known she'd be alone? Known that Wayne would be planting and the children in school? She glanced around to find something to make her less alone, but even the dogs were off exploring for the moment.

"You knew I would come."

She made her face impassive. "I hoped you wouldn't."

"I checked the hospital records. Your son Darrel is twelve, almost twelve and a half. Don't you think I know what that means?"

She took a deep breath before replying. Years of being with Wayne had taught her to think before she spoke. Words could wound too deeply for later repair. "What I know is that you left to work in Boston where your parents lived. I know I stayed here and married Wayne."

"He's not the father of your child."

There. It was out in the open, though she hadn't expected to feel the words so forcefully. She had made her peace with God and with herself and even with Brandon's memory. She had paid the price of security. She had made a promise to Wayne.

"And you think you are." She made the words flat, a statement, not a question, and was pleased to see him flinch.

"The timing's right. We were together then."

"We made a terrible mistake. You have no right to come back now." She hoped he didn't notice the trembling in her voice or the way her fist clutched the gardening spade.

"No right?" He flushed, his nostrils flaring. "You should have told me."

She studied him, eyes wandering over the familiar planes of his face and investigating new ones. The angles were sharper now, harder looking. It was a face that had seen trials. Had they been as severe as hers?

Wordlessly, she turned and began walking to the covered back deck that Wayne and Austin had built for her after she'd given birth to Scott. She'd wanted to be able to sit there rocking her new baby while watching the other boys play in the yard.

Brandon followed her. "This isn't going away."

She whipped around to face him. "Would it have made a difference? Would you have stayed if I'd told you?"

"I had a right to know!"

"You should have known it was possible. You're a doctor, for crying out loud. And for all that I was twenty-six, I was as innocent as a teenager. You knew what my life was like growing up! How my father controlled everything. You knew me and my dreams and what I'd hoped for us. The fact is, you didn't care, and now you have the gall to come back after all this time and tell me I should have told you? Well, you know what, I probably should have. But what would it have accomplished? You left! You left *me*. It was *your* choice." She was breathing hard, barely able to hold back the emotions and memories. How dare he come to her like this? How dare he confront her when she was alone and vulnerable!

Then again, he had always been a master at using her vulnerability and aloneness against her. She took the deck's two stairs in one leap and turned again to face him, glad to have the advantage of height but unable to look him in the eye. She gripped the spade in her hand more tightly.

"I thought you'd call," he said after a pause. "I thought you'd come to see me."

She gave a derisive laugh. "Without an invitation? I was pregnant, Brandon."

"I didn't know that."

"You should have figured it out. Why didn't you call me?"

"Your number was disconnected. If you'd called me . . ."

So he had at least called, though weeks too late to catch her at the apartment. "What would that have done? Forced me into your life? If you think I could do that, then you never knew me at all. My mother wasted her life following my father like a puppy dog. I would never let myself fall into that trap. You didn't want me so you certainly had no right to want my son."

"I loved you!"

"Not enough." She folded her arms, hating the pleading, piercing way his eyes met hers. *Go away,* her mind screamed. *Go away and leave me alone. Leave* us *alone.*

"I heard you were married. I couldn't believe it."

"I waited six months, and every day my stomach grew bigger. I had to hide out here on the farm."

"You waited?" That seemed to puzzle him. What did he think, that she'd gone out the week he'd left and started dating again? As far as that went, he was the one who'd seemed to go on so easily without her.

He started again. "If you'd told me, things might have been different."

Could he really believe that? "Not a chance," she retorted. "You made it clear you weren't ready for marriage, much less a child. How can you think otherwise? You would have wanted me to take care of it."

He didn't respond, and she felt some satisfaction, knowing she was right.

"So I did take care of it. Just not in the way you would have wanted me to. It was my way and my choice." Her tone changed with the next words, which came more softly. "Besides, even when all was said and done, when you had broken my heart into so many pieces that I thought I'd never be whole again, even then I wanted our child."

He looked around in confusion. "I don't know what to say. I need to think."

"What you need to do is pack up and leave Wyoming."

"No, wait! Please, Mercedes. Please! You don't understand."

He raked a hand through his hair. "Maybe you're right about what I would have done if I'd known before I left. I don't know. I was a different person then. But I'm sorry for what happened. I've asked myself a million times why I let things slip away. I guess . . . well, we seemed to have forever. But the one thing I do know is that I don't want to make another mistake. You said you wanted our son. Well, now I want him too."

Mercedes felt faint and had to remind herself to breathe. She took a few backward steps and sat in a chair, bringing one knee up to her chest in an instinctive urge to shield herself from the man who'd once torn her life apart and from all appearances had every intention of doing so again. The spade in her hand fell to the deck.

Brandon took her action as an invitation and quickly came onto the deck and settled in another chair. They sat in silence for long minutes, staring at the huge log swing Wayne had built for the boys in the backyard. It was so tall and sturdy that Mercedes herself often swung on it when playing with the boys.

"It's too late," she said, forcing a calm she didn't feel.

"For us, maybe. But not for my son."

Her jaw clenched. Why would he have even included "us" in the equation? At the moment, she wanted nothing more than to see him as far away from her as possible.

"There is no us," she snapped. "And you can't come in here and dump this on my son. He doesn't know you exist. Wayne's his father. He's listed on the birth certificate."

"I don't care what's listed there."

"Then you'd better get a lawyer, because I will fight you with every bit of life in my body. Darrel is not your son, and he never was."

"That's a lie."

She lifted her chin. "Prove it!"

He jumped to his feet and began pacing. "Look, I'm not saying I want to come here and dump anything on Darrel. I just want to see him. Talk to him. I want to know . . . I want to know that he's okay."

"Okay? Of course he's okay! He's okay because I made him that way. You didn't even want him to exist. Look at you, Brandon. You're here chasing something you had no desire to start in the first place. You have no part of him. Darrel is mine. He was mine and only mine the minute you walked out. You have no rights here." She was forcing the words between her teeth, trying hard not to burst into tears. This man, the one she'd loved so desperately, the one she had wanted to spend the rest of her life with, the one who had made her feel so alive, was once again trying to break her heart.

"If he's my son, maybe he won't be happy with this." He swept his arm around to indicate the rolling fields.

"He's *my* son. And I love it here." She said this, though both she and Wayne already knew Darrel wouldn't be taking over the farm. No matter his love for the place, his mind was already searching far beyond Walker Farm, destined for something else. Perhaps not better or greater, just different.

"You weren't happy here when I knew you."

"Turns out you never knew me very well at all."

His lips tightened, masking the emotion she'd glimpsed there for an instant. "He's my son."

"Please, Brandon, don't do this." Mercedes felt her control

slipping. She came to her feet. "I'll make sure he knows later, when he's older, but for now leave us alone. Please!" Tears began, falling fast, blinding her. "If you want a child, you can get married and have one. Don't try to take mine. You didn't want him or me then. It's not fair to want him now."

In three steps he was standing directly before her. "Mercedes, it's not like that. I'm not trying to take him. Well, maybe I thought I could—I don't really know. But being here now . . . seeing you . . ."

"Go away!" She pushed at him, but he grabbed her hands. "Mercedes, listen! I can't have more children. I had cancer. For a while there I didn't think I was going to make it, and now even if I do find a woman who will love me, I will never be able to father another child."

"They have ways to plan for that!" She ripped her hands from his. "You should have prepared for the future."

"I tried, but everything went wrong at the lab. And frankly, I was too sick to care. For a long time I told myself it didn't matter. But when I overheard your brother telling my boss that he had a nephew who was twelve, I—I felt . . . I don't know. Hope, I guess. I knew I had to find out. I jumped at the chance to present at this seminar for that reason. Look, I don't want to take your son away from you, I simply want the chance to be a father to my son."

"No," she moaned. "No." This was far worse than she'd expected. If Darrel was the only child Brandon would ever have, he wouldn't give up easily. "You could still marry and adopt."

"Maybe someday. But that doesn't change anything. Darrel is my son."

Mercedes couldn't take any more. Sobs shook her shoulders

and shuddered through her entire body. She was dying. He was killing her all over again.

"Don't, Mercedes."

He reached for her hands once more, and she didn't stop him from taking them. She felt hopeless. Darrel, her son, her firstborn. Her golden child. What would Brandon's appearance do to him?

There was a movement in the fields beyond the garden. Wayne, she saw, coming at a run. It was early for him to miss her yet, but she wasn't surprised to see him. He had always shown an uncanny awareness of what was going on at the farm, as though the lifeblood that pumped through the earth also brought him news of anything amiss.

She pulled away from Brandon, and with only the slightest resistance, he let her hands drop. She met Wayne on the lawn, and he enveloped her in the hug that made her feel safe. She was still shaking, but the sobs subsided almost immediately. Wayne would know what to do. He'd keep his head, if nothing else.

After her shaking stopped, he guided Mercedes back to the deck where Brandon waited, looking both nervous and defiant. "What are you doing here?" Wayne asked in a voice that wasn't ugly yet demanded an answer. He looked much older than Brandon, but stronger, and Mercedes took comfort in his strength.

"It wasn't what it looked like."

Wayne chuckled, and Mercedes felt distinctly sorry for Brandon. He had no knowledge of her husband or what he might think. As far as she knew, Wayne didn't have a jealous bone in his body. He trusted her completely, as she did him. In all their years of marriage he had never second-guessed her actions, and the fact that Brandon had hold of her hands would never seem a betrayal. Wayne would know there was a reason.

Or would he feel differently because it was Brandon?

"It looked to me like you were trying to comfort my wife after you told her you were here because of Darrel," Wayne said.

Brandon swallowed with apparent difficulty. "You know?"

"She told me yesterday you were in town. We both suspected why."

Mercedes bit her lip hard. She was clinging so tightly to Wayne that her fingers ached.

"Look, can't I just meet him?" Brandon asked. "I—I need to see him."

"To see that he's okay," Mercedes muttered bitterly.

Brandon sighed. "I get it—I know this is hard on you. On all of us. But seeing him isn't an unreasonable request."

The pleading way Brandon was looking at her made her feel uncomfortable, though with Wayne present, Mercedes had regained her strength. Still, Brandon wasn't backing down. What should she do? Maybe she could stall for time. "Later this week, then."

"Why not today? It's just a look. Please. I've been waiting more than twelve years."

Mercedes' thoughts raced. Wayne was gently urging her to a seat, but until she sank down, she hadn't realized her knees had been trembling. "He's a smart kid," she said. "It has to seem normal."

"That's not going to be easy, seeing as we don't exactly let strangers wander around our land." Wayne came around behind her chair, resting his large hands on her shoulders.

"I'm not a stranger," Brandon said. "I'm—" He stopped

talking, and Mercedes was glad. If he'd said he was Darrel's father one more time, she'd scream!

"We knew each other for a year, Mercedes," he said instead. "How would we be acting if things were different?"

"They aren't different." She didn't want to hear any of this. She wanted him to leave.

Wayne squeezed her shoulders. "Generally when our friends come to town, we have dinner together." Usually at the farm, though Mercedes noticed he didn't add that information, leaving it for her to choose where to meet with Brandon—on her own land or in a neutral setting.

Her heart rebelled. Brandon wasn't an old friend, and she certainly didn't want to cook for him. Or to eat anywhere with him, for that matter. She'd put a stop to the idea this instant.

"Would that be okay?" Brandon asked her. "I'll pay."

His expression was her undoing. In that instant he reminded her so much of the man she'd loved. "I guess we could try," she said, hating herself for not finding some way out.

"Today? There's a nice restaurant or two in Riverton. But I know that's an hour's drive for you. Don't know if there's anything closer."

Suddenly Mercedes didn't want to be in a situation where she had so little control, nor did she want to disrupt her family on a school night. "No, there's nothing close, and the boys have to get up early for school," she said stiffly. "It would be better here." She glanced at Wayne, who nodded, though his reluctance showed he liked this as little as she did. She refocused on Brandon and added, "You're an old friend visiting. If you bring up anything else, I'll have Wayne throw you out."

Brandon's mouth twisted in a forced half smile. "I assure you. That won't be necessary. I promise not to say anything to him for the time being." He nodded at both of them and started down the deck stairs.

"At six, sharp," Mercedes added.

"I'll be here." Brandon started across the yard.

"And I'll thank you not to come again when I'm not here," Wayne called to his retreating back. "Unless Mercedes asks you to."

Brandon stopped, turned, and met her eyes. His looked so green against the blue of his sweater. He didn't seem like an enemy. "Fair enough. Thank you both for the invitation."

Mercedes held herself erect in her chair until Brandon was out of sight, then she slumped back, glad Wayne's hands were still on his shoulders.

"Thanks for coming." Her eyes were teary again. "I really lost it there for a minute. I needed you."

"I know," he said simply, sitting next to her and taking her hand. His skin felt warm against her cold flesh.

"What are we going to do?"

"We're going to put in some wheat, and then we're going to have dinner with the boys and our guest."

"He came to try to take Darrel. I could see it in his eyes. He backed down when I got upset. But what on earth made him think I'd hand over my son?"

"I don't know."

"Darrel doesn't deserve to have things change like this. It's not his fault!" Guilt oozed from the words. If only she'd understood all those years ago how her choices would affect her children, her family. She would give her life now to have Darrel be Wayne's son.

"You cared about him once," Wayne said. "You thought he was a good man. Maybe we ought to wait and see."

"I won't let him take Darrel."

"If it comes to that, we'll fight."

His quiet words strengthened her. "I love you." She felt it perhaps more than she had felt it since she'd agreed to marry him.

"I love you too. Everything is going to work out." He kissed her and arose, taking the few steps to the kitchen door. "I'll get my lunch and take it to the fields. You don't need to come out today. I can manage on my own. You have enough to deal with here. Just send Darrel out when he gets home."

"But—"

"It's okay. Really." He smiled, one side of his full mouth rising higher than the other, forming the crooked smile she loved. Moments later, he returned with the lunch bag she'd already packed, filled with roast beef between thick slices of homemade bread, fresh milk from the cow, carrot slices, and his favorite apple pie.

He nodded, and she watched him go, experiencing a distinct sadness. She loved Wayne, but she had always felt she didn't love him as much as she should, that perhaps something inside her had broken after Brandon left, so she couldn't love fully. Or perhaps because too much of her heart was still in the past, no matter how she yearned for it to be otherwise. Wayne deserved so much more.

She sat in the chair on the deck and watched until Wayne became a small dot that soon disappeared. Then she pushed herself awkwardly to her feet, still shaky from the encounter with Brandon. Inside her bedroom, she went to the closet where she kept her most private possessions in several large boxes. In one of these was the baby quilt she'd made for Darrel. Each square was intricate, the stitches perfect. But it had been created from the darkest, ugliest material she'd owned, though she hadn't realized it at the time. Now she understood that creating it had been a way of pushing her grief out, a way of exorcising her anger at Brandon and at the world in general. Even at Wayne for not being Brandon.

By the time her baby was born, the darkness in her soul was gone, and she'd seen the quilt for what it was. She hadn't wrapped her precious boy in it but instead used the one her neighbor had made for her. She rarely looked at this one now.

Every time she held it, she was pulled into that faraway world of sadness. Her fingers traced the black square with the fractured heart, made the first month of her engagement to Wayne when she was more than four months pregnant. The purple triangles bordering the heart looked like shark's teeth, and the plaid design below now called to mind a person being tortured. All the ugly feelings in her heart had gone into this quilt, a repository for her suffering and remorse. But Wayne's love and Darrel's miraculous birth had made it all go away. She kept it now only to remind herself of how good her life was compared to then. Besides, it was hard to throw away emotions.

Underneath this quilt was the one she'd been making for Brandon. Dark blues intermingled with the occasional yellow, bordered with a blue patterned piece. The top was finished, but she'd never done the stitching that would have taken days to do by hand. Her friend Geraldine now had a quilting machine, and sometimes Mercedes used that, but it wasn't as satisfying as making each individual stitch herself. After Brandon had left, there was no reason to finish the quilt. She couldn't even bear to look at it. The truth was, the rare moments when she was brave enough to admit it to herself, she wondered how her life would have been different if she'd told Brandon about the baby. If she had followed him when he'd left Wyoming. Or even if she'd stayed here and sent pictures. It might have taken a year or more, but was it possible there would have been a happy ending for them? He did marry eventually, and she believed he'd once honestly loved her. Could she have been the one who gave up on them too early? She would never know.

"Why did you have to come back?" Mercedes whispered to the empty room. She sat on the bed clutching Darrel's baby blanket, despair swirling around her.

CHAPTER 4

Diary of Mercedes Walker
June 11, 1994

I took Brandon out to the swimming hole at the farm and showed him the rope swing. He got a real kick out of it, and we ended up in the water. We were kissing when Wayne found us there. I think he'd come to cool off in the water himself. He looks tired. I know he's working too hard without Daddy here to help, but I'm not sure what to do about that. Though the crops were good last year, there is so much debt from other years that there isn't any money to hire anyone else. Maybe after I get an education, I could pay someone. Really it's my father who should be helping, but who knows where he is. Texas, last I heard. I wonder if he thinks about Momma.

Sometimes I wonder why Wayne doesn't leave. Surely he can't feel loyal to my father after all he's done. And with Momma gone, what's the point? I have to admit, though, I'm glad he stays. As much as I hate this farm, something inside me stirs when I look out over the fields of wheat and alfalfa. It's as though the childhood I'd always dreamed of lurks there somewhere, if I can only find it.

Wayne went through the motions of planting without experiencing any of the joy and satisfaction his work usually gave him. His mind worried at the problem of Brandon and Darrel. And Mercedes. He had the distinct feeling Brandon hadn't come only for Darrel. Oh, perhaps he'd started out that way, but the way he looked at Mercedes, with his heart in his eyes, boded ill for their family.

Wayne had never had a reason to mistrust Mercedes. She was an honest, upright woman who kept her promises. He'd known when she married him that her heart had been given to another man, but he'd loved her so much, and he believed he could change her feelings by simply being there for her. And he had. He'd given her back her smile, her laughter, and her will to live. His entire life was dedicated to making her happy, and he knew he'd succeeded. She'd come to love him as he'd hoped and prayed she would.

Yet always there was the unspoken "he" between them. The tragic, romantic figure of a girlish past that remained locked onto a piece of her heart. It didn't usually matter because the rest was enough, but now that Brandon had returned, Wayne experienced a fear too terrible to contemplate. The time had finally come. He would now lose Mercedes or win her forever. His job would be to let her make the choice, because if it wasn't hers, it wouldn't be real. He had never doubted her with any other man, but Brandon wasn't just anyone.

Darrel did not worry him so much. Darrel was a smart child, and he would take this in stride. If it came to a court battle, he would never choose to leave his mother and the farm to live with Brandon, exactly as Mercedes wouldn't force him to stay when it was time for him to leave for college. However, it did wound Wayne to the heart that the boy would finally know he wasn't his birth father. Would their relationship change? There was really no way to predict that, though he'd done his best to teach Darrel well. Sometimes he found himself spending more time with Darrel than with the other two, as though to prove to the world—and himself?—that he loved him every bit as much.

Whatever the cause, he loved Darrel with his entire heart, just as if the boy had been his own son. He'd been there for his birth, his first fever, his first steps. He'd given him his first and only spanking and had lain beside him at night studying the stars. They'd read hundreds of books together, first because Wayne had felt intellectually inferior to Mercedes and wanted to please her, and then because he and the boys simply loved to learn together.

Opening the cab and jumping down from the tractor, Wayne knelt in the freshly turned soil, picking it up in his hands to examine the texture and content. The lovely, rich smell brought memories rushing back.

"You watch after my girl," Lucinda Walker had said to him at the kitchen table while her husband, Jed, was out in the barn checking up on Austin. Jed could never seem to trust the boy, though at sixteen Austin did the work of a man and had for years.

"I do, Mrs. Walker," Wayne said, as he always did when she brought it up.

"It's more important now since she's grown. I don't want her being her daddy's slave." Like herself was what she meant. "She deserves a man who loves her. A man like you."

A flush crawled over Wayne's face. Had he been so transparent? Since Mercedes had started studying at the local college, his feelings about her had begun changing. He felt tongue-tied, and the familiar ease between them had vanished. She was no longer the little girl who'd built maze houses in the alfalfa fields. Of course, she'd never be able to return his feelings, so he made it a point not to be around when she came home. Unless he knew Jed was drunk. Then he would make sure to be there to run interference.

"I'm sure she'll find someone," he told Lucinda. "And so will I. That reminds me. I won't be here Friday night. I'm going on a date."

Lucinda studied him. "You got it bad, don't you? Hang on there, Wayne. Mercedes still might wake up before it's too late. She belongs here, not out there. Not like Austin." She looked down at the linoleum floor. "Not like me."

They both jerked as Jed stomped into the kitchen, railing on Austin as they came in together. "You ain't never gonna amount to nothin' if you don't listen to me," he bawled. "You gotta stop being so blasted stupid!"

Austin's eyes went to his mother's, pleading for assistance, but she looked away. Wayne took a breath. "I'm going to pick up something in town. If you're ready, Austin, I'll drop you off at school so you don't have to take the bus."

"Thanks! I'll get my books." Austin paid no attention to the breakfast on the table, only too glad to accept the escape offered him.

Jed gave Wayne an icy glare. "Thought you fixed the steering yesterday."

Wayne ignored his tone. He was bigger than Jed, and besides, Jed needed him. No other man knew as much about this farm as Wayne did or would work for such an irritating man. "The part they gave me don't fit." Don't fit. That was how he talked, though *Mercedes and Austin teased him about it.* Doesn't fit, *he corrected himself mentally.*

"Those people are idiots!" fumed Jed.

"No, just young. They don't pay 'em much."

Wayne left Lucinda cowering beside Jed in the kitchen like a frightened hen. He didn't know why she stayed. The only reason he did was because of Austin and Mercedes and even Lucinda. And because he loved the land. But no one could deny that things were quickly falling apart for this family. The minute Austin turned eighteen, he'd get his scholarships and be gone. Mercedes was already talking about sharing an apartment in town with friends. With no love lost between Jed and the children, they wouldn't be back, and Lucinda was dying little by little under her husband's neglect and abuse.

Shaking aside the memories, Wayne let the dirt slide between his fingers. He stared up at the sky, not caring as his hat fell from his head. *I don't know that I have strength for this. I love her so much.*

How long he had knelt, Wayne didn't know, but a touch on his shoulder brought him back to himself. "Dad?"

"Hey, Darrel." Climbing to his feet, he briefly hugged the boy. "Glad you're here, son. I hope you don't have much homework because I really need the help."

"I had math, but I did it on the bus. It's too easy."

"Well, we'll have to look into that, won't we?" It wouldn't be the first time they'd had him moved to a different class or supplemented at home.

"Is everything okay?" Darrel asked. "Mom looks like she's been crying."

How much to tell him? Wayne felt at a loss. This wasn't like book learning where he could give Darrel as much as he could absorb. "She's all right. Just a little sad. She saw an old friend today, and it brought some sad memories of the old days. Hey, that reminds me, this fellow's coming to dinner tonight. He's a doctor. You might think of some questions to ask him."

"If he makes Mom sad, why's he coming to dinner?"

"It's not him so much. Just that time in her life. She was actually good friends with this guy. But you know your momma had a difficult upbringing."

Darrel nodded. "Sometimes it's hard to imagine Grandpa being so mean."

"Well, he's changed some." Wayne was glad to say it, though the change wasn't near enough and had come far too late in life to help Jed's children.

Mercedes had forgiven Jed when he'd asked nearly five years ago, but her brother had gone seventeen years without seeing his father. Only last year Austin had finally visited Jed at the assisted-living facility in Rock Springs, where Jed had lived for twelve years. Things weren't perfect, though they were all at least on speaking terms. But Wayne noticed Mercedes didn't offer to have Jed move back in, nor would Wayne have permitted it. Jed was trying to be nicer, but he was still a grouchy old man with a tendency to abuse others, especially those who loved him.

"Should I drive the tractor?" Darrel asked.

"If you want. We'll need to fill the drill with more seed." Wayne pointed down the road where he'd left the seed truck.

"Oh, wait, I just remembered—my teacher gave me an article on nanotechnology." Darrel stopped halfway up the side of the tractor and looked back at Wayne, his face alive with eagerness.

"Good. We'll read it later tonight. I hope we don't have to look up so many words in the dictionary like last time."

Darrel laughed. "I read a little bit. I think we will."

Wayne gave an exaggerated sigh. "Good thing your momma insisted on getting the Internet. I bet half the words aren't even in our dictionary."

Darrel laughed again as he settled into the seat. He was a small, thin kid, who hadn't yet come into his height or bulk. Given Brandon's build, he'd likely never be as muscular as his younger brothers, but he should at least get the height and the looks. Both Brandon and Mercedes were beautiful people, and their genes ran clearly through Darrel's body. Yet his thirst for knowledge was also shared by Wayne, though he was content to do it from an armchair, for the most part. Darrel would need to seek it out and touch it. Experience it. That was who he was.

I love you, son, Wayne thought, *and no matter what genetics say, you are my boy.*

CHAPTER

5

Diary of Mercedes Walker
June 21, 1994

Daddy came back from Texas as poor as ever after more than two years away. His dreams of making it rich on a Texas ranch were as elusive as the love Austin and I craved from him as a father. As I suspected, he didn't even know Momma was gone. When he heard, he lay down in their bed and didn't get up. He's really ill. I don't know what's wrong with him, and he won't go to the doctor.

Good thing Wayne is still here to keep the farm running, or we'd lose it for sure. I worried that he'd leave when Daddy returned so suddenly. Wayne is so much more than a hired hand, no matter what Daddy may have said in the past. The farm is still in our family only because of Wayne. If I had any say, I'd give it to him. I know he'd always let me visit, if I needed to.

Grandma actually owns the farm on paper, but she's too

heartbroken over Momma to care about anything other than her charity work. But there was nothing she could do to stop Momma. Nothing any of us could do. She was sick. I understand that now, but it doesn't take away the pain of being deserted once again.

Brandon was nervous as he drove off the main highway and onto the dirt road leading to Walker Farm. The sun hung halfway down on the horizon, and fields stretched for miles around, beckoning as the short stalks of wheat or whatever was growing there bent and swayed in the evening breeze. Something here was absolutely foreign to him; he'd felt it every time he'd been to the farm, even with Mercedes all those years ago. He knew it was because he didn't belong. He'd once thought she didn't belong either, but he'd been wrong. Seeing her this morning in the garden, she was every bit as much a part of the farm as the peas she was growing. A quiet partnership existed that even he couldn't deny.

What if his son had the same connection Mercedes did to the farm? Brandon had come to entice him away, but after Mercedes' emotional pleas, he wondered if he'd have the strength. If his son belonged here, would there even be a choice?

He's my son.

What if the child took an immediate dislike to him? What if Mercedes had said something that made him hate Brandon? But she wouldn't do that, would she? Brandon simply didn't know the woman she'd become.

Yet he wanted to know her.

How had things gone so wrong? He should be driving home to his house in California now, with Mercedes and their children awaiting him. Or maybe he'd be picking up their son to meet her at the office where she was helping a late psychiatric patient. That was how they'd talked about it, and he knew it hadn't happened mostly because of him. He'd learned during his marriage that women needed to be told and shown often how important they were. He should have told Mercedes he'd come back for her or send for her. If he hadn't been so arrogant, so assured of her love, so completely absorbed in his new career, he would have understood her mind. He would have put aside his own hurt at not hearing from her and realized something was wrong.

Yet would he have done the right thing even then? He had no way of knowing, and the truth was—the truth that hurt deeply, like a wound that would never heal—it didn't matter for them now. Their relationship was over. She had gone on with her life, even if he found himself back at the beginning.

Regret every bit as painful as the treatments he'd endured for his stomach cancer rolled through him in a terrible, blinding wave. There was nothing here for him.

No, that wasn't quite true. There was still his son.

He pulled to a stop before the low-slung farmhouse that had been built a little at a time as the family who resided in it grew. Mercedes told him there had been only one bedroom when she was a child, and she'd slept in a small alcove built into the hallway. Her brother slept in the kitchen by the stove until a room had finally been added. Mercedes and her husband had made more new additions in the years since he'd first visited, though he couldn't be sure how much from the outside. One of those rooms Mercedes shared with her husband. They had loved and lived and created two more children there. In another room, Darrel slept, dreaming . . . of what? Brandon wanted to know that more than anything.

Taking a deep breath, he opened the car door. This time he was greeted by a red retriever followed by at least five puppies.

The dogs began barking, keeping him from coming onto the porch. The front door opened, and Mercedes emerged. "Di, down. Come on, girl. He's invited."

She was wearing a buttercup yellow dress that skimmed the tops of her brown bare feet. The yellow contrasted with the dark hair that fanned out over her shoulders. Her eyes looked black in her face, which was tanned despite the silly hat she'd been wearing that morning. She was so exactly like his Mercedes from the past that he found it impossible to do anything but stare.

The dogs had stopped barking, and now he was being attacked by warm, wet black noses as the puppies investigated his dress pants.

"Shoo!" Mercedes scolded. Her head turned. "Joseph! Scott! Come get these dogs."

Seconds later two young boys shot from the door behind her and tumbled into the array of puppies, giggling all the while. They cast shy glances at Brandon but didn't speak to him.

"Take them around to the barn and put them in the empty stall," Mercedes said. "Not the one with the baby goats."

"Aw, they hate that."

"It's only while we eat. Now go."

Whistling for the dogs, the boys raced around the side of the house. The puppies' mother looked between her retreating offspring and Mercedes, as though trying to make a decision.

"You can go too, Di," Mercedes encouraged, but Di, giving a low bark, chose to stay with her mistress. "Well, that's fine then," Mercedes said with a smile. To Brandon she added, "She considers herself my protector. Come on inside. We'll be eating on the back deck. It's nice out this evening."

"So many dogs," he said, for something to say. "What are you going to do with them?"

"We're only keeping one. We've promised the others to neighbors. Tomorrow, in fact. They're in high demand around here. Di and Thunder—that's the father—have good pedigrees. I'm letting the boys pick one because they lost their other dog, Jellybean, last year when he deserted us for my brother's wife."

"Deserted?"

She laughed. "Jellybean is a very self-centered, lazy dog. A disgrace to his parents. He knew he'd get more attention there." She led him through a front room, down the hall where he saw the alcove where she'd once slept—now filled with sewing paraphernalia—and into the kitchen. Delicious smells reminded Brandon he hadn't eaten since breakfast.

Mercedes pointed to the door leading to the deck. "Why don't you go through there and have a seat? I have to check on a few things, and then I'll be out."

Where's Darrel? he wanted to ask.

As though reading his mind, she added, "Wayne and Darrel are washing up. They've been in the fields until now."

"How did you know what I was thinking?"

A faint smile touched her lips, her dark eyes luminous and sad. "I live with four men. I've learned to read between the lines."

He felt a distinct disappointment. She hadn't guessed because she knew him or felt anything for him. Anything but perhaps resentment and hatred.

I'm really sorry, Mercedes, he told her silently. *I don't know what else to do.*

"Go on," she urged, as though talking to the dogs.

He did as he was told, amused that Di followed him out

to the deck. "Keeping an eye on me, are you?" he asked the
creature.

Di sat near the door and studied him, her demeanor regal.
Only once, when they heard one of the boys shout happily
from the distant barn, did she glance away from him.

The backyard was exactly as it had been that morning, with
the exception of the clothesline that was full of damp clothing.
Socks, pants, shirts, little boys' underwear, but nothing notably
Mercedes' except one dress and maybe a pair of jeans. If he
hadn't been coming, would there have been more? A dressy
blouse perhaps? A pair of nylons? Of course there would be
nothing he would recognize, not after all these years.

The table on the deck was set with matching dishes. Six
places. A green salad in a plastic-covered bowl, a basket of
rolls, and a pitcher of milk sat in the middle. A normal family
dinner. Brandon remembered his wife, Hannah, arranging a
similar table and how he'd loved to come home and find everything ready.

*"Oh, you're home!" Hannah met him in the hall, lifting her
face for his kiss. Her blond hair was cut short, and he liked the
way it followed the curve of her head.*

"How was work today?" he asked.

*She wrinkled her cute, slightly uptilted nose. "You don't want
to be anywhere near a grade school during the first week of a
new year, much less in the principal's office. My phone didn't
quit ringing today. Half the calls were from teachers looking for
missing supplies, and the others from concerned parents wanting
to move their children to other classrooms."*

"Thank heaven schools have regular hours."

*"Yep. No emergency operations for me." She pulled him into
the kitchen. "Come on. I have dinner ready. It's your favorite."*

"You made pizza?"

"No, your other favorite."

"Ah, shrimp." He took her hand. *"You're so good to me."*

The cancer and the treatments had changed all that. He didn't blame her—he was the one who'd taken out his frustrations on everyone around him, including Hannah. Before he realized what he was doing, it was too late.

The story of my life, he thought bitterly.

Mercedes and Wayne came onto the deck, carrying steaming dishes. They moved with the familiar rhythm of those who knew each other well and were comfortable together. Wayne was wearing clean jeans and a polo shirt, his white-laced red hair wet from the shower. His face was gentle, but his eyes were cautious. Brandon had the impression of great power within the man, this man who had probably never studied further than his high school diploma, and he looked away uncomfortably.

The boy emerged next, carrying a set of small dessert plates. Brandon stared. The child looked younger than twelve. He was thin everywhere, from his face under the dark brown hair to the narrow bare feet sticking out under his stiff, new-looking jeans. His eyes, so dark as to be nearly black, were Mercedes', and the oval curve of the face as well, though his cheeks had a sharpness that had never touched his mother's. His skin was tanned, and a few stray freckles scattered over his nose. There was nothing of himself that Brandon could see in the child. The hair was darker than his own and would likely darken even more to the same color as Mercedes'. He was his mother's child through and through.

Darrel's eyes met Brandon's, and in that moment he felt something more. The intelligence and curiosity were immediately apparent, but they had also been obvious in Darrel's brothers. What, then, was Brandon experiencing?

My son, he thought. *I know him.* He wanted to reach out

and touch the boy on the shoulder. To caress his face and ruffle his hair. To make up for all the lost years.

I would have told her to take care of it.

No, he couldn't believe that. If she'd waited, had placed Darrel as an infant in his arms, and Brandon had stared into those intelligent eyes . . .

Stop, he told himself. There was no going back. Not Ever. The past could not be undone. Only the future could be shaped. But would he make the same mistake he'd made with Mercedes and Hannah? No, he had to make this work with Darrel. It was his last chance.

"Hi," he said aloud, his voice sounding rusty and unused.

"Brandon, this is my son Darrel." Mercedes put a hand on the child's shoulder. "Darrel, this is an old friend of mine, Brandon Rhodes. He was a resident at the hospital in Riverton many years ago."

"Hi," Darrel said, staring at him frankly. "You're a doctor, huh?"

Brandon grinned, impressed that he understood what a resident was. "Don't I look like one?"

Darrel considered a moment. "I guess I'd expect you to be wearing a white jacket or green scrubs."

"And wearing a stethoscope?"

"Something like that. But if I were a doctor, I guess I probably wouldn't go around wearing that all day."

"I do get rather sick of green and white."

"I'll bet."

In the ensuing silence, Mercedes said to Darrel, "Would you go get the boys?"

"Can I ring the gong?"

Mercedes groaned. "If you must."

"Yes!" Darrel sprinted across the deck and darted into a tool shed at the far end. Inside, Brandon spied a gas grill, a hedge trimmer, and other odds and ends people usually stuffed into such structures. The boy pulled out an object that could only be the gong, held up on a homemade frame by a sturdy rope.

"He made it for a Boy Scout project," Mercedes explained. "All by himself. It's pretty creative, actually."

"I can hear it in all the fields but the north one," Wayne added, seating himself at the head of the table. "If I'm late to dinner, you can be sure the boys'll ring it."

Darrel grabbed the wood mallet tied to the frame and gave the metal sheet three strong hits in succession. The sound reverberated through the yard. In seconds, the younger boys bolted from the barn, followed by another full-grown red retriever, whom Brandon assumed must be the father of the puppies. He loped with the same regal air as Di, his good breeding showing in every movement.

"I'm starving," complained the larger of the two boys as they reached the deck. He had bright red hair, from his father, and a face covered in freckles. His eyes, like his brothers', were as dark as their mother's.

Mercedes grinned. "This is Joseph, our resident bottomless pit. He's always starving."

"Especially at bedtime," Wayne added.

"Or in the middle of the night," Darrel said.

Joseph giggled and started to sit at the table. "No," Mercedes told him. "Go wash your hands. You too, Scott."

The boys tumbled into the house to obey without the smallest protest. Brandon had no doubt they'd played out this same scene many times and had learned their objections wouldn't get them very far.

Darrel finished replacing the gong in the shed as the younger boys returned. They sat still in their seats while their father prayed over the food, and then for a while, everyone was busy loading their plates.

As Brandon took his share, he peered across the table at Darrel every time he dared. This was his son. His child. With his wide smile, honest face, and intelligent eyes. Mercedes' eyes. Brandon looked at her to be sure, though he already knew it was true, but her eyes were lowered and she didn't glance his way. Her face was locked into an expression of endurance, one he'd almost missed identifying. This was torture for her.

Wayne, on the other hand, met his gaze steadily, unflinchingly, and without a visible sign of stress. He was in control here, no doubt about that, no doubt at all. "So," Wayne said, "tell us, Dr. Rhodes. How are your lectures going?"

"Okay, I guess," Brandon began without enthusiasm. He didn't want to talk about himself. He wanted to hear what Darrel was studying, what he wanted to be when he grew up. If he liked the farm. If his brain was getting all the opportunity it needed to stretch and grow. "At least they haven't kicked me out."

"Mom said you were a heart doctor," Darrel said. "Do you operate on people?"

Brandon turned perhaps a little too eagerly toward the boy. "All the time. Hearts are the most fascinating of all the human organs. Over the past five years, I've developed a new procedure that is particularly effective on children with heart valve problems. I predict it'll become fairly routine with time."

"Did you ever see someone die?" This from Scott, the youngest, whose eyes looked huge in his round face. He had brown hair like Darrel, though not nearly as dark. Both the younger children would likely be as tall and broad-shouldered as their father, and Brandon wondered what Darrel would think when they began to develop. Would he begrudge his own genetics? Would he understand why he was different?

Brandon meant to see that he did. He would fight for a place in his son's life. Mercedes must be made to understand that his involvement would be for the best. *I can give him what they cannot.* He could educate the boy, show him the world and all its endless possibilities. He could not let the child get stuck raising grain.

Yet what if that was Darrel's desire? Farming was an important occupation; food was vital in any economy. In fact, food was more vital than heart valve surgery to the general population. Who was Brandon to look down upon that? Who was he to take away his son's dreams? But he didn't really believe Darrel would want to be a farmer. Surely there was something of Brandon in him, something not as obvious as the color of his eyes or the shape of his face.

He became aware that everyone was staring at him, waiting for him to answer Scott's question. "I've seen people die before," he said slowly, "but only after everything we can do. Many more live than die."

"We saw a dead calf," Joseph volunteered. "There are lots of dead things around here. Birds and animals. But we've only seen one dead person."

"That's enough, Joseph," Wayne said, the words clipped but not harsh.

"But I was just—"

Wayne gazed at him. "No."

Joseph nodded. "Yes, Dad." He glanced over to where his mother sat. She'd stopped eating, her face still and her eyes looking past the garden and the orchard at something Brandon couldn't see. Something in the grove of shade trees beyond.

Darrel dug Joseph in the arm with his elbow, making a stern face at him.

"Darrel," Wayne said.

"Sorry," the boy muttered.

Brandon had no idea what was going on, but this was something more than talking about dead animals at the dinner table. Had Mercedes suffered another loss he was not aware of? What was out behind those trees? Before he could consider the matter further, Mercedes came back from wherever she had been in her mind.

"Hey, boys," she said. "Did I tell you what I made for dessert?"

"Apple pie?" Joseph asked eagerly.

"Chocolate cake?" Scott guessed.

Darrel smirked. "Nope, I saw it. You're both wrong." At his mother's nod, he added, "It's strawberry ice cream. Not the store kind, but the good kind Momma makes."

"Yum!" Both Joseph and Scott fell to shoveling in their food as quickly as possible to be ready for the ice cream, and the tenseness Brandon now thought he might have imagined was completely gone.

The pork roast and potatoes were excellent and kept Brandon eating, though he was bursting with questions he knew he shouldn't ask—yet. He didn't want to alienate Darrel by seeming overly interested or pushy. Nor did he want to worry Mercedes. She had a little color back in her cheeks now, though her eyes were still wary and avoided his.

"So what happened in school today?" Wayne asked the younger boys.

They listened as Joseph and Scott recounted the day's events in detail. Joseph told a long story about a baseball game that went into all three recesses, and Scott told a story about a king who couldn't seem to find his cow, or some such nonsense, and then how Bradley Pyne had thrown up all over the floor during math.

"Not exactly great dinner conversation," Wayne reminded him.

"Well, it's better than what happened to Tim McDonnell during the test last week," Joseph said. He, Darrel, and Scott burst into laughter, and even Mercedes and Wayne couldn't hide their smiles.

"Enough of that," Mercedes said, and the conversation went on before Brandon could work up enough nerve to ask them to let him in on the secret.

The younger boys stopped their constant narration every so often to take a huge bite of food, and Mercedes would have to remind them not to talk with their mouths full. Wayne appeared to take great interest in every story the boys rehearsed. Was he always like that, or was it a show for Brandon? And why didn't he ask Darrel any questions? Even eating slowly, Brandon was almost finished before the boys fell silent.

"Any homework?" Wayne asked.

"Momma already helped us." Scott stabbed his last piece of meat. "But we still have to read tonight."

Wayne nodded. "I need to check on the cattle after dinner, to see if they're ready to move to a new pasture, but we'll read when I get back. By then Darrel will have finished the milking and you boys will be done with checking the animals."

"I'm done," Joseph said, pushing away his plate. "Can I have some ice cream now?"

Mercedes grinned. "In a few minutes. Wait for the rest of us. But you can take your plate to the sink."

With an exaggerated sigh, Joseph grabbed his plate, utensils, and cup and went inside the house.

Brandon was still waiting for Wayne to question Darrel about his day, but he didn't. The incongruity bothered him. Did Wayne treat the child differently because of his parentage? Brandon felt a sliver of justification. If his son were being neglected, he would make up for it.

"So," Mercedes said to Darrel, "did you tell your dad about the article your teacher gave you?"

"Yeah. That's what we're going to read. And Dad says we need to talk to the math teacher about getting me in a different book. It's too easy."

"Yeah, even I can do it," Wayne joked.

"I got all the states and capitals memorized," Darrel said. "Dad tested me on the way home."

Of course, Brandon thought, feeling like an idiot. Darrel and Wayne had spent hours together in the fields after school. They would have covered all the usual topics while they worked, took breaks, or were returning to the house. Likely Wayne spent far more time alone with Darrel than with the other two boys.

Mercedes began stacking dishes. "I'll get the ice cream. You men stay here. Boys, help me carry these inside."

Within minutes they were all enjoying freshly made strawberry ice cream. Mercedes had made ice cream often for him and their friends in the old days. He remembered the long summer, cooling off in her apartment with the windows wide open to let in the breeze as they bantered back and forth with his friends about the meaning of life.

The meaning of life.

Whatever it was, Brandon felt he'd missed it completely. "When did you decide you wanted to be a doctor?" Darrel asked him.

"I think I was just born knowing. Sometimes it's like that."

"I was the same way," Wayne said.

"Not me." Mercedes' spoon poised over her bowl in an oddly appealing manner. "I tried a dozen things before I knew I wanted to be here at the farm."

He knew she'd studied many occupations, and it had puzzled him, her lack of focus, when she'd always seemed so sure about where their relationship was headed. At the same time, her wide knowledge of subjects had fascinated him. She was a continual mystery. In their early days together, he'd worried that one day she'd wake up and consider him old news, like her hair-cutting days or her year-long stint in construction.

The meal was over before Brandon was ready for it to be, and he felt them looking at him, waiting for him to leave. They had work to do. *But I haven't even really talked to Darrel,* he wanted to protest. A look passed between Mercedes and Wayne and Darrel, and Brandon acutely felt his outsider status. This family didn't need or want him.

"Hurry and check on the cattle, okay, Dad?" Darrel said. "I can saddle a horse for you before I get to the milking. I can't wait to read about nanotechnology."

Nanotechnology? And apparently Wayne checked on his cattle using a horse and not in their old truck sitting out front. This surprised Brandon, though he really had no idea of how things were done on a farm, much less this one.

Wayne smiled. "Thanks, son."

Again they all looked expectantly at Brandon. "Well, it was nice to meet you, Darrel," Brandon said. "I enjoyed our conversation."

Darrel shrugged with a carelessness that bruised Brandon's ego. "Yeah, me too. See ya." He ran off, heading to the barn, the dogs and his little brothers taking up the chase.

Brandon proffered a hand to Wayne. "Thanks for having me."

"You're welcome."

There was much to say, but Brandon didn't want to press his luck after such a nice meal. He started to offer his hand to Mercedes, but she clung to Wayne's arm and nodded at him. The wariness in her face hurt him, though he knew she was right to maintain it. This little time with Darrel did not begin to fill the craving in his heart.

"Goodbye," she said.

He left them standing on the deck and went around to his car. He started the engine and pulled around in the gravel beyond the front lawn until he was facing the long dirt road out to the main highway. In his peripheral vision, he saw a movement to the left of the house, a horse galloping along the edge of the field with Wayne atop.

Like a scene from an old western, he thought.

Brandon shut off the car. Darrel would be milking now. His son milking a cow! He couldn't bear to pass up the opportunity to see him one last time tonight. Did he milk well? Did he complain? Was it dangerous?

Slipping from the car, Brandon made his way around the side of the house. No one was in sight, and he would have to hope that Mercedes wasn't looking out her kitchen window as she cleaned up from the meal. Or that she didn't return to the deck to gather the few items remaining there. He skirted the log swing and began traversing the considerable space to the barn. This was a backyard he would have loved when he was growing up. Plenty of room for baseball, or hide and seek, or watermelon seed spitting contests.

Inside the darker interior of the barn, he could hear the voices of the children, but he could only see unfamiliar shapes.

As his eyes adjusted, he spied the younger boys playing in a stall with the puppies. Where was Darrel? Brandon took a few steps into the barn, unnoticed by the boys. He was glad the older dogs were nowhere in sight, or he would likely have been discovered upon entry.

A black horse lifted his head from the hay he was munching and eyed him. Brandon walked down the middle of the barn, which had stalls on one side. Three more horses were in stalls that opened to a pasture beyond, and at the far end of the structure he could hear chickens clucking in an adjoining coop.

Brandon peered around the thick post that made up one corner of the last stall. There was Darrel with a huge black-and-white Holstein cow. She had short horns, though Brandon remembered reading somewhere that milk cows often had their horns cut off for safety.

"Come on, move!" Darrel was saying. He threw his thin body against the side of the cow, who turned her head in his direction with boredom, as if wondering what this tiny annoying creature was trying to do. Darrel pushed again and again. Finally the cow moved over, and Darrel whipped out a stool and sat down. He looked vulnerable next to the cow, as though at any moment she would move, squishing him flat against the far side of the stall.

Unconcerned, Darrel placed a bucket under her udder, burrowed his head into her side, and started milking. After a little effort, the *swish, swish* of milk sounded as it hit inside the bucket. Brandon kept his head hidden behind the post, not wanting to alert the boy to his presence.

"Meow, meow." Two small kittens appeared, seemingly out of nowhere, weaving their way around the cow's hooves, heedless of any danger. Darrel lifted his head and chuckled. With a deft twist of his wrist, he squirted a thread of milk at first one kitten and then the other. The animals jerked as the milk hit them but settled down immediately to lick their paws. Within seconds, they were meowing for more.

The bucket was nearly full when Brandon became aware of someone moving toward him. He turned to see Mercedes, still in her yellow dress. On her feet she wore white tennis shoes, her ankles bare. Her face was flushed with anger.

"What are you doing here?" she hissed.

His gaze swung back to Darrel. "He seems so small compared to that cow. One step, and he'd be squashed. But he has no fear. Or maybe he doesn't know what might happen."

"Nonsense. Darrel knows how to take care of himself. Besides, he and that cow grew up together. She'd sooner hurt one of her own calves than do anything to him. I asked what you were doing here."

"I don't know. I needed to see him with the cow. I couldn't imagine it." He was whispering, but now his voice dropped further. "I've missed out on so much." Their eyes met, his begging her to understand.

Mercedes relaxed, the anger noticeably seeping away. Passing him, she put her bare arm on top of the stall gate in plain view of Darrel if he were to look their way. Brandon felt a strong and inappropriate desire to run his hand along her arm.

"Look," she said.

Brandon glanced back into the stall and saw that Darrel had placed the milk some distance away from the cow and was now rubbing her neck. The animal turned her head lazily in his direction, and for a moment he stood between the big head and body in a sort of hug. He buried his face in her neck.

"Good girl," he murmured. "You're a good cow."

"Reminds me of my brother," Mercedes said. "He was the same way with this cow's grandmother."

Brandon's eyes fell again on her arm, a few short inches away from his own hand that now tightly gripped the wood. Might as well be a mile apart. Following his gaze, she dropped her arm to her side and stepped away, a clear message.

"I'd better go," he said. "I'm sorry for intruding. It won't happen again." It was a promise he didn't know if he could keep.

Mercedes nodded, her expression unreadable—she who used to be so open with him. Her black eyes glinted in the dim light. "Good night."

He turned and left the barn.

CHAPTER

6

Diary of Mercedes Walker
July 1, 1994

    I hate having Daddy back. That's the truth. I hate the way he orders me around when I visit. I hate how he treats me like a backward child. But as I've said before, he is my father. There is duty in that even if I don't want to accept it. Unlike Austin, I can't seem to get completely away. At least Daddy isn't often drunk. Wayne won't give him the money, and the farm funds are going through Grandmother. She is still not talking to my father, and she never goes to the farm. I can't blame her. I wouldn't go if I didn't feel I had to. On top of everything, Grandmother's been ill. I've finally convinced her to go to Arizona to stay with her sister. A change of scenery should do her good. I'd rather do without her for a time than lose her altogether.

    Brandon is sweet to go with me to the farm. I think he might be hoping for a repeat of our romantic swimming day, but I'm too nervous that Wayne will find us there again. Silly, I know, but it made me feel weird. Next time we go, I'm going to make sure we take friends.

Mercedes breathed a sigh of relief as Brandon's car disappeared down the road. She'd followed him out to the front to make sure he'd really gone this time. Why had he stayed? Obviously, he'd felt compelled. Was it in the same way she felt compelled to check on the boys each night? She didn't like to think of him like that, to assign him any emotion. He had no right to be there.

Yet Darrel is his son.

She'd seen the longing in Brandon's eyes when he looked at Darrel, and it frightened her.

The almost forgotten pain gripped her chest, squeezing nearly past endurance. At first her younger self hadn't believed he wasn't coming back. She'd had enough sadness in her past, too much to anticipate any more. Brandon was her future. He loved her. Or so she'd thought at the time. In the end he'd been like every other guy she'd met—except for Wayne, who now had to endure this heartache with her.

I'm sorry, Wayne. She gazed toward the fields where he'd disappeared, imagined him checking the cattle to make sure the new calves were coming along. They represented a way to continue the farm, the cash from selling them promising to help pay the farm expenses. She couldn't remember a time in her life when they hadn't struggled to make ends meet, first with her parents and now with Wayne. It was part of farming. Her grandmother had offered Mercedes and her brother the farm shortly after Mercedes had given birth to Darrel, but it had only become entirely official at her death two years ago.

Austin had immediately signed the deed to the farm over

to Mercedes. He knew he'd always have a place here, but the title was meant for her and Wayne. Their children alone would inherit.

Joseph or Scott. Not Darrel. His craving for knowledge of the outside world had told her he would not always stay on the farm.

What might he become?

She felt a longing to jump on Windwalker and ride out after Wayne, to let him reassure her that everything would be all right. To feel the wind rushing through her hair and cooling her heated body. But she had the milk to take care of and the boys to get ready for bed. She would have to wait for him here.

Slowly she went back into the kitchen where Darrel had placed the milk bucket on the counter. "You want me to strain it, Momma?"

She shook her head. "Call the boys and wash up. Your daddy will be here in a while." *Your daddy.* How ironic those words were.

If she could take it all back, if she could make Darrel Wayne's son, she would. In a heartbeat. Yet if it hadn't been for Darrel, would she have married Wayne and had the other children? Regret might have lodged in her heart for how she had come to this place in her life, but she could never regret the lives of her children. Or her time with Wayne, though she wished she could love him more.

Stemming the panic bubbling inside her, Mercedes settled to work straining the milk. Many people now thought it unsanitary to drink milk fresh from a cow, with no preservatives or pasteurization, but to her there was nothing as natural and delicious. Each morning after it had sat in the refrigerator overnight, the cream would be at the top, and she'd mix it back in so the boys would get the full advantage of the nutrients. Of course she strained the milk for stray bits of straw or dust, and Darrel was careful not to let anything fall into it. On days when she planned to make whipped cream for dessert, she'd skim off some of the cream and save it to sweeten later with powdered sugar. The boys would live off whipped cream if she let them, and Mercedes felt satisfaction at passing down to her children one of the few traditions that her mother had passed to her.

She put the milk into the refrigerator. The gallon saved last night for her neighbor and another from that morning were still there, reminding her that Geraldine hadn't yet come for them. What could that mean? Geraldine was expecting again, her eleventh child, but she wasn't due for weeks. Maybe she'd gone to visit her mother, as she did sometimes. Mercedes thought she recalled her mentioning such a thing on Sunday, but so much had happened since she saw Brandon in Safeway three days ago that she could be mistaken. If Geraldine had gone, her husband would likely remember to send someone for the milk this evening.

"Momma, I'm hungry," Joseph said as the boys burst into the kitchen. The younger two were dirty and needed a bath.

"Of course you are," she said, laughing, "because we only just ate. There are leftovers in the fridge." Then, already knowing what he'd ask next, she added, "But you can't have more ice cream."

"Mom, do you think it's really possible to travel faster than light?" Darrel picked up a book he'd been reading earlier at the table. Something with a cover that looked like science fiction. Mercedes smiled weakly. Brandon had loved science fiction too.

"Probably. But I don't know when people will discover it. Maybe you will."

He considered her proposal seriously. "Maybe I could do that after I develop molecular nanotechnology."

Sure, all in a summer's work. Or maybe a year, tops, Mercedes thought with a smile. The sheer power of youth was beautiful. She remembered what it was like to have such dreams. She'd once dreamed of saving lives, especially of women like her mother who were abused and thrown away. A mere session or two with her and the women would see the light and change their lives. Now Mercedes knew different. Her mother had been an educated woman, but she had a destructive element within her that would have taken years of help. Years that had not been available to her.

Mercedes entered the house, but she wasn't greeted with the aroma of cooking food. "Momma? I'm home." She'd stayed the night with a friend in town so they could cut each other's hair and then go out for a movie. Her mother had been having one of her better days yesterday and was content to let her go. "You have a good time," she'd said. "I'll be fine."

Usually this late in the morning, Momma should have been in the kitchen whipping up a hot lunch for Wayne.

The house was quiet. Too quiet. "Momma?"

Could she be out in the fields with Wayne? She didn't often help, but with Father gone, he sometimes needed a hand. Her mother didn't love the farm, but she knew the jobs as well as anyone.

Mercedes entered the kitchen. Everything was in place, except a single cup and saucer in the sink. That was odd. There should have been either no dirty dishes or many left from breakfast.

Mercedes' heart thumped loudly in her chest. "Momma, are you here? Are you sick?"

A sense of foreboding made Mercedes' feet slow as she walked down the hallway to her parents' bedroom, the room her mother had been sleeping in alone in the months since her father had

disappeared. She stopped at the closed door, unwilling to open it.
"Momma?"

Her hand touched the door, and it fell open under the pressure. Her mother was lying in the big bed, a sheet covering her body. Mercedes rushed to the bed. "Momma, you are sick! Why didn't you call? I would have come home earlier."

Momma didn't move. She lay more peacefully than Mercedes had ever seen her. "Momma!"

No answer. And no breath lifted her chest.

Mercedes finally understood that there would never be an answer. The empty bottle of sleeping pills sat upright on the dresser, with even the lid replaced. Everything in order.

Mercedes sat on the bed and took her mother's hand, pulling on it slightly, like a child unwilling to believe. "Momma," she whimpered. Then she crumpled on the bed, sobbing into her mother's neck as she had never done when her mother was alive.

Her body was cold. So cold.

How much time passed until Wayne found her there, Mercedes never knew. She ran the few steps to the door and fell into his arms. "She's dead. I can't believe it. She's dead!"

Wayne held her tightly. "I'm sorry. I'm so sorry." He held her, smoothed her hair until her tears lessened and finally ceased. "He can't hurt her anymore," he said softly. "Think of that." Mercedes let her head lay on his chest, glad to feel his warmth seep through her. "He's not even here. He's in Texas or wherever. How can he still be hurting her?"

"You know as well as I do. She's been hoping he'll come back. She loved him."

"She gave up, didn't she?" She drew in a shuddering breath. "Why couldn't she love me more than him? Then she wouldn't have hurt so bad."

He lifted her chin and stared into her eyes. "That ain't the way it works. Leastwise not with women like Lucinda. You're not like that, Mercedes. You're strong. Remember that. You will never lose yourself to the point where you feel there's no hope left."

"How do you know? What if I'm just like her?"

"You aren't." He said it with such conviction that she began to believe. "But if you ever need someone to talk to, I'll be here."

"Thank you, Wayne." Mercedes sniffed hard. She would probably have stayed in his arms longer if he hadn't set her firmly away from him.

"We need to call the doctor."

"We'll be the talk of Riverton."

"I don't think so. No one ever needs to know."

And no one but Wayne, Austin, Grandmother, and the doctor ever did. And Daddy, but that wasn't until two years later. After the funeral Mercedes lived in town with her friend because it wasn't appropriate for her to stay alone with Wayne on the farm, and he was needed there more than she was. Besides, in Riverton she could work full time. On weekends she visited her grandmother, but neither of them went to the farm the rest of that year.

The doorbell drew Mercedes' attention from the memories. *Brandon,* she thought.

No, it was probably Geraldine or one of her children. Sure enough, a pimply teen was waiting at the door. Geraldine's middle son, Jimmy.

"Oh, good," Mercedes said. "I was wondering when you'd come. You must be out of milk."

She looked for the bag of quilt fabric he was scheduled to bring, but there was nothing in his hands. For the first time, she noticed his face appeared anxious. "Is something wrong?"

"No. Least I don't think so." He tossed his head so the

longish blond hair in front fell back from his eyes. "But we was up at my grandma's today helping with the planting, and we just got back. Momma's started to have pains."

"Is the midwife there?"

"We called, but Momma says she ain't gonna make it, and my dad's still in the fields."

"I'll go back with you, but first I'll get the milk. It'll only take a second." Mercedes felt the rightness of being there for Geraldine. She'd attended most of Geraldine's births. They lived only four minutes away by car, and Geraldine's labors rarely lasted longer than thirty minutes. No time to get to the hospital. After having her first three babies in a truck on the way to Riverton, Geraldine had taken to having Bridget, a midwife friend, stay at her house for the last week of her pregnancy, usually calling on Mercedes to assist.

"Geraldine's having her baby," Mercedes told the boys in the kitchen. "Joseph and Scott, after you eat, get yourselves a bath and brush your teeth so you're ready when Daddy gets back." Fortunately, at eight and almost ten, they were capable of bathing themselves. "Darrel, you're in charge. If your father gets back before I do, tell him I'm at the Pinkhams', okay?"

"Okay."

"I'll be back to tuck you all in." As she talked, she was loading the Pinkham boy with two gallons of milk. "There's another in here for you as well. Still warm from the cow. You go ahead and put these in your truck and come back for the last one. I'll get my first-aid kit and go on ahead in my own truck so you won't have to drive me home later."

When she arrived at the Pinkham house, she found Geraldine attended by two young daughters, Grace and Camilla, who were twelve and fourteen. Their faces were more excited than nervous. Birth to them was as it is for any farm child, a natural event in life, perhaps even more so for these girls because their mother had ten children already and such short labors. Unlike Mercedes, who had struggled for more than fifteen hours with each of her babies, except for the last, which had only been four.

Given the outcome of that pregnancy, she would gladly have suffered the additional eleven hours if it would have helped her child survive.

"Oh, Mercedes, you made it." Geraldine was lying on her side on the large bed, her forehead glistening with sweat and her white-streaked blond hair lank and flat against her head. "Looks like this baby won't wait another week. Probably all the excitement at my mother's."

"Don't tell me you were driving a tractor," Mercedes teased. Geraldine managed a smile. "Momma and I were quilting, actually. And cooking up a storm. My sister was there. I brought back a lot of new material for you. Three bags."

"I think we'd better look at it later." Mercedes eyed the birthing supplies at the foot of the bed. "Do you have everything we'll need?"

"I think so. We'll have to use an old umbilical clamp, though. I've got a metal one left over from one of the others. The girls are boiling that and some scissors." Geraldine's face crumpled as another pain set in. Camilla held her mother's hand, while the younger sister, Grace, watched, biting her lip and tugging a hand through her tangled blond hair.

"Go check on the clamp, Grace," Mercedes told her. "It has to boil at least five minutes—ten is better. Then get the little kids in bed, okay? Read them a story or something."

"But I want to be in here. Momma said I was old enough this time."

"We'll make sure to call you before the baby comes."

"Jimmy'll be back. Tell him to take care of the kids," Camilla offered. Grace nodded and left the room, looking slightly relieved, despite her plea to stay.

Mercedes scanned the supplies lying on the edge of the bed: linens, towels, pads, a plastic sheet, olive oil to smooth on the skin around the birth canal to prevent tearing. The girls had been thorough in gathering what was needed. As soon as the contraction passed, Mercedes would spread the sheet under Geraldine and have Camilla find a heating pad to warm the baby clothes for the impending arrival. There wasn't much time.

"Now, Geraldine, stop clenching your jaw." Mercedes sat down next to her friend, who was still lying on her side, and began pushing with her thumbs on the pressure points on her back to help cut the pain. "Breathe with me. In, out, in, out. Good. That's the way. Keep it up. Let the pain roll through you. After the contraction, I'll need to see where we are." Mercedes had helped numerous calves, kids, kittens, and puppies into the world, but none of those were quite like a human baby, and human mothers needed much more care. Over the years, Geraldine's midwife had been generous with her knowledge, even requesting Mercedes' presence at other births, and Mercedes felt confident she could help Geraldine alone.

As if they had a choice.

The contraction subsided, and Geraldine turned on her back, sighing with exhaustion. "It gets harder when you're old, like me."

Mercedes grinned, pulling on a disposable glove from her first-aid kit. "Doesn't everything? But at least you'll have a sweet little baby here when it's all over." She shifted her position to better check Geraldine. "Sure enough, you're all dilated. Whew, that was fast! But your water hasn't broken."

"Remember that time when the baby came out in the sack?" Geraldine asked.

Mercedes remembered all too well how the baby had come so fast that the midwife barely had time to catch the infant as it slipped into the world, how she had frantically ripped the sack so the baby could take his first breath. Mercedes remembered staring with a sort of horrified fascination and then felt the tears of relief on her cheeks as the baby choked and began to cry. That had been her second experience at a home birth.

"I'd rather not repeat that," Mercedes said. "I know how to break the water. We need to get this sheet on first."

Geraldine shifted her weight. "Let's wait a bit to break the water. Maybe Jacob will be back in time. I sent Hyrum to the field to get him."

"He probably went to the wrong field," Camilla said.

"He's only nine," Geraldine reminded her daughter. "It may take a while, but he'll find him."

Mercedes hurriedly finished smoothing out the plastic sheet on one side of the bed, covering it with a white cloth sheet for comfort. "Here. Roll over on this side, and let me finish." She topped the sheets with several towels before letting Geraldine roll back to the middle. It was all they had available to soak up the impending fluids.

"Ohhhh," Geraldine groaned.

The pains had returned, only a minute apart. "I think we need to break the sack," Mercedes said.

"Next contraction, then," Geraldine panted. Breaking the water sack was easier and safer during a contraction when the bag usually bulged, especially when Mercedes wasn't as experienced as she'd like to be.

Mercedes felt a fleeting desire for the hospital and the constant monitoring that showed the baby's heartbeat, but

Geraldine wouldn't make it five miles down the road, much less an hour's travel. Besides, Mercedes knew Geraldine likely wouldn't go even if she could make it. Giving birth for her had become as natural as for the cows in the field.

"Let me know when you have the urge to push." Once the baby was in the right position, the transition would come and Geraldine wouldn't be able to hold back. "I hope Jacob hurries, or he's going to miss this one."

"He'll be here." Geraldine lay back. Her face was drawn but flushed and pretty. Crow's feet gathered around her eyes, and there were deep grooves at her mouth. She looked older than the forty-five she was, but her life was full and rewarding. Eleven children would keep her happy in her aging years.

Mercedes wished she had a stethoscope to check the baby's heartbeat. If only Jimmy had come when Brandon was still at the farm. He would have had his doctor's bag, full of sterilized equipment and emergency supplies, and surely he'd assisted with at least a few deliveries before specializing in heart surgery.

But even if she had a stethoscope, what would she do if she learned the baby was under stress? It wasn't as if she could do anything to help the child. Anything but what she was doing now.

Geraldine began another contraction, so Mercedes pierced the water bag with a curved quilting needle, hastily sterilized in alcohol. The needle did the trick and soon they were changing the towels. Then she propped pillows up behind Geraldine to raise her until she was half sitting, half lying.

Another contraction, and Geraldine began keening, a high-pitched cry that made Mercedes reach around her to dig into her pressure points.

"It's not helping." Geraldine pushed her hands away, and Mercedes knew it was almost time.

"Go get your sister," Mercedes ordered Camilla.

"I need to push," panted Geraldine.

"I know."

Geraldine took a deep breath and pushed as she held it. The baby's head began its descent.

"Good one," Mercedes said, checking the position of the baby. "Another one or two like that, and it'll all be over." She squirted olive oil onto the new glove she was wearing and began rubbing it in.

The girls entered the room, followed by their father, who was out of breath and still in his dirty overalls. Only his hands looked clean.

"Jacob!" Geraldine shut her eyes momentarily. "Thank you, God."

Jacob hurried to the bed where he sat next to his wife. "Is everything going well?"

"Perfect." Mercedes said. "Your child is almost here. During the next contraction, you'll be able to see the top of the baby's head. Maybe."

The next contraction came quickly, and Geraldine pushed with apparent great effort.

"Not so fast," Mercedes cautioned. Too fast often meant ripping tissues, and Mercedes had stitched up a lot of animals but never a human.

"I can't stop," grunted Geraldine.

"Head's coming." Mercedes pushed gently against the top of the baby's head so it would emerge more slowly. "There, the head's out. Checking for a cord." This part was much like with her animals. The plump, ropy cord was around the neck, but Mercedes deftly hooked it with her finger and pulled it over the baby's head. "All clear. Push whenever you want. Or with the next contraction."

"Oh, my goodness," Grace squealed, bouncing on her feet by the bed. "It's a baby. A real baby!"

"Of course, it is," Camilla said, laughing.

Geraldine gave another push and the baby's face rotated upward as the torso slipped out and onto the bed, guided by Mercedes' hands.

"A girl," she announced, wiping the baby's face with a large square of gauze. "I need a—" Before she could finish, Camilla handed her a bulb syringe.

"It's boiled," Camilla said. "We didn't have a new one."

"That's fine."

Mercedes cleaned out the baby's nose and mouth. Still no breath. Her little face was quickly going from ashen to a bluish tinge. Mercedes' chest tightened with the beginnings of panic. *No!* she thought. *Please, no!* She rubbed the baby's chest, toes, held her upside down, all the while talking to her encouragingly. "Come on, sweetie, breathe. Come on. We're all waiting. Take a breath. You can do it."

Nothing.

"Why ain't she breathing?" Jacob stared, terror frozen on his face. Everyone stared at Mercedes anxiously.

Geraldine gave a broken sob. "Help her. Please. Dear God, help her!"

"She's still getting some oxygen through the cord," Mercedes said, though by the bluish tinge, she could tell it wasn't much. The placenta must already be pulling away from the uterine wall. She had to act. The next few minutes would be critical.

She tilted the baby's head slightly. *Not as far back as an adult,* she reminded herself. Babies' airways were small, and tilting too far back would only make it worse—that's what they had told her with Lucy. The tongue didn't seem to be in the way. What was wrong?

"Is she dying?" Grace backed up against the wall, a hand across her mouth. "Momma? Will she be okay? Momma?"

Geraldine didn't answer, her anxious eyes fixed on her newborn.

"They just take time, that's all." Camilla put her arms around her sister.

"What do we do?" Jacob knelt beside Mercedes, his big callused hands trembling.

Mercedes had no time to respond. She placed her mouth over the mouth and nose of the newborn. Was that the right way? She couldn't remember for sure. She blew a tiny puff of air into the baby's lungs, using only the air in her mouth. The chest filled. She lifted her head, allowing the baby to exhale on her own. But she didn't take a new breath. Mercedes gave her another short puff of air. She felt desperate to do anything to prevent Geraldine from knowing the pain she herself had known all too intimately. The midwife would have had oxygen, but Mercedes had no such equipment. Though it wasn't normally needed, today it might mean life.

Still no breath.

"We should call the ambulance," she said.

"I will." Camilla ran from the room, dragging Grace with her, but Mercedes knew, as did Jacob and Geraldine, that the ambulance would arrive far too late.

"Her heart?" asked Geraldine. Tears streamed down her face and her fingers grasped at one of her baby's limp hands.

The heart, that strong but amazingly fragile organ. Mercedes placed two fingers on the inside of the baby's upper arm, checked the pulse at the brachial artery. *One, two, three, four, five,* she counted. No pulse. She would have to do chest compressions. This she was more familiar with, the memories rushing back to guide her actions. Two middle fingers on the baby's chest, one-half inch compressions. Five times, then a breath. Repeat. Again.

Come on, baby! Tears streamed down Mercedes' face, falling onto the newborn's velvety skin. Inside Mercedes was shaking and sobbing, but her hands on the baby were sure and deliberate. She'd worked similarly on calves—rubbing them, talking to them, encouraging them to breathe. But this was far different.

Where was the midwife? Shouldn't she have arrived by now? Surely Mercedes had been doing this for hours. Should she tell the girls to get ice water? She'd heard sometimes it worked to put the baby in cold water for a few seconds when all else was lost. Or maybe Mercedes should try spanking the infant, a concept she'd always vehemently opposed.

What was wrong with the child? Maybe she wasn't merely a week or two early, though her size seemed about right. Possibly her lungs weren't yet developed enough to work on their own. But why would her heart stop beating? Because of her breathing problems? Mercedes wished she knew more.

"Please, Lord," sobbed Geraldine. Jacob reached one hand out to his wife to comfort her, his own expression one of agonized disbelief.

Mercedes checked the brachial artery again. This time there was a faint pulse. "Her heart is beating," she said, leaning down to give the baby another puff of air. Three seconds and then another breath. Pulse still there, though faint. "Come on," she murmured.

The infant gave a little gasp and began to cry weakly. Immediately her color turned from blue ash to pink and then red as she balled her fists and began crying with more effort.

Mercedes picked her up and held her close to her chest. "That's it," she said, her voice scarcely a whisper. "I knew you could do it."

"Thank God. Oh, thank you, God!" Geraldine wept tears of relief as her husband held her, his own face slick with tears.

A part of Mercedes didn't want to let the baby go, wanted to hold her and nurse her and see her grow up, to watch her running through the fields with the boys. But this was Geraldine's baby, and Mercedes had long ago come to terms with the fact that she wouldn't have another child, much less a little girl to restore what had been lost. She had her boys, and that was enough. She no longer lived in the days when knowing she wouldn't have another little girl had brought her nothing but despair.

Brandon's face shimmered in her mind. Was that how he felt? Despair at never having a child. If so, he wouldn't give Darrel up.

I wouldn't if I were him.

Trembling now for another reason altogether, Mercedes placed the infant in Geraldine's waiting arms. Then she collapsed on the floor near the wall, grateful for the support against her back. She felt weak, as though she couldn't possibly move ever again. The clock on the nightstand told her she'd been in the house less than twenty-seven minutes. So little time for such a big miracle. She let her head fall into her hands and sobbed silently in relief. Camilla and Grace had returned, and the family talked together softly, jubilantly, over the newborn.

After a few minutes, Camilla said, "Uh, there's a lot of blood. Too much, I think."

Camilla had been at other births and probably knew enough to judge, so Mercedes forced herself to check on Geraldine. "I think you're hemorrhaging, but not a lot. Let's get the placenta out. Try to nurse the baby. That will help." Mercedes tugged the cord a bit to see if the placenta had torn all the way free.

"I feel a contraction," Geraldine said.

Mercedes continued to keep the cord taut as the placenta was delivered. But the blood didn't stop as it should have. "Well, at least the ambulance is on its way."

"I told the ambulance we didn't need them after all." Camilla's face was abruptly devoid of color.

Mercedes hadn't noticed her leaving the room again. "Well, it looks like more than it is, I think," Mercedes reassured her. "A little blood goes a long way. Keep nursing, Geraldine. Jacob, massage her stomach here. You should feel the uterus shrinking. If it doesn't, we'll have to take you to the hospital right away." Mercedes tried not to think about the hour and five minutes it would take to arrive there.

"I feel fine." Geraldine stared down into her baby's face with so much love that Mercedes had to look away. She knew that feeling, and it was so private and deep that it couldn't be shared with anyone, not to any meaningful extent.

"Wait! Is that the door?" Camilla ran out of the room and came back seconds later with the plump, gray-haired midwife in tow.

"Bridget!" Mercedes said, relief flowing through her. "Glad you're here. We can use a hand."

"Got here as fast as I could." The older woman took in the situation at a glance and immediately went to work, mixing an herbal tincture in juice for Geraldine to drink. Then Bridget placed cloths soaked in ice water on Geraldine's lower stomach. With Jacob's help, she elevated the foot of the bed by shoving numerous pillows and blankets underneath the mattress.

"Put pressure here," Bridget told Jacob, placing several sanitary pads on Geraldine's perineum. "I'll massage the pressure points on her feet. Camilla, go see if that tea I had you put on is ready. Shepherd's purse has a lot of Vitamin K, which is good for this sort of thing."

The worrisome blood flow eased under Bridget's competent care. Now turning her attention to the baby, Bridget checked every inch of the small body, pulling out a stethoscope to listen to her heart and lungs before pronouncing her completely healthy.

Mercedes knew her job was over and that the midwife would stay as long as she was needed. Less than two hours had passed since she'd left the boys at home. They would be finished reading now and in bed. Unless they'd convinced Wayne to read more.

"I'd better get back home," she said to Geraldine. "I'll come check on you tomorrow. I'll bring dinner." She'd also spread the word among the neighbors so the family would have meals brought in for the next week.

Geraldine grasped her hand. "Thank you. Without you . . ." She trailed off.

"You'd do the same for me." Mercedes smiled sadly. "You rest up, okay?"

Mercedes started shaking again in the truck and had to sit there for a few minutes in the darkness before she could drive. So easily things could have gone wrong. But nature had a way of continuing on, and in reality, this birth was easy compared to many. Compared to those of her own children, in fact. She had simply been in the right place at the right time to help her friend.

Wayne met her at the front door. A quirk of his eyebrow showed he was interested in the outcome.

"A girl," she said to his unasked question. "She wasn't

breathing. I had to do CPR. I don't know what would have happened if I hadn't known how. If I hadn't learned with Lucy."

He held her then, and Mercedes drank in his warmth, the smell of the fields and the horse that clung to his clothing. But she didn't let herself fall apart again. Better to let the numbness take over.

"I think it was the shock, being born so fast. Or maybe there was something in her lungs."

"But she's okay?"

"Yes." Mercedes made a face. "If Geraldine has any more, I'm going to urge her to rent a place in town near the hospital, just in case."

"Good idea. But maybe this is the last one."

"Probably." Eleven children. Mercedes would have liked to have even half of that. A daughter to teach how to cook, another son in the fields.

They went down the hall holding hands in silence. Mercedes stopped to check on the boys and found the younger ones already asleep in their shared room. But Darrel, who had his own room, was still awake reading a book with a flashlight that he clicked off when she came through the door.

"Give it to me," she said, stifling a smile. He reluctantly handed it over, and she placed it out of reach on his dresser. Unlike the younger boys, he'd put away the clothes he'd worn that day, and his belongings were neatly stored. There was an order here that was comfortable to her. This he'd gotten from her—or perhaps from Brandon. Wayne had a tendency to let his clothes lie where they dropped and to misplace his belongings.

"You have to milk early tomorrow," she reminded her son.

"I know. What did she have, a girl or a boy?" "A girl. A pretty little girl."

"Like Lucy?"

"Yes. Like Lucy." She leaned over and kissed his cheek, her heart full enough with him that she didn't feel any other longing. "Good night, honey." She stood to go.

"Momma, I liked your friend. He seemed pretty nice. Kind of like Uncle Austin."

What should she say to that? "I hoped you'd hate him" or "Good, because he's your father," or "I hope we never see him again." Or even, "Don't trust him. He's good at breaking hearts."

No, none of these were appropriate, and Mercedes, after seeing the miracle of birth and the fragile nature of life, couldn't seem to continue the hatred she'd been feeding in her heart. She understood why Brandon wanted Darrel.

"That's good," she said. At the door, Wayne was watching them. Mercedes held out her hand as she walked toward him.

In their room down the hall, Mercedes sat on the bed with a soft sigh. Wayne helped her off with the sweater she'd thrown over her yellow dress, which she now saw was spattered with blood. A good soak in cold water would likely remove the stains if she did it tonight.

"What are we going to do?" she asked. "He's not going away. I know him."

Wayne sat next to her, his big hands resting on his knees. "The way I see it, we have two options. We can forbid him to see Darrel and be prepared to fight legally, which we could probably draw out for months or a year or more."

Mercedes had gone over that option in her mind, but each time she knew it would lead to a court battle. That didn't seem the way to protect her son, especially because tests would show Brandon had at least some claim on him. "Or?"

"Or we let him get to know Darrel—and us in the process.

We show him that leaving Darrel's life intact now is a step toward building a future with him later."

"I don't know if he'll be willing to settle for that." She spoke slowly, sluggishly, as her eyes wandered over the familiar room. The double dresser and huge mirror, the queen-sized bed that was barely big enough for them because of Wayne's bulk, the chair she'd rocked her babies in, draped with Wayne's pajamas from this morning. Above the chair, the three pictures of lilies that she'd bought on a trip to Nevada to visit Austin. And lastly, the small closet which held their few clothes. Simple things for simple folk. Likely Brandon would consider it impoverished.

"What if this life isn't good for Darrel?" She felt a pain in her chest similar to the one she'd felt when Geraldine's baby had refused to breathe.

"What better place could there be? Growing up here won't limit him. Look at Austin. It's just a matter of making sure he has the right opportunities."

Wayne was right. If nothing else, *she* was best for her son.

She couldn't let Brandon's appearance and the memories of the past confuse her. She'd loved Brandon—loved him too much. Perhaps she still loved him in some way. Regardless, she couldn't allow that to interfere with Darrel's here and now.

"I'm going to move the herd on Saturday," Wayne said. "If he asks to see Darrel again, send him along. In fact, he's welcome to help with the planting after school as well."

"He's still lecturing this week, I think." She sighed. "Seems unlikely he'll leave even after the seminar is over. But he'll have to, right?" For all they knew he might have months of vacation saved up.

"If he wants to see Darrel, it'll be on our terms." Wayne stood, pulled off his shirt, and reached for his pajamas.

"I can't lose Darrel."

"I know. I know." He took her in his arms and kissed her.

Passion flared in Mercedes breast, pushing out the tiredness. She arched toward her husband, returning his kiss. Each nerve in her body came alert, humming with anticipation. She took the pajamas from his hand, tossing them back onto the rocking chair, then broke away, turning so he could unzip her dress. He kissed her neck as it dropped to the ground and for once she left it there.

She sighed as his strong, callused hands ran down her body. He knew how to love her, this man of hers. He knew all her secret places, her greatest pleasures. She turned to him again, her mouth seeking his. Their bodies fit together perfectly, their passion honed with years of experience and familiarity. Still kissing her, he eased her back onto the bed. For long, blissful moments, Mercedes forgot her worries in the joy of loving her husband.

Later, she lay in Wayne's arms until he was asleep. Usually she tried to fall asleep first or his snoring would keep her awake, but tonight sleep failed her. Gently, she wriggled out of his grasp and slid from the bed. Guided by the light of the moon filtering through the sheer curtains she had made last year to match their new quilt, she padded on bare feet to the closet and pulled down the box she'd been looking at earlier. She ran her fingers over the different fabrics of the unfinished queen-sized quilt. Maybe it was time to finish what had been meant to be Brandon's gift. Maybe if she did, she'd understand why she'd kept it all these years.

Her hand rested for a fleeting moment on the baby quilt, so dark and filled with despair, a vessel for her heartache. Somehow, with Brandon's return, the emotions had escaped. It was up to her to find a way to trap the pain inside the squares forever.

CHAPTER 7

Diary of Mercedes Walker
July 23, 1994

I went out to the farm again yesterday with Brandon. He is so kind to go with me. I know he hates visiting my father as much as I do. Wayne was in the fields, but I could tell he'd been taking care of Daddy. He'd bought groceries and apparently washed dishes. Daddy was in bed, the bed he shared with Momma, the bed where she died. I wonder if he ever thinks about it as he lies there, too sick with the consequences of his life to be of use to anyone, even himself. Austin and I blame him for her suicide, though my studies have taught me that maybe we will never know all the issues. How desperate she must have been to swallow those pills! Sometimes I find I'm still angry that she could have been so selfish.

I have to realize that Wayne won't be at the farm much longer. He's a good-looking, kind man, and I know most of the single women around here are in love with him. I suppose he'll settle down soon enough. It should be sooner, though, since he's already nearing forty, if my calculations are correct. I will miss him.

*T*he annoying ring of his mobile phone forced Brandon to consciousness. *Bling, bling! Bling, bling!* He cursed whatever mad impulse had possessed him to download the same ring tone used on the hit television series *24*. Too often, instead of waking right away, he began dreaming of someone shooting at him.

He rolled over and grabbed the phone from the bedside table. He squinted at the number but couldn't make his eyes focus in the bright morning light streaming through the white curtains.

"Hello?" His voice was thick with sleep.

"Hi, Brandon," said a female voice. "It's me. Sorry to wake you." Then as though realizing there might be another "me" in his life, she added, "It's Hannah."

Hannah. Of course. Hannah was the only one who would recognize his sleepy voice. *Mercedes might,* came a thought, but he dismissed that. Mercedes didn't know him at all anymore, and he shouldn't assume she did.

"Hannah." Why had his ex-wife called? They had kept in touch in the two years since the divorce, but she couldn't know he was in Wyoming. They hadn't talked in several months.

"I hoped to get you before you left for the hospital. I wanted to see how you were doing."

"I'm fine. You?"

"I meant the checkup. Did it go okay?

The concern in her voice and the fact that she'd remembered touched him. "It was fine. No cancer."

"Thank heaven!"

"Well, I'm not considered in the clear until five years."

"Yeah, but every year means more of a chance."

Brandon didn't see it that way, but he didn't want to ruin her hope. Hannah was one of the few people who was genuinely interested in his welfare. Oh, his friends at the hospital cared, but not in a way that would change their lives if he died.

Darrel would care, he thought. *If he knew.* Or would he? Perhaps his death would be such a relief for Mercedes that Darrel would be grateful for it.

I'm not going to die.

If he said it enough, maybe he'd believe it was true. Hannah was saying something about a mutual friend—or rather, a woman who had been his friend before the divorce but remained close only to Hannah afterward. That was the way of divorce. Divide the friends along with the furniture. Hannah had gotten most of both. Her voice rolled on, comfortingly, stirring up all kinds of emotions. Happy and sad memories. Melancholy leaked through the phone and into his heart.

"I'm sorry," he said during a lull in her narrative. "I want you to know that. You didn't deserve the way I acted. I had a hard time dealing with it all, and I know I took it out on you."

She was silent a long moment. "You did treat me badly, but I understood what you were going through. It was the other I couldn't deal with."

The "other" was her insistence that he held a part of himself back from her. Which was ridiculous. He loved her and shared more with her than with anyone. Well, except for Mercedes.

Except for Mercedes. Where did that come from?

"You were probably right about that too. I'm sorry. I really wish . . ." He couldn't finish the thought because what he wished—that he'd never left Wyoming—would only hurt her.

"Brandon, what's happened? Are you sure your tests were negative?"

He swallowed hard, wondering how much to tell her. She'd never craved children the way some women did, but they'd talked about having a child of their own one day. "Hannah, I found out I have a son."

"A son?" her voice rose an octave.

He lay back on the bed, pushing the pillow under his head. "He's twelve. He lives in Wyoming—that's where I am at the moment, by the way. I'm speaking at a seminar here this week. I dated his mother before I went back to Boston."

Boston was where he'd first met Hannah, though at the time he'd been dating a woman his parents had lined up for him. They'd wanted him to marry her, a daughter of their friends, and for a time after he'd learned about Mercedes' marriage, he'd entertained thoughts of going through with it. Eventually he'd broken it off—and not to spite his parents, as they insisted. He and the woman simply weren't right for each other.

Even before Mercedes had married Wayne, he'd begun wishing he'd never left Wyoming or at least had taken Mercedes with him. Who cared that his intended father-in-law had helped him get his high-paying job at the local hospital? He realized too late that no job was worth what he'd given up. He hadn't planned on the chance of never seeing Mercedes again.

Fool, he thought.

"A son," Hannah breathed. Did the knowledge hurt her? If so, he was sorry.

"I know. Blew me away when I found out. After the cancer, I thought I'd never be a father."

"There's always adoption."

"Yes." He forced a laugh. "But not for a single man."

"You might marry again."

"I don't know, Hannah. I might be too used up." He felt sorry for himself.

"That's up to you," she said without sympathy. A pause and then, "So is she the one?"

The one. The one Hannah had imagined standing between them. Well, if there was anyone, it would have been Mercedes.

"Yes."

"Is she single?"

Brandon couldn't tell if there was jealousy in her voice. Surely not. He couldn't expect her to still care about him in such a way. "She's married. Has two other children."

"So what now?"

"I don't know. She's not happy to see me."

"I imagine not."

Was that disapproval in her voice? "I have a son, Hannah. I can't just walk away."

"You can't appear after this long and expect to take him home, either, Brandon. Think of the boy."

"He's smart. He doesn't belong on a farm. He belongs in a good school, researching, discovering things."

"You mean being a doctor."

"Maybe. I don't know. But not planting wheat. He's more than that."

"Only if that's what he wants."

"I want to be a part of his life."

"Does he know?"

"Not yet."

"I'd like to meet him," Hannah said.

That was unexpected. "I'm sure you will, once it's all settled."

"Let me know if you need anything." A pause. "Well, I guess I'd better run. Take care of yourself."

Suddenly he didn't want her to hang up. He wanted to tell her about Darrel, about how he looked and what he said. He wanted to share Darrel with someone who didn't judge him for wanting a relationship with his son.

"Do you have to hang up now?" She had transferred to the administrative offices of the school district and likely had a backlog of business awaiting her attention.

"Not really. I have time."

So he told her about Darrel, about the farm, and the dinner. About Darrel milking the cow. "That cow was huge," he said. "Huge. I thought it would squash him. But he cuddled up to it like it was a kitten."

"Sounds like a good life."

"He needs more opportunities."

"I'm sure that will happen. At least now with you in the picture."

He felt good at the comment. Hannah seemed to understand he couldn't walk away from his responsibility—that he didn't want to walk away. Not anymore.

His eyes rested on his watch, uncomprehending, for a few minutes. "Oh, no. Hannah, I've got to go. I'm going to be late for my presentation."

"Call me later then." She sounded amused. "For what it's worth, I'm glad you found your son. I hope he gives you enough reason to keep fighting."

For his life, she meant.

"Thank you."

Before he hung up the phone, he thought he heard her say, "I love you." But no, that was an echo from the past, from the time when she had said those words every time they'd talked on the phone.

"I'm sorry, Hannah," he whispered to the empty room. "I

wish I'd never hurt you." It seemed he was saying that a lot
these days.

For most of Wednesday, Thursday, and Friday, Brandon was
stuck in meetings, presentations, and business dinners. Every
spare moment he was thinking about Darrel and Mercedes. In
fact, people began asking him if he was all right. He responded
to their queries as best he could, but his thoughts were definitely affecting his work. Fortunately, after Saturday morning's
closing remarks, he'd be free. He planned to stay at least another
week in Wyoming but could extend that another two if needed.
Several times he drove by a local grade school, but he had no
way of knowing if Darrel was there. He didn't catch sight of the
boy but imagined him playing with the others.

He was tempted to call Mercedes and ask for another visit,
but he was reluctant to face her. He'd hurt her so much. But
he was a changed man now. Didn't that count for something?
Should he be required to pay for his past choices for the rest of
his life?

On Saturday morning, he could no longer bear the waiting.
He ditched the last day seminar, begging one of the other
doctors to fill in for him. His son would be at the farm and
not in school. He might be able to see him. Or at the very least
make plans with Mercedes to visit on another day.

The hour ride out to the farm went faster than expected.
Brandon's heart beat hard in his chest. *Typical flight-or-fight
reaction,* he told himself. His heart pumped all the more.

He found Mercedes in the barn, emerging from the door
leading to the chicken coop, a basket of eggs in her hands. She
froze when she saw him, as if she'd been holding her breath all
week, wondering what he planned next.

"Hi," he said, marveling at how this woman version of the girl he knew was so familiar to him now. She was wearing old jeans again and an oversized blue shirt that might have been one of Wayne's. Her eyes were black as night in the dark barn, holding him in place. A chicken squawked, and from somewhere came the bleating of a goat.

She blinked, and he was free to look away. But he didn't.

"Hi," she said. That's all. No welcome, no casual conversation. The girl he'd known had gone out of her way to make him feel wanted, to make him feel he belonged. Obviously, this woman didn't feel obliged to offer such niceties now.

"I want to see more of him." A statement of fact without challenge.

"You want to see more of him," she repeated without emotion.

He wondered if she was thinking about how thirteen years ago he wouldn't have been pleased to have Darrel interfere with his so-called bright future. Well, he would have been wrong then, but he didn't feel wrong now. Darrel was his flesh and blood—his only flesh and blood. That gave Brandon rights, didn't it?

"Wherever, whenever," he said. "Just a little time until we figure out what to do."

"I knew you wouldn't leave." Her words said she still understood him. But he nearly tore apart when she added, "But then, I thought that once before."

Before he could protest, she shook her head, indicating that he shouldn't answer. "Darrel's helping Wayne move the cattle to the east field today. They're short a hand. You could help them."

"Does Wayne know about this?"

"It was his idea." Still no emotion. He'd seen her speak

this way thirteen years ago whenever she confronted her father or talked about him. Brandon had understood then that her manner had been to protect herself from the abusive Jed Walker, but now it was directed at him.

I don't want to hurt you, Mercedes, he thought. He'd never wanted to hurt her. Yet wasn't that what he was doing now?

"Well?" she asked. One hand rested on the eggs in the basket, reminding him that she was a farm woman, accustomed to hard work and hours in the sun. She should have been old and worn before her time, but she was as beautiful to him as she had been thirteen years ago. Her hair was dark and vibrant, her face, freckled by the sun, showed the peace of a happy life. Dark eyes sparkled with depths he could only begin to imagine. She belonged here. He felt it as he had when he saw her in her garden. The pulse of her being was in sync with the vibrations of the land. But once she'd belonged at the hospital, in his world. Could she again? He knew he had no right to hope, and yet, strangely, he did. He'd left her, but apparently his heart, or at least part of it, had stayed behind.

"Thank you," he managed. "Am I dressed okay?"

Her gaze rested on his jeans and long-sleeved T-shirt, and he felt himself grow warm under her impersonal stare. He could have been a horse or a chicken she was examining for flaws before purchase.

"You're fine," she said finally, "but I'll give you a sweatshirt to put on under your jacket. It's still nippy out in the mornings. You can take it off later if you need to." She could have let him freeze out there, but that wasn't Mercedes' way. She was a nurturer. He'd known this from the beginning. He'd probably taken advantage of the quality in the past.

I've been such a fool. The loss hit him again, so forcefully that he felt dizzy.

"Are you all right?"

He nodded, stifling the urge to reach out to her. "I'm fine."

"I bet you haven't eaten breakfast."

"No."

"Come on. After you eat, we'll saddle the horses, and I'll ride out with you to show you where they are."

Mercedes on a horse? He found the idea unsettling. Of course, it made sense that she'd ride, and he remembered, as though it was a memory belonging to someone else, that they had gone riding together at least once or twice years ago. He'd forgotten until now.

"With nanotechnology, kids would never get sick," Darrel said. "The nanobots in their bodies would fix them before they even showed signs of being sick." The boy had stayed close to Brandon as they drove the cattle along in front of them. Brandon worried that Wayne might become offended, but he seemed to understand Darrel's interest stemmed from natural curiosity, not filial affection. Of course, they'd hired hands before, and Darrel must have treated them the same way. Brandon was simply one more in a long line.

I'm different, Darrel, Brandon longed to say. *I'm your father. Your real father.*

After questioning Brandon about his life as a doctor and briefly about his friendship with his mother—the reason Brandon had given for being asked to help with the cattle—Darrel had begun to talk about nanotechnology, a field that fascinated Brandon, but one he'd never thoroughly researched.

"Medical nanobots would be an incredible leap for medicine," Brandon said. "Nearly instant regeneration."

"Yeah, but not everyone would be happy about it." Darrel

urged his horse to the side to head off a cow from straying. The ease and grace with which he accomplished his task made Brandon inexplicably proud, as though he'd personally had something to do with it.

Darrel reminded Brandon of Mercedes. When she'd ridden up to the fields with him, she had shown the same innate grace as her white horse galloped across the fields.

In seconds the boy returned and took up the conversation as though he'd never left. "I mean, doctors like you need to make money. Why would they want nanotechnology? They'd be out of a job. Like when I jumped off the haystack and broke my arm, if I'd had nanobots in my bloodstream, they'd have fixed it right away. I wouldn't even have had to get a cast."

"Well, it might depend on how broken the arm is. If it was out of place, it'd have to go back in before it could be fixed."

"But people would be really strong, almost like cyborgs, so they probably wouldn't get hurt much."

Brandon thought a moment. He remembered reading about engineering super humans, especially in regard to futuristic soldiers. The idea was both frightening and exciting.

"Okay, think of this," Brandon said. "Someone needs to put all those nanobots in the people, program them and so forth, and invent new ones. Then there would likely be some diseases that even nanocites couldn't cure."

"Well, I guess so. But anyway, I think there will be a lot of people not wanting anything to do with it. They're too afraid of the gray goo."

"Gray goo?" Brandon's horse stepped into a depression, and he was knocked off balance, falling forward over his saddle horn. He struggled to right himself before Darrel noticed. While the child was as at ease in the saddle as he was on his own two feet, Brandon's backside already throbbed with pain.

He suspected it would be worse if Mercedes had chosen a more spirited horse for him to ride.

"Well, this is how it would work," Darrel began. "There would be nanofactories where things would be built. You'd have certain codes or programs that would tell the nanocites what to make. They could be programmed to make anything. *Anything*. Like a space rocket. Only it wouldn't be made of pieces welded together. It would be one piece—seamless. You could make anything. Or even program it to change its shape to whatever you needed."

"Seems rather impossible."

"Yeah, but no one has proven scientifically that it can't work," Darrel said, "so I think that means it will work—eventually."

"And the gray goo?"

"Well, some people think terrorists might be able to use the nanocites as a weapon to create a goo that would be self-replicating and would spread throughout the world using up all the resources."

"And that couldn't happen?"

"Only if someone did it on purpose. That's why the government needs to make rules about nanotechnology now before we really get into it."

"Did you know that nanotech is already used in a lot of stuff?" Brandon asked. "Mostly to make really small things for computers and such."

"Yeah, but the kind I'm really interested in is molecular nanotechnology. That's the kind that could make self-cleaning dishes, or change someone's whole face. Could you imagine that?"

Brandon grinned. Other twelve-year-olds he'd met couldn't even say the words *molecular nanotechnology*, much less understand what they meant. "That might not be all that good. Think of all the movie star look-alikes we'd have around."

"You can say that again." Darrel smiled back at him.

"Isn't there anyone you've ever wanted to look like?"

"No, just myself." Darrel glanced over to where Wayne had galloped after a stray steer. "Well, sometimes I'd like to have really bright red hair like my dad used to have. And I wouldn't mind being tall like you."

"I'm only regular height. About the same as Wayne—your dad." Brandon experienced a sour taste at the words.

"Yeah, I guess. You probably look taller 'cuz you're skinny. Like me."

That much was true. Wayne's muscles had been built up by years of hard physical labor; the only exercise Brandon's body received was what he managed to work in at the gym. Brandon wouldn't stand a chance in an arm wrestle with Wayne.

Did Mercedes like to feel Wayne's strong arms around her? Brandon didn't know where the thought came from, but he pushed it away.

"A lot of guys don't come into their height until sixteen, eighteen, and even twenty," he told Darrel. "And that's me talking as a doctor. I've seen it time and time again. You'll shoot up in a few years. Both your parents are tall."

"Well, it's not fair 'cuz all the girls are taller than us guys. But at least we're stronger." Darrel held up his wiry arms.

"That's because of hormones, you know. So's the growing taller." Brandon launched into an explanation, surprised that Darrel actually listened and asked intelligent questions. He was a good kid, and smart, and again Brandon felt a swell of pride he knew he had no right to feel.

"Hey, Dad's calling us." Darrel turned his horse and galloped toward Wayne, who was motioning for them. Brandon hurried to catch up. His backside was on fire, and they'd only been out here a little over an hour.

"I think this is good," Wayne said. "There's enough new grass here to keep them for a while. But we'll need to fill the water troughs. The stream doesn't pass by these fields," he added for Brandon's benefit.

"I'll do it!" Darrel was off his horse in an instant, running toward two huge troughs that stood by the fence.

Wayne watched him go, an indulgent expression on his face. "He likes operating the well. He helped me dig it a few years back, so it's kind of his baby."

"I don't see a well." Brandon scanned the area. Darrel was kneeling between the two troughs, doing something on the ground.

"It's in the ground there. Rigged up with a pump and hose. The pump's only needed for a bit—the pressure actually brings up the water. Slowly, but it works." They fell quiet for a moment as they watched Darrel drink from the short hose before putting it into the trough.

"He sure knows a lot about nanotechnology," Brandon said. "More than I do."

Wayne's ruddy, weathered face cracked into a slightly lopsided grin. "I bet you've heard more about that today than you ever thought you'd hear from any kid."

"Where'd he learn it all? Don't tell me it's in the regular sixth-grade curriculum."

"We read a lot. I do my best to keep his mind filled." The smile left Wayne's face. "He doesn't belong here. He doesn't know it yet, but Mercedes and I do. For the future, I mean. So we're preparing him. We want to make sure he has the world to choose from."

This was news to Brandon. Mercedes had given him the impression that Darrel was happy here. Or maybe he'd jumped to that conclusion himself. "You don't want him to stay on the farm?"

"Want?" Wayne arched a white brow. "More than anything I want Darrel to be happy, and the farm won't give him that forever. One of his brothers, maybe, and Darrel will always want to come back to visit, but his mind—" Wayne shook his head. "He needs more. So we try to make those opportunities available, regardless of the cost."

"You've done well with him," Brandon admitted reluctantly. How much easier this would be if he'd found Darrel's education lacking or his curiosity stifled. But then, Mercedes had endured too much of that as a child. She would never allow her children's minds to suffer.

"Nanotechnology," Wayne said. "Self-cleaning houses, soldiers who are never weary. Stuff of science fiction, it seems. But who knows? I've seen a lot of changes in the past fifty years. Darrel will see much more."

"Maybe he'll be a part of it."

"Probably." Wayne took a deep breath before letting out a slight chuckle. "Of course, I don't know how long this nano-tech stuff will last. Last year he was into geology, and before that medicine."

"Medicine?" Brandon couldn't help but feel pleased.

Wayne nodded. "He's like his mother. Has a lot of interests. Do you know she used to build houses?"

Brandon's chest began to ache, as though something vital had been taken from him. He'd never met a woman who knew so much about everything.

And now she lived on a farm.

Wayne didn't wait for an answer. "Eventually he'll find his

place and settle on it. Meanwhile, we'll keep giving him the information he craves—and we'll all learn a thing or two along the way." Wayne's smile was back. "I think he's heading toward rocket science now. He wants to go to space camp."

"I'll pay for it," Brandon said without thinking.

For the space of five heartbeats, Wayne didn't respond, and then he said with more grace than Brandon knew he'd have shown in the same position, "Thanks for the offer, but I think we'll be able to swing it."

"Dad!" came Darrel's excited voice. "Look! An eagle." Darrel was pointing to the sky. "Can we follow it for a while? Maybe we can get a peek at where it has its nest."

Wayne looked at his watch. "Sure, son. But don't forget we have the north field to plant. We've got to finish the spring wheat by next week. It looks like rain in a few hours, so we won't have as much time as we'd like."

"Wa-hoo!" shouted Darrel, as he ran toward them. "I'm for sure going to find that nest!"

Brandon looked into the blue sky, where there was no trace of a cloud. "It doesn't look like rain."

Wayne gave him an easy, confident smile. "No, but it's coming all the same. Just a good warm wash, probably about ten or fifteen minutes is all, and after it'll be perfect timing to spray one of our wheat fields that's having a bit of trouble."

"Bugs?"

"Maybe."

"We can't see anything yet," Darrel explained as he mounted his horse, "but if Dad says they're there, they are. He just knows." He laughed. "I've been trying to learn how he does it, but it doesn't make sense. So don't even try to understand." With an admiring look at Wayne, Darrel started his horse after the eagle that was still flying high in the air.

Brandon knew this detour would likely mean working late for Wayne, but he also felt that whether or not he had been there, Wayne's response would have been the same. Wayne seemed to be the father Brandon had wished for himself. If his own father had been like Wayne, caring more about his son's happiness than prestige or appearances, Brandon might have been the one teaching Darrel about rocket science.

CHAPTER 8

Diary of Mercedes Walker
August 13, 1994

Brandon and I went riding today for the first time. He is hilariously bad on a horse. But so cute too. I hope I can teach him to ride without looking so funny. I plan to have horses wherever we end up, though it might be challenging in a city. Hmm, I'll have to think about that. Maybe we won't live in a city after all. It doesn't really matter as long as we're together.

ercedes gave Windwalker a final loving pat and left the barn. Thunder followed her, watching her carefully, her silent guardian. He'd whined when Mercedes had ridden off with Brandon half an hour before, as though worried she wouldn't return. Of course she had, and Thunder had been waiting for her.

She had experienced a mixture of emotions as she led

Brandon out to the fields, as though time had been turned backward somehow. After all these years Brandon looked even more out of place on a horse. His feet stuck out awkwardly, and his back tilted at an odd angle. By contrast, she'd grown up in the saddle and loved riding. On a horse she had power. She had the ability to get away fast to a place where she couldn't hear her father's derogatory words. The sting of the wind hitting her face was far more pleasant than his hand. She'd tried to explain, but Brandon had never understood her love of the animals. He'd never even seen a horse up close until he met her.

"Who'd imagine I'd end up in Hickville riding a horse," he said with a laugh. It was their first ride together on horseback, and Mercedes was glad to have him alone, away from his hospital friends.

"You wouldn't be here if your father hadn't known Dr. Clark." She shivered at the thought of never having met Brandon.

"Well, that's true, and to give my old man credit, Dr. Clark is exceptional. I'm glad to learn from him."

She lifted her face to the sun and laughed. "Even in Hickville?"

"Especially in Hickville—if that's where you are." He tried to urge his horse closer to her, but all he managed was to make it move away. "Help! Where are the brakes? Or the steering wheel, for that matter?"

Mercedes caught up to him. "What were you saying?" She leaned close.

"I'm saying I don't care where I am as long as I'm with you." He kissed her, and Mercedes felt happiness explode inside. This was her future; she felt it with every sense she possessed.

"Race you," she said after a long moment. With a clicking sound and forward movement, she urged her horse into a gallop.

Brandon's horse followed quickly, with Brandon gripping the saddle so he wouldn't fall off. "I'll get you for this!" he called. "You wait and see."

Mercedes couldn't wait.

The memory faded. She'd been so sure about her future that summer and where they were headed. Was love really so blind? Why hadn't she seen signs of his upcoming betrayal? They seemed so obvious to her now. He hadn't made a firm commitment, he hadn't introduced her to his parents when they'd come through town, and he'd left without promising to return. He had given her nothing solid to hold onto. Nothing that had any substance.

Except Darrel, and he hadn't meant to do that.

What was Brandon doing with Wayne and Darrel now? She couldn't help wondering. Would Brandon keep his word about not telling Darrel the truth? Had he challenged Wayne or said something to offend him? If so, Wayne would keep his cool, but she hated to put him through this torture. Probably everything was going well, though by the poor manner in which Brandon sat his horse, he might have been thrown by now. She smiled at the thought. *Serve him right.*

Of course, if an accident were to happen to Brandon, a serious accident, it would only mean Darrel would be safe. With a disgusted snort at this thought, Mercedes hurried up the porch stairs. She had bills to take care of and lunch to make before her weekly shopping trip.

Thunder barked a brief greeting to his mate, who was on the back porch with the younger boys and her one remaining puppy. All the others had gone to good homes nearby, but Di didn't appear to notice. Joseph and Scott and the puppy seemed to be enough young things for her to look after.

"Chores done, boys?" Mercedes asked.

"Yeah," her sons chorused.

"Even the weeding?" She could see by their faces they'd forgotten. "Get to it. We may need to go out and help Dad with the planting later."

"I wish we could've helped move the cattle," Joseph complained. "Darrel gets to do everything fun."

"That's because he's older. But don't worry, you're nearly ten, and that's when he started."

"Cool!" Joseph jumped off the deck.

"No fair. I wish I was going to be ten." Scott jumped off and fell on his face. When Joseph laughed, Scott tackled him, and they wrestled on the ground. Scott held his own pretty well, but Mercedes noticed Joseph was careful not to hurt his little brother, as Darrel had been careful not to hurt Joseph when he was little.

"Boys, the weeding." She gestured to the garden. "Getting out those weeds means bigger peas. They'll be ready to eat soon." They loved fresh, raw peas so much that she could always inspire them to work by reminding them how good they tasted.

"Can we go to the swimming hole today?" Joseph asked.

"We'll see. Maybe for an hour after lunch. It looks like it'll get warm enough." Warm enough for them, not for her. But maybe she could read a book or work on the unfinished quilt she still thought of as Brandon's. She had a portable frame her neighbor had made for her, about the length of her arm, that resembled a square embroidery hoop. If she took extra care, it worked well enough to hold the small areas taut as she made the tiny stitches by hand. It was a simple pattern, and she had already managed to finish a third of it over the past few days.

The boys headed to the garden, and Mercedes paused in the doorway to watch them wrestle each other to the grass again. There was something so constant about their friendship and the concept of family that for a moment she felt rooted to the spot.

These two boys were all hers. Hers to love, to teach, to spoil, to discipline. At least until they grew up. Even then, they wouldn't go far. Not like Darrel. Not like her brother, Austin, who she still sometimes ached for so terribly it was like missing an arm.

Mercedes went to the room she kept for Austin. They'd moved the computer in there only recently, since Austin and his wife, Liana, had cleaned out all the boxes of records from their grandmother's charity. When she'd passed away two years ago, she'd left the charity to Austin, but he'd been so occupied with work of late that Liana had mostly taken it over, aided by employees in Ukraine where most of the charity's work took place in overcrowded orphanages.

The room had been Austin's for years, and every time she entered it, she was forcefully hit by his presence. Mercedes picked up a corner of the quilt she had made for the bed last year. It smelled faintly of musk and detergent.

Smiling at her sentimentality, she switched on the computer and brought up the accounting program Liana had installed eight months earlier. An accountant by profession, Liana had promised Mercedes that the computer would simplify the farm finances. Since her sister-in-law had also set it all up, Mercedes had nothing to lose, and it remained the best thing she'd done since getting the Internet.

The bills this week were simple. Payment for the new tractor—higher really than she'd hoped they'd be paying, but the old tractor had given out last year—and payment for the seed Wayne was planting. Utilities were the least of the bunch. She set aside a few dollars for Darrel's space camp and calculated what she had left for groceries. They had plenty of meat in the freezer and grain she could grind into flour. In the summer, she'd have fresh produce from her garden and might be able to skip the store visit altogether. Living on a farm had advantages. But that payment for the tractor worried her. If some of the other equipment were to break, or if the crops failed, or if the cattle contracted a sickness, they'd have to use the tiny savings she'd managed to put together over the years, and then what would happen to them when it was time for Wayne to retire? She couldn't think about selling the farm; she might as well give up a child.

As she was finishing the last bill, the phone rang. "Hello?"

"Hi, sis."

"Austin!" She settled back in the chair. "I was just thinking about you."

"So that explains why I kept having the urge to call."

"Where are you?"

"Work. I had a minute before a meeting."

"How's Liana?"

"That's part of why I called." His voice took on a jubilant note. "She's going to have a baby! We just found out. I know we've only been married four months, but we're not getting any younger, and we figured we'd better get started."

"Liana's what, thirty? That's not old."

"Thirty-one next month. You'd had your third by that age, hadn't you?"

Mercedes thought a moment. "I guess I had. Well, congratulations! And to think last year I was beginning to fear I'd never be an aunt."

Her brother laughed. "It's because of you and Wayne that I even dared try marriage. Thank you." He was always doing this, calling her and thanking her. Usually for something she had done for him as a child when they lived under their father's harsh rule. She had done her best to look after her little brother. Sometimes she'd been able to get it right.

"Mercedes?" Austin asked when she didn't reply. "Is everything okay?"

She tried to swallow the impossible lump in her throat. "He's back."

"Wayne? Let me talk to him for a moment. I want to be the one to tell him about the baby."

"Not him. Brandon Rhodes."

"Who is—oh, him." Austin was silent a moment. "What does he want?"

"Darrel."

"But how did he find out? Did you call him?"

"Actually, your company sold some stuff to the hospital where he works in San Diego. He saw you there."

"I thought one of them looked familiar. Wait a minute, do you think he found out about Darrel from me? Mercedes, I would never . . . Oh, no." His voice took on a tone of shock. "I remember telling the hospital administrator I had a nephew the same age as his son."

"Brandon overheard you."

"Oh, Mercedes. I'm so sorry. I'm such an idiot."

"You couldn't have known. He's the one who shouldn't have been listening. Or at the very least, he shouldn't have come here. For crying out loud, he had his chance thirteen years ago."

"I'll make this right, Mercedes. I swear. Whatever you need. If this goes to court—"

"I'm hoping it doesn't come to that. Frankly, our finances can't handle it."

"I have savings, and it's all yours. Look, I'm coming up there. I should have been more careful."

"Austin, it's not your fault." Mercedes almost wished she hadn't told him, though a little part of her was happy that he was taking responsibility for his error, however unintended. "You couldn't have known you'd run into him. And you've already been up here way too much lately to help Wayne with the planting. We're doing fine, really. I'm not sure where this is headed yet. If I need your help, I'll call."

"Promise?"

He knew she didn't give promises lightly. Neither of them did. It was part of the upbringing they'd shared. "Yes."

There was a brief pause before Austin asked. "So how are you holding up? I bet it's weird seeing him again."

"Really weird. He's still him, you know? I feel like we should . . . I know it's crazy, but there's a part of me that feels like Brandon never left, that this life I have now is fake somehow. A lie."

Austin was silent a moment and then, "That's absolutely not true, Mercedes, and if you think about it a minute, you'll see that. You and Wayne and the boys—what you have is very special. Something every person in the world wants."

Tears leaked from Mercedes' eyes. "But I should have told Brandon then. I should have been truthful. I was so scared. I've regretted not telling him all these years, despite what Wayne and I have here. I'll never know what might have happened."

"You made the choice you did, and you've been happy. Haven't you? Remember Dad and how he had it all, but still he kept looking so long and so far that he lost everything."

Austin's words were sobering to Mercedes. Was she like her father, who couldn't see the happiness that had stared him in the face? A growing farm, two healthy children, and a wife who loved him. None of it had been enough for her father. Her mother was just as bad, waiting for a man who would never change. Sacrificing her happiness and the welfare of her children to an alcoholic.

Whenever Mercedes went back in time in her mind, she played out numerous scenarios that might have happened. But always the one where Brandon didn't come back, when he told her he wasn't ready to be a father, was most prominent. Yet with his reappearance, she'd begun to suspect her own motives. Maybe she'd been wrong.

Or maybe she'd been right. She'd never know.

The point was she'd made her choice and couldn't go back. That was life. You could choose to do anything you wanted but not what happened afterward. The consequences, good or bad, were set, and sometimes, as in her case, there was no way of determining exactly what road you would be walking down once you took the first step. Marrying Wayne had been a good thing for her and for her family. In fact, it had been the only thing that kept her alive. And they'd been very happy together. She clung to that knowledge.

"You're right," she told her brother. "I'm just so scared of losing Darrel."

"It'll be okay. You're not alone. Remember that. You have Wayne and me and Liana and the boys. We're a family, and family means a lot more than what blood runs through your veins."

"Thank you."

"You're welcome." He paused. "Hey, did I ever thank you for sneaking dinner to me out in the barn the night Dad banned me from the house because I lent my horse to the neighbors?"

"You did," she said softly. "At least a hundred times."

When she hung up the phone, Mercedes was feeling slightly better. She turned off her computer and went to the kitchen to start lunch. The men would be coming back to the house soon, and she'd better be prepared—in more ways than one.

Outside, it began to rain.

CHAPTER

9

Diary of Mercedes Walker
September 3, 1994

I love Brandon, but sometimes he's so infuriating. We talk about the future, but we really have no plans. I feel . . . worried somehow. It's like he wants us to act married without a real commitment. My girlfriends tell me that's the eternal problem between men and women. We long for security—which to us means marriage and commitment—but men want . . . well, I don't know exactly what they want. Brandon and I have talked about the family we might have someday, but it's nothing tangible. Meanwhile, he's pushing for us to sleep together. But I'm not ready. For me, a commitment like that should be lasting. I think I should focus more on my studies and less on Brandon. I'm nearly finished with yet another two-year degree. I need to decide if I'll continue at a real university and become a psychologist. I'd hate to leave my new receptionist job, but it really doesn't pay all that well.

"So what do you want to be when you grow up?" Brandon asked. They'd spent the last hour planting wheat and were now heading back to the house for lunch.

Darrel thought a moment. "I want to be a lot of things, but mostly I want to be a farmer like my dad."

Brandon tried to hide his surprise. He should have expected this; children often wanted to be like their parents at this age. Not like at sixteen when they generally wanted nothing to do with their parents. "Well, you might change your mind."

"That's what Dad says."

"He's right. It's a big world out there. You can always come back to visit."

"That's what Momma says. I can visit a lot like my uncle Austin."

Brandon looked away from Darrel's intent stare, the dark eyes so like Mercedes'. Who was he to tell Darrel he should leave the farm when he himself was wishing he'd been the one who stayed with Mercedes?

Darrel scratched his head. "Do you know my uncle? He says there's always a part of him here but he can't live here all the time because there's so much other interesting stuff out there. Sometimes I feel that way. Like I really want to go to space camp. I want to learn how to make a rocket ship, though I probably can't learn that in only a week."

"I think space camp actually teaches more about being an astronaut."

Darrel's eyes shone. "That's way cool. I hope I get to go."

"I think you will."

"You never answered my question. Do you know my uncle? I mean, if you knew my mom, you probably knew him."

"I met him a few times. But that was a long time ago. I did see him a couple months ago in California at the hospital where I work. He was setting us up with some equipment. But we didn't talk. At first I wasn't really sure it was him."

"So how did you meet my mother?"

"At the hospital. We ran into each other in the cafeteria. We . . ." Brandon knew he couldn't go any further with the truth, so he finished lamely, "We became friends. A group of us hung out together."

"Momma says you came here to teach other doctors. That's really cool. If I was a doctor, I'd want to invent new ways to do things and then teach them to others so we could save a lot of lives."

"You've thought about being a doctor?"

Darrel nodded. "When my sister died. She was really sick, but nobody could help her."

Brandon was quiet as he absorbed this information. Mercedes had lost a child? He hadn't realized that. Then he remembered the boys' cryptic comments at dinner the other night, followed by Mercedes' aloofness and Wayne's abrupt ending of the conversation. A child's death explained everything. It also meant Mercedes would fight extra hard to keep Darrel. She wouldn't want to lose him too.

Which was what I came to make happen—at least in the beginning. Brandon felt sick at the thought. "When did she die?"

"Let's see. I was nine, so it was about three years ago. She was only two. So little. It was her heart that was bad. Momma had to learn to start her heart again in case she had problems. They tried to fix it, but . . ." He shook his head, his face somber. "She was really cute. But after she died, Momma was . . . well, it was awful. I didn't ever want to see her like that again. That's why I thought about being a doctor. Maybe I still will be one. I'd do anything to make sure nobody else in our family dies. Momma doesn't deserve that." He turned his face away from Brandon to hide his emotion, then clicked his tongue, touched his heels to the horse's sides, and galloped up to where Wayne was riding several yards ahead.

Mercedes had lost a baby. He could only guess at how hard it had been.

"Brandon, they're adorable. You should really be a baby doctor, not a heart doctor." Mercedes stood in front of the window where the newborns slept peacefully under the care of soft-spoken nurses. One nurse was rocking a crying infant to sleep.

"It's called a pediatrician, not a baby doctor."

"Oh, that's so clinical! These are babies, for crying out loud." She punched him playfully. "Next you'll be telling me that a heart doctor is a cardiologist."

"Well, yeah."

"I want at least half a dozen children. I hope that's all right with you."

"Well, you'll be the one having them. But that's not for years and years. I'm not ready to be a father yet."

The smile on her face faltered. He knew why. She was worried about the future. He wished he could tell her she didn't have to worry. They'd spend some time apart, which he knew she'd hate, but he'd come back or send for her when everything was taken care of. He couldn't take her with him right away, and he didn't want to tell her why. The fact that a fiancée was waiting back home—well not a fiancée, really, but a girl his parents wanted him to marry— made things difficult. That her father was a prestigious doctor in the hospital where he wanted to work made things even worse. But Mercedes didn't need to know any of that. He loved Mercedes, loved her more than anyone, and he'd make it right in the end.

"When we do have children, I hope they look like you," he whispered in her ear. *Her smile returned, dazzling him with its brilliance.*

"I love you, Brandon."

"I love you too."

When Brandon and the others arrived at the farmhouse, Mercedes had a hot lunch out on the table. Thick slabs of meat, homemade bread, mashed potatoes, and a fruit salad. "I'm out of lettuce," she said apologetically. "I haven't made it into town yet."

"This is great." Wayne heaped his plate high.

"Really great." Brandon felt so hungry that the seed they'd been planting had started to look appetizing. On top of that, every muscle in his body ached with weariness. Maybe all this farm work would be good for Darrel as he grew into his height. No one would ever be able to accuse him of being a weakling. "This box was in the mail for you." Mercedes set a small priority mail package in front of Wayne.

"It was me who got the mail," Scott added importantly. "All by myself."

"That's a long walk out to the highway," Wayne said. "Thank you for going. But I hope you stayed away from the cars once you got there."

"I did." Scott bounced in his chair to emphasize his point. "Well, actually, I only saw one car pass."

"Good job. I knew I could trust you."

"So what's in the box?" Darrel asked. "Something for the tractor?"

"Maybe shoes," Scott guessed. "It's about that size."

"You'll see soon enough. It's a surprise." Wayne took the box and placed it under his seat, ignoring the curious stares of his wife and sons.

"Daaaad," whined Scott.

Wayne grinned. "Later."

The guy knows how to drag out a mystery, Brandon thought. *Or is he hiding something?*

Joseph had been washing his hands in the kitchen, but now he practically exploded outside, landing on a chair at the table. "Hey, we're going swimming in a minute. The rain's almost all dried up on the grass. And can Darrel come, or is he going out to plant again?"

"I think he has time for a swim." Wayne's eyes shifted to Brandon. "I think we all do."

Brandon was relieved. He couldn't imagine going out to the field immediately after lunch, though he knew Wayne could do so easily.

"And then, Joseph," Wayne continued, "I think you can come help us plant while Momma goes into town with Scott." Joseph bristled with importance until he realized Scott was getting the better end of the deal.

"But, Dad," he complained.

"Would you rather we go out to plant right after lunch instead?" Wayne's tone brooked no nonsense.

"There'll be plenty of Saturdays with nothing to do this summer." Mercedes set her hand on Joseph's shoulders. "And other days too. The planting will be over next week."

"Yeah, but then there's harvesting." Darrel's eyes gleamed with the joy of teasing his brother.

"Oh?" Brandon asked, interested in what his son would be doing—had been doing for all these years. "What comes first?"

"Alfalfa begins in June," Darrel said. "Then comes the winter wheat in July and the spring wheat in August. After that, it's sugar beets in late September. We finish with the alfalfa again in October."

"And the grain corn's in October too," Wayne added. "Or thereabouts. All of it depends on the conditions and how much water we get."

Brandon was impressed. "Sounds like a busy summer."

"Good thing we get lots of light." Darrel shoved a forkful of meat into his mouth.

"And we have our fun." Mercedes' eyes met Brandon's.

He could tell she was worried at what he might be thinking. Something in the way her brow creased. But he thought harvesting was likely better for a child than hours of video games, movies, and hanging out with friends while their parents were at work. "I'm sure you do."

After the meal, the adults followed the boys, now clad in old cutoffs, as they set out toward the river. "They should probably wait half an hour," Brandon said. "After eating, that is. Could get a cramp." His voice trailed off, and he wished he hadn't spoken. He bet none of these boys ever had a cramp in their lives.

Wayne smiled more lopsidedly than before. "Don't worry. It's a good fifteen-minute walk, and they finished eating ten minutes ago. By the time we get there, the food'll be as good as gone."

"And they'll be starving again," Mercedes added.

"I'm starving right now," Joseph said.

"Tag, you're it!" Darrel touched Joseph on the shoulder, and they were off, bounding nimbly over the stalks of alfalfa as though their feet instinctively knew where to land without damaging the plants.

"I'm thinking of keeping Darrel home from school on Monday and Tuesday to finish the planting," Wayne said to Brandon. "If you'd like to come help, you'd be welcome. Unless you're still teaching your seminar."

Brandon wondered if he really needed the boy's help or if he was taking him out only for Brandon's sake. "The seminar is over now, but can he miss school like that?"

"He's far ahead in most subjects," Mercedes answered, switching the large black plastic bag she carried from one arm to the other. "A day or two will make no difference."

Brandon didn't need to think twice. "I'll be here." He had a sneaking suspicion he was being used, but he didn't blame them. He wanted to see his son, and they needed help planting. Although if the truth be told, he doubted he was even as much help as Darrel.

At the river stood the giant, ancient oak tree Brandon remembered from his few visits there with Mercedes. The tree's best feature was the large flat branch, ten feet high and more than a foot and a half in width, that ran parallel to the water and could seat at least ten children side by side. Children and adults alike would leap from the branch, holding onto a rope hung from above, and fly out over the river, finally letting go to plunge into the water. Years earlier, Mercedes and her brother had dammed up the river with rocks to make the swimming hole deeper. It was a child's paradise, and it looked good to Brandon as well, with his aching muscles—until he dipped in a hand and felt how cold it was.

These farm children must have skin made of whale blubber, he thought, as he settled down on the grass. *No way am I going in there.*

Apparently, Mercedes shared his opinion. She promptly set out the folding chair Wayne had carried and sat down. From her black bag came a half-finished quilt with a section clamped in some sort of frame. Her needle began flying in and out faster than he could follow.

Wayne got the job of climbing the tree and pushing the

children out on the rope so they'd go higher and faster than they would on their own.

"He's a good sport," Brandon said, glancing at the branch above their heads. He'd had a slight case of vertigo since the chemotherapy and didn't relish the idea of climbing the tree at all.

"Wayne's always been a good father."

I can be too, Brandon wanted to say, but that would sound petty. Like a child trying to best his rival.

"Aaaaaaaaaaah!" screamed Joseph as he slipped from the rope into the water. He came up gasping. "Cold!"

Darrel laughed from the tree limb. "You wanted to be first."

"Me next!" Scott cried.

"I'd better go wait for you in the water, just in case," Darrel said.

"Okay," Scott said, as Darrel climbed down the tree and jumped into the cold water to wait for his little brother.

Brandon tore his eyes away from his son. "He's so . . . wonderful."

Mercedes smiled. "Yes, he is. Well, they have their moments of fighting like all brothers, but he's really matured a lot in the past year."

"You've done a great job with him."

"Thank you." Her face creased with worry, and Brandon wished . . . What? Well, that he wasn't the cause of so much heartache. Or at least that they could leave it for another day. This place held good memories for them. Couldn't she feel that? Couldn't she leave the present for an instant and remember?

"Brandon, don't you dare!" Mercedes struggled in his arms. "If you throw me in, I swear I'll drown you. Don't think I won't!" He tickled her, causing her giggles to change into shrieks of laughter. Then he tossed her into the river.

"You'll pay for this!" Mercedes said when she came up gasping.

"She sounds serious." This from his buddy Rob, a fellow resident, who sat with the others on the bank.

"I'll help her." Sandra, Rob's date, launched toward Brandon, grabbing his arm.

"So will I." Their friend Micky took Brandon's other arm. She was bigger than Sandra, and her hands were strong from the daily work she did as a nurse at the hospital. It was all he could do to fend them off.

"Oh my, look at that," said Micky's husband, Chad. Everyone looked down the river in the direction he pointed, and in that moment Chad pushed both his wife and Brandon into the river.

Screaming and water-choked giggles filled the air.

"That's it, Chad!" Micky shouted. "I want a divorce."

Chad pulled her from the water. "Never." He kissed her deeply while everyone hooted.

"Okay, okay," Sandra said. "Knock it off, you two. Chad, you're forgiven already. Can't you tell by that kiss?"

"Well, at least I'll wait until his residency is over," Micky said, wrapping her arms lovingly around her husband. "That way there'll be more money." No one paid the threat any mind. The two had been married three years and were practically inseparable.

Still in the river, Brandon felt himself being pushed under the water. "I told you I'd drown you." Mercedes was laughing, and he was surprised at how strong she actually was. Farm girl. He should have known. But she let him up after only a brief dunking.

"Promise to be good?"

He took her in his arms. "Do I have to?"

"Of course. I only show good boys how to use the swing. Come on." She slipped from his arms.

Afterwards they all lay on the bank, talking and eating. It was the first of several wonderful days with the group at the river, but Mercedes never took Brandon there alone. Not since that first time when Wayne had found them there together.

"Remember Rob and Chad and the girls?" he asked.

"Michelle—Micky, I mean—and . . ." She clicked her fingers. "The girl from admissions. What was her name? Sandra, I think. Yeah, that's it."

"I seem to remember you dunking me."

She laughed exactly as she had in his memory of that day. "You threw me into the water. You deserved everything you got."

"Couldn't have been me. Residents don't do stuff like that. They need to protect their hands."

"Oh, never the residents. Not them." She rolled her eyes. "You guys were so full of yourselves."

"Those were fun times."

"I used to wonder when you'd all wake up and realize that I didn't work at the hospital like you all did."

"Are you kidding? That was what was so fun." Brandon pulled a piece of new grass from the bank. "We were all so boring, but you had studied so many things, and you owned a farm."

"Well, not me exactly, though I do own it now."

They were quiet for a moment, watching the boys play. Brandon studied her face, now peaceful instead of worried. He was glad he still had the power to do that much. She smiled at something Scott was doing, and Brandon saw fine lines at the corners of her eyes, reminding him of the years that had passed. So much had happened to both of them.

"I heard about your daughter," he said quietly. He wondered

if the child had taken after Mercedes, as Darrel had, or if she'd resembled Wayne.

Mercedes' needle stopped. She turned her face slowly in his direction, her smile becoming wistful. "Lucy."

"What was she like?"

"She was . . . a fireball. Even had her daddy's red hair. She got her way with all of us, knew exactly what she wanted. Always wanted to do everything herself."

He understood without her saying that losing Lucy had been bad. Worse than being deserted by him? Worse than being alone to give birth to a fatherless baby? He thought it must have been much worse, and yet throughout the ordeal she'd had the support of Wayne and the children. He hoped that had made Lucy's passing more bearable.

"What happened? I mean, if you don't want to talk about it . . ."

She swallowed several times. "Maybe it's something you should hear. For a year after her death I blamed you."

He sat up. "But I wasn't here."

"Exactly."

What was she saying?

When she saw that he didn't understand, she continued. "She had a heart defect. The doctors tried everything, but they couldn't save her. They gave her two weeks to six months if we didn't find a donor heart. I knew you had planned to do research on the heart, so I looked you up on the Internet. I found an article that said you'd made great progress with children like Lucy. I thought if I called you . . ."

She shrugged and looked down at the quilt in her hands. The needle started moving as though of its own accord, and the growing tenseness in her face relaxed slightly. "I did a bit of searching, found the number and called, but I couldn't get through. For weeks I called, left at least a dozen messages. They said you were out of the country and they would pass on my message to you later. I begged them to give me your contact information there, or to call you and tell them who I was. I thought because you knew me, because of what we'd been to each other . . ." She glanced over at the boys to make sure they were all out of hearing range. "I was even prepared to tell you about Darrel, so you'd help."

It took a moment to sink in that she had thought he might have needed an incentive to help her. Did she think he had cared so little? He found it suddenly difficult to breathe properly. He remembered being in Brazil around that time on a charity mission, principally to do heart work on patients who didn't mind being the first to receive his new, unproven treatments because they were dying anyway. He'd accomplished a lot of good there. When he returned to the States, the hospital had told him a lady had called repeatedly, but he'd been so busy he'd never followed up. She hadn't called again. A few months later he'd been diagnosed with stomach cancer, and his whole life had changed.

"The last time I called," Mercedes went on, struggling to keep her face impassive, "I told them not to bother telling you. I knew it was too late. She died that night." A single tear escaped, sliding down her left cheek. Mercedes didn't look at him but concentrated on her needle as though it was the only thing keeping her from falling apart.

"And I failed you again." The enormity of missing those calls washed over Brandon. He stared at her miserably, wanting more than anything to wipe the sadness from her face, to comfort her in his arms. But he'd given up that right on the day he left, or maybe even before that when he failed to put her welfare before his own in their relationship.

The needle hesitated as Mercedes' eyes met his and held. "You might not have been able to do anything. Besides, you didn't owe me."

"On the contrary. I'll owe you forever. For Darrel."

"You can't take him." More tears flooded her eyes, and her voice was low and urgent. "I know you have a lot of money, and I know you could sue for partial custody. But please, don't think about taking him away from here. Let him have an untroubled childhood. He deserves that much."

Brandon was saved from answering as a big splash drew their attention. Wayne had joined the boys in the water. "Hey," he called to them, "it ain't half bad." Arcing his hand across the water, he sent out a spray of droplets that pelted Mercedes and Brandon.

Mercedes wiped her face with the edge of her quilt and laughed. Brandon could no longer tell her tears from the water. "Wayne, you aren't dressed for swimming," Mercedes said as he swam to the bank.

"So what? Aren't you going to join me?"

She looked down at her jeans and T-shirt. "Dressed like this?"

"That never stopped you before." There was a playfulness in Wayne's tone that belied his age, a tone Brandon had heard hints of that morning in the fields.

Rising from her chair, Mercedes set aside the quilt and met him at the bank. Wayne touched her chin, bringing his lips briefly to hers, and Brandon had the sense they'd completely forgotten him.

Yet he remembered all too vividly a day when his role and

Wayne's had been reversed in this very place. He'd been the one with Mercedes and Wayne the one on the outside.

He had to look away.

In a few seconds the private moment was over, so brief that it hadn't been anything to speak of—or wouldn't have been if Brandon's heart had been in the right place. But he found he envied Wayne and, yes, Mercedes for the life they had together.

He's my son, he told her silently. *That counts for something.*

He couldn't—wouldn't—let anyone take that away from him.

CHAPTER 10

Diary of Mercedes Walker
October 1, 1994

Brandon has been sending me roses almost every day all week. That's because I broke up with him. But I'm going to make up with him because it's been the longest, most dreadful week of my life. I even went out to the farm alone. Daddy was there, and he started complaining about how I never cleaned the place. I don't even live there! That doesn't mean anything to Daddy, though. I thought he was going to hit me, but Wayne walked in the room and asked me to come out to the barn to see a cut on the cow's side that she got from barbed wire somewhere. He said he was worried about it getting infected, but I know he said it only to take me away from Daddy. I hate him. Daddy, not Wayne. I'm glad Brandon seems to have realized how important I am in his life. Maybe now he'll finally get down to asking me to marry him.

*S*unday morning Brandon hurt more than he'd ever hurt in his entire life. If he'd thought his muscles ached yesterday, today every movement was pure torture. How would he ever be able to work two more days in the field? Wayne was like a machine in his ability to endure, and Brandon felt like a weak child around him. Maybe in the old days of all-nighters at the hospital, Brandon could have kept up, or maybe before the cancer he'd have been able to muster more energy, but he'd grown soft in the past years. Worse than a child. Darrel had shown no signs of overexertion.

Brandon had thought at least he'd be far ahead intellectually, but Wayne and Darrel had read a lot together and were well versed on many subjects. Gone were the days of the stereotypical uneducated farmer, at least where Wayne was concerned. And his intuition was uncanny, something Brandon wouldn't have believed possible. It was similar to Brandon's instinctive ability to feel his way through a heart operation, giving the patient a greater chance of survival.

He'd long ago accepted this "knowing" as part of his profession, though not all doctors he'd worked with possessed it, but that farming should have an equivalent was not something he'd ever considered. Did every profession have such a thing? Construction work? Mail delivery? Book writing? No, he couldn't believe it. That would mean he wasn't unique, as he'd always believed.

Mercedes, if she could see his thoughts, would say his ego was showing again. Hannah might say the same thing. Good thing he was alone to nurse both his thoughts and his aching body. The only reason Brandon figured he was alive at all this dreadful morning was that yesterday afternoon Wayne had sent both him and Darrel back to the house early.

"I don't like him to spend all his Saturday out here working,"

Wayne had said, as he refilled the planting drill with seed. "And you've no reason to be here if Darrel isn't."

Brandon had been grateful and took his leave without even glimpsing Mercedes again. At least she wouldn't guess what a wimp he'd become.

His first course of business now was to take something for the pain and then to soak in a hot bath. Tomorrow he'd call his attorney and start feeling out his options. Mercedes wouldn't likely concede anything except permission to visit Darrel at the farm, but he wouldn't settle for that. He craved more. He'd missed out on the first twelve years of his son's life, and he wasn't about to let more time escape them. He wanted to have a say in his son's future, to be seen as more than a family friend. Surely custody on holidays and summers would be a fair agreement, and California held a lot of wonders for a boy his age. Perhaps Darrel would choose to attend high school there. Or at least a university. For a moment Brandon lost himself in the vision of himself and Darrel, sitting by the sea and talking about Brandon's growing up years. Of course, the only way Darrel would ever care about Brandon's stories was if he knew the truth.

But first Brandon had to get his foot in the door.

And endure these next days at the farm without making a fool of himself.

Or dying.

His throat felt suddenly dry. After the cancer, death jokes didn't seem so amusing, especially when he told them to himself.

An hour later the phone rang as he was climbing gingerly out of the bath. Pulling on a robe, he hurried to his phone, hoping without real hope that it was Mercedes calling to ask him to dinner. Any time with Darrel would be welcome.

"Hello?"

"Hi, it's me."

"Hi, Hannah."

"I wanted to see how it was going. Have you resolved anything yet?"

"No, I spent most of yesterday with him. Well, with the family. But nothing's resolved. I think they're hoping I'll go away, or maybe they plan to work me to death."

"Work you?"

"It's planting time, and Darrel's helping. If I want to be with him, I gotta plant."

She laughed. "How barbaric. I would give a lot to see that."

"Every inch of me hurts. But you should see Darrel's stepdad. He's impossibly strong. Has the endurance of a bull."

"Well, you know farmers."

"That's just it. He isn't like any farmer I ever imagined. I thought all they knew were crops, but this guy's smart. He could have been anything."

"Apparently, he chose to be a farmer."

"Apparently." *He stayed where Mercedes was,* he added silently. He couldn't fault Wayne for that.

"Must like the job."

"Clean air, hard work, nice family. Why not? I think he really does."

"You sound almost jealous."

"There's peace in knowing where you belong." Brandon sat down on his bed, feeling again every sore muscle. "One thing's for sure, I'd never survive this life. Physical work aside, there's a lot of stress. I gather last year's crop wasn't very good, and they have some heavy bills. For the past few years, they've been trying their hand at raising cattle, which seems to pay better, but that comes with a whole new set of worries. Do you know they actually immunize cattle against diseases?"

"It's good for you, the money thing. If they don't have funds, they won't want a long court battle, right?"

He'd had the same thought, but hearing it out loud seemed crass somehow, like he was plotting against Mercedes. "I guess. But they do have the farm. I get the sense they'd sell the whole thing if that's what it took. Then I'll have been the one to take that from Darrel."

Hannah was silent for few seconds. "Maybe you can come to a peaceful arrangement."

"I hope so, because as much as I want my son, I don't want to hurt them."

"Them or her?"

Brandon stared down at the quilt on the hotel room bed. He'd thought it beautiful when he'd arrived, but now the varied colors made him dizzy. Hannah's question had merit. As much as he was coming to respect Wayne, it was Mercedes he didn't want to hurt.

"It would be easier," he said slowly, "if they were bad parents. But they seem quite perfect. I keep wondering if I could do any better."

"They're probably on their best behavior."

He was relieved that Hannah let him dodge her question. When they were married, she wouldn't have let him get away so easily. "So am I, I guess. But honestly, they're just so stinking normal. No dysfunction—not like with my parents."

"Hey, your parents did the best they could."

This was generous, given what had happened the first time he'd taken Hannah to the house. Four years after he'd left Wyoming, he met Hannah at the hospital when she brought a group of school children for a tour. She seemed so alive, like Mercedes had been, and yet so different that he'd been enchanted and followed the group out of the hospital to the bus where he'd gotten up the nerve to ask if he could see her again. They had dated steadily for two months before he decided to introduce her to his parents.

"This is Hannah," he said, swallowing his nervousness. "She teaches school."

"Actually, I'm an assistant principal," she corrected.

"That's what I meant." He mentally berated himself for the mistake. Something about being around his parents made his brain go soggy.

His mother offered her hand. "Nice to meet you." Her voice was icy.

"Has Brandon introduced you to his fianceé?" his father asked. Hannah blinked, caught by surprise. "Ah, no. I didn't realize he was engaged."

"I'm not." Brandon's smile was strained. "Dad, we've talked about this. I told you Hannah and I've been dating for two months."

His father sighed. "I'm sorry, but I'm going to have to excuse myself. I have a headache."

They watched him go up the stairs.

"Have a nice time, dear," Brandon's mother said to him. "Thanks for dropping by." She gave a tight smile as she ushered them to the door.

His parents had come around during Brandon and Hannah's three-year courtship, albeit slowly, and they now acted as if Hannah had been their choice all along. He bet they called her more often than they called him. They still hadn't forgiven him for the breakup. Or for leaving them and Hannah when he moved to California.

"And so will you," Hannah was saying.

"So will I what?" He'd completely lost track of their conversation. That happened more often, since the chemo. He didn't have the ability to focus as well on two lines of thought.

"Do your best with your son. I only wish . . ."

"What?"

Her voice was quiet as she answered. "I wish he were my son too."

There. It was out in the open, as Brandon knew it had to be. "I'm sorry, Hannah." He wished he could say, "So do I," but he didn't. If Darrel were Hannah's it would make him another child altogether, and he couldn't wish that. Besides, wishing was for people who didn't act to change their own lives—and he planned to act.

He cleared his throat. "I'm going to call my attorney."

She laughed. "The one who gave me the house, the car, half your savings and alimony? I think you'd better find someone else."

"You have a point."

They were silent a moment, and then she said, "Brandon, I miss you."

He thought of holding her in the night, of seeing her face every morning, of secret looks exchanged at his parents' house, of dinners awaiting him after an exhausting day at the hospital.

"I miss you too, Hannah."

CHAPTER

11

Diary of Mercedes Walker
December 25, 1994

No ring, no proposal. I'd thought for sure both were coming. Just a stuffed animal that I threw out my apartment window into the garbage bin below. Not in front of Brandon, though. I probably should have. I hate stuffed animals. They're completely worthless.

Still, I love Brandon—so much. He's like the air that I breathe. Why do I keep thinking something terrible is going to ruin our chance together? He's going away next spring to a hospital in Boston where his parents live, and I've been waiting for him to say he's taking me with him. No word so far. I'd bring it up myself, but I don't want to be like Momma and love a man so much that I lose myself, my values, and my dreams. Doesn't real love mean he should support my dreams as well as his own?

Maybe I've got love all wrong. Maybe love is an emotion you

can only learn if your parents show you how it's supposed to be.
And honestly, I can't say for sure if my parents ever loved me.

*W*ayne walked into the kitchen, and the boys' chatter stopped. Mercedes heard Scott hop up from his chair. "Dad, what did you do with your hair?"

Mercedes turned from the stove, spatula in hand. There in the doorway stood her husband, looking the same as always except his hair was a bright red—almost the exact color she remembered from her youth.

Her free hand went to her mouth as she tried to mask her smile. "Wayne, what have you done?"

He strode to the table. "Do you like it?" The question was all too casual. The boys gaped, unsure how to respond.

Mercedes burst out laughing. "You dyed your hair? You? That was what was in the box?"

Wayne flushed a deep telltale red. She could see him struggling to pretend he was upset at her laughter, but he never managed to be really angry at her.

"You mean the box I got from the mail?" Scott was grinning widely. "I like it, Daddy. You look just like Joseph. Well, except a little taller . . . and a little bigger . . . and older."

"Thank you, Scott." Wayne said. "I think." All three boys giggled.

"A lot bigger and older," Joseph added. Their laughter grew louder.

"I get the point." Wayne poured a tall glass of milk and helped himself to the bacon and eggs on the table. "Are there hash browns?"

Darrel nodded. "Momma's cookin' 'em."

Still chuckling, Mercedes carried the potatoes to the table.

"Honestly, Wayne, what gave you the idea? I thought you said you'd never dye your hair."

"A man can change his mind."

"So we see." She winked at the boys, who immediately started laughing again. Her own laughter bubbled up inside her. Every time she glanced at one of the boys, she laughed harder. They fared no better. Scott had tears coming from the corners of his eyes, Joseph slapped his leg as he laughed, and Darrel had a hand over his mouth in an attempt to support Wayne.

Mercedes sat down to catch her breath, purposely avoiding her sons' eyes. When they began to calm down, she said faintly, "It just looks so . . ."

"Red," Darrel finished.

They exploded into laughter again. Wayne studiously focused on his breakfast, trying to ignore them.

The laughter slowly died, and then Joseph said. "Reminds me of tomatoes. Yum." And they were off and laughing again.

"Knock it off," Wayne said grumpily. "Or I'll go shave my head right now."

Mercedes took his hand. "Actually, I like it. You look . . . well, I guess you look younger."

His smile returned. "That's what I'd hoped. But it's only semipermanent. It washes out after a week or two. Of course, I can always give it another dose."

Mercedes caressed his hand, sensing a vulnerability in her husband that she hadn't felt since Lucy was diagnosed. For him to order hair dye the same week her old boyfriend returned from the past was no coincidence.

"I love the hair, Wayne. It's perfect. And you can bet that when I start going gray, I'll do the same thing."

"You, gray?" He shook his head. "Your grandmother's hair was dark till the day she died."

Mercedes grinned. "Hate to break it to you."

"She dyed her hair?"

She nodded, and they laughed together with their boys around them. Everything would have been perfect but for the looming threat of Brandon's presence in Riverton. Mercedes wanted to wish him away, but wishing had only ever brought her false hope. No, somehow they had to face Brandon as a family and put the past where it belonged, once and for all.

After breakfast was finished, Mercedes left the boys to wrangle themselves into their church clothes while she went outside to pick a bouquet of daffodils from the front flowerbed. Their bright yellow color cheered her heart as she walked past the barn and garden to the small grove of trees where the family cemetery had been in use for more than a hundred years. Besides her Walker relatives, her grandparents on her mother's side were here, out of the way enough to not be stumbled upon casually but close enough to talk to when Mercedes needed comfort.

She visited her grandparents first. She didn't remember her grandfather well, because he'd died when she was young, but her grandmother had been a stalwart in her life, more of a mother than her own mother had been.

"You can't let it bother you, Mercedes." Grandmother put a loving arm around her shoulders. *"Your momma doesn't see what kind of a man he is. She'll love him until the day she dies."*

Mercedes shivered. "I just want her to tell him to go easier on Austin. I don't care about me. I do okay. But Austin gets more trouble than he deserves."

"He has you, and he has me. I know it's not perfect, but he'll

be fine. At least she got him to take Austin to the hospital when you found him with that cut on his head."

"I think he would have died if she hadn't." Mercedes searched her grandmother's face. "You told him you'd sell the farm if he ever hurt Austin again. Can you really do that?"

"I sure can. He's borrowed enough money from me that I own it now."

"I hate the farm." Mercedes put all the anger she felt into the words, and they came out ugly.

"Shush, child." Grandmother's hand stroked her hair. "It's not the farm. It's your father. Someday you'll understand. But until then, I want you to know I'm always here for you."

Mercedes understood now. Understood that she'd needed love from her father and mother. Understood that a lack of love had driven her into Brandon's arms without the hint of a safety net. When he'd left, she wasn't really surprised. Everyone she loved left in one way or another. Even Austin, though he came back now and again. Everyone left but Wayne.

"Oh, Grandma, I wish you were here." Mercedes pushed away the dried daffodil she'd left on the headstone last week and set out a fresh one from her bouquet. Moving to her mother's grave next, she set one there as well. "What made you stay?" Mercedes felt she understood that a little better now. It was the same reason part of her was happy to see Brandon again. "But I won't let him take Darrel."

She passed over the place left for her father. He was still in the same assisted-living facility that Wayne had put him in shortly after they'd married—to prevent further abuse to her and their children. Over the past years he'd mellowed to the point where she loved him now for the man he was, though she still didn't understand the man he'd been before. She usually drove to see him twice a month but had missed her last trip.

He'd wonder why, but with Brandon here, the memories of the past had made her angry at him all over again.

Later, she thought. *I'll see him later. When it's over.*

Or would it ever be over? Did the pain of one generation always have to be visited upon the heads of the next?

Only if you allow it to continue.

Her grandmother's voice rang in her mind as memories converged on the present. Mercedes smiled and looked back at her grave, nodding. She passed her father's older brother and his parents, whom she'd never known, and their parents, and several other relatives, including some small children. She left flowers on the graves of the youngest ones, knowing only too well how their mothers had grieved over them.

She stopped beneath a tree where a mound of grass-covered dirt was still raised, even after so long. She'd chosen this place for the slight rise, how it seemed to look over the others. Lucy would have loved to play in this spot, especially since Wayne had tied up a rope swing with a wooden seat where Mercedes could sit when she visited her daughter.

Look at me! Look at me! Lucy would have called from the swing as her short legs churned over the grass. Mercedes could almost hear the words on the light breeze.

She brushed the old bouquet from the simple headstone and arranged the rest of her flowers on top, smiling when she thought about how much her baby would have loved them. Lucy loved anything bright and happy, especially flowers in the hospital. For that reason, Mercedes always wore bright clothes when she came here.

"How do you like my pink skirt, sweetie? Daddy says it makes me look like a teenager. That's until you see the wrinkles in my face, of course."

Tears welled up in her eyes. "Oh, Lucy girl, I miss you. But

Grandma's taking good care of you, I bet—like she did me." Though Mercedes had accepted that the pain of losing Lucy would never fully leave her heart, the thought of all the relatives who had gone before comforted her.

Sitting next to the mound, she placed her hand on the soft grass she so lovingly tended. "Lucy, I can't lose Darrel too. First you, my youngest, and now my oldest. I can't. Please, if you have any pull up there, talk to God." She smiled through the tears. "Or get Grandma on it. She knows how to get her way."

A hand on her shoulder startled her. She looked up. "Wayne." He was the only one she knew who was so much a part of the land that he could sneak up on her, however unintentionally.

His smile was gentle. "She would have loved those flowers."

"I know."

"Right up until the point where she tore them apart to see what was inside."

Mercedes laughed.

He sat beside her on the grass in his Sunday suit, his red hair bright against the backdrop of the tree.

"I think Lucy likes your hair."

He grinned and reached for her hand. They sat quietly a moment. Then he offered her a handkerchief from his pocket. Her husband, still so old-fashioned in many ways, always the gentleman. One of the things she loved about him. She wiped away her tears.

"You ready?" he asked.

She nodded, and he drew her to her feet. Hand in hand they walked slowly back to the house.

CHAPTER 12

Diary of Mercedes Walker
April 14, 1995

I'm pregnant. I can't believe this is for real. I feel so sad and devastated, which is not the way one should feel at this time. I'm so angry with Brandon. He's still planning to leave at the end of the month. He mentions us, but it's always so far in the future. I think his parents are putting pressure on him, but he won't talk about it. I wish we could run away to another state and forget Massachusetts. I've finished my course now, and I didn't sign up for another. I think I've been waiting for Brandon to ask me to go with him. I'm not going to tell him about the baby. I know he doesn't want to be a father yet, and I have no intention of forcing him to love me. I'm mostly afraid if he learns about the baby, he'll talk me into doing something I'll regret, and that's what got me into this in the first place.

Wayne lifted the cup and drank the water in one gulp. He filled and drained the cup three more times before his thirst was slaked. His eyes took in the dirt he'd passed over again with the field cultivator and deemed it ready to plant. It would be the last field they'd plant with the spring wheat. The feed corn would be easily taken care of in the next couple mornings.

In the next field over, he could see Darrel and Brandon inside the cab of the new tractor, pulling the planting drill over the prepared soil. They were nearly finished and could work the last field in less than an hour, or maybe Wayne would send them back to the house and he'd finish up himself. He didn't really need them at this point.

He was tired. Dead tired. He felt as though he hadn't slept in a week. It was normal to feel tired at planting time, but this seemed something more. There was an odd feeling in his right hand, probably due to his long time at the wheel on the ancient tractor he'd been using today instead of the one Brandon was driving. He hadn't used this machine since replacing it last year just before harvest time, but over the winter he'd been able to make it run again, and it saved time to have Darrel use the new one while he battled with this creature.

He'd been torn about letting Darrel ride with Brandon, even while knowing it was the right thing to do. Wayne had to be vigilant whenever Darrel was using the equipment. Darrel was competent, but he was still a child and had a tendency to daydream at times, as all boys did. Not a good thing. Improper use of the equipment could relieve a man of his arm, as it had the neighbor down the road last month, or worse, his life, as it had Wayne's own father when he was a baby. Wayne had made sure Brandon understood the dangers, and with Brandon watching Darrel carefully, and Darrel directing their work, Wayne was able to work harder himself without as much worry.

Darrel's a good boy, Wayne thought, *and he knows farming.* They would be finished on schedule now, not running behind. Better yet, this time with Darrel might soften Brandon's heart toward their family.

Or it might make his longing take more drastic measures. Only time would tell.

They were coming toward him on the tractor. They'd be nearly out of grain, so he'd top up the drill with seed before starting on this field. Wayne rubbed his chest, feeling the sweat underneath and the way the shirt stuck to his skin. He needed a long, hot shower. At least he didn't feel hungry, though he was normally starving by now. Mercedes had gone all out for their lunch today, as she often did when Darrel spent the day with him in the fields.

It's not because Brandon's here, Wayne told himself, though he didn't know this for sure. She was different since Brandon's arrival. More fragile, younger. Wayne wondered if he was losing her, if she had ever really been his.

Pouring a little water over his hair, Wayne shook his head vigorously before shoving his hat back on. His hair was still a bright red, and he was more comfortable with it now, but he wondered what Brandon thought. He had stared yesterday but hadn't commented.

Wayne felt a shortness of breath as Darrel jumped off the tractor and ran toward him, full of energy despite their long day. Wayne poured him a cup of water.

"Thanks, Dad." Darrel chugged it down.

"How's he doing?" Wayne asked, motioning his head toward Brandon, who was coming slowly toward them.

"Pretty good, I think. But he doesn't get the rows quite straight."

"That takes practice."

Darrel grinned. "Yeah, I remember."

Brandon moved as though doing so caused him discomfort but better than he had at the close of the previous day. Wayne had to admit he'd worked hard and had been easy to teach. He had a quick mind like Darrel's and years of adult experience at learning that made him open to new ideas.

His questions had been endless: Why are farmers required to use treated seed? How does the drill put the dirt back over the seeds? How many times do you have to go over the soil with cultivators before the fields were ready for planting? How much seed do you use? How much water is needed? Wayne had answers ready, but some things you simply had to feel. Or you had to learn by making mistakes.

"You've been a good sport," Wayne said, handing him a cup of water.

Brandon smiled. "Do I look like a truck hit me? Because that's how I feel."

"I do too." It was the truth.

"Yeah, right. Like I believe that." He drank the water and then filled it again from the jug. "Wayne, I think you're going to live forever by working so hard."

"Maybe."

Darrel touched Wayne's arm. "Dad, we forgot." He took off his hat and held it to his heart.

"Oh, right." Wayne pulled his hat off and bowed his head in the direction of the field they'd just planted. "Lord, we thank you for the work that's been done and ask you to look after this field." It was the same prayer he'd offered over every field he'd planted for the past thirty years, and he believed it was a big part of why the farm had held its own while so many had gone under.

"So, is this one next?" Brandon gazed at the field before them.

"You two can head back to the equipment barn with this old thing, and I'll finish up here."

"What about that field?" Brandon pointed to a field beyond the one they'd finished planting.

Wayne shook his head. "That one and those beyond it remain fallow this season."

"It's good for the crops," Darrel added. "The land has to rest sometimes, then the crops are better."

"Oh, yeah, I've heard of that."

"Some people try to get around it by using new fertilizers and stuff, or rotating crops," Darrel said. "We do that some here, but there's nothing like resting for a season."

Brandon nodded, looking impressed at Darrel's knowledge. "So, shall we head back?"

Darrel shook his head. "I think I'll stay. It won't take long to do this field. I can help fill the drill and keep my dad company."

Wayne felt a burst of pride at his son's offer. He knew Darrel wasn't staying because he loved the smell of the earth as Wayne did or enjoyed the satisfaction and comfort of a planted field but because he wanted to be with his dad. Did he feel Wayne's absence on the new tractor as acutely as Wayne did his on the old one? For the past two days they'd worked near each other but never close enough to talk, to share feelings. Always Brandon had been there, in the way. A hired hand but not quite. The difference must confuse Darrel, even if he wasn't aware of it on a conscious level.

Wayne looked at Brandon, who gave a short nod, acknowledging both Wayne's generosity in having Brandon with them these past days and Darrel's desire to be alone with Wayne now.

"Well, I can still take this old tractor back to the barn," he said, "if you'll point me in the right direction."

Wayne lifted a hand toward the south. "Go out to that dirt road there. Follow it until you see our grain bins on the right. The equipment barn's behind them. Just leave it in the yard. I'll put it away when I get there. To get to the house and your car, head east from there."

"And east would be . . ." Brandon thought a moment. "That way, right?"

"Right." Wayne smiled, amused at how city people had to think out which way was east or west. In the country east and west, north and south, were as familiar to them as right or left, day or night.

"I'm assuming this tractor has more or less the same controls as the other one, even though it doesn't have a cab. Right?"

"Basically. The controls are a bit simpler." On the pretense of giving Brandon further instructions regarding the old tractor, Wayne walked with him for a space. "You won't be going to the house." A statement, not a request or an order.

Brandon met his eyes. "No. But I do need to talk with you and Mercedes."

"Tomorrow, then. Or the next day."

They stared at each other a few moments before Brandon nodded. "Okay."

They shook hands, and Wayne felt as much admiration for him as he did dislike. What would he do in Brandon's place?

I would never have been in that position. That was the truth. Wayne could as soon have left Mercedes or put her in such a predicament as cut off his own foot.

Wayne's chest tightened with the desire to protect Mercedes and Darrel. He had to make things right for his family. He had to. Even if it meant losing the farm and going to work at Safeway. He'd sacrifice anything.

He strode back to the new tractor. Darrel had driven the truck with the seed into position. Forcing down his emotions, Wayne reached for the funnel that would fill the drill with seed. The smell of the wheat and the feel of it against his fingers were calming.

Darrel came to stand beside him. "So," Wayne said casually. "What do you think of Brandon?"

"He asks a lot of questions."

Wayne grinned. "I noticed."

"Reminds me of the little boys. Annoying sometimes. But at least he has some good stories to tell."

"About?"

"Mostly about being a doctor. He doesn't shout loud enough over the tractor, though. Could barely hear him even in the cab."

"Guess that's a learned trait."

Soon they were on the tractor again, Darrel driving while Wayne watched, taking a rest for the first time that day. Darrel grinned over at him. This was how it was supposed to be: father and son together.

Yes, this was how it was supposed to be.

Diary of Mercedes Walker
May 4, 1995

A year ago I met Brandon. Now he's gone. He hasn't called yet. Should I have told him about the baby? I don't think it would have changed anything. My heart is dead. There is nothing left. I wish I could die.

I missed work too much because I've been sick, and they fired me, so I had to move back home. Daddy is up from his sickbed a little but mostly just around the house and the yard. Living with him is impossible, worse than when my family all lived here together. I'm under his thumb all the time.

Wayne is the only thing that makes being here bearable. If it weren't for him, I'd go down to the tree by the river and go to sleep forever. I wish Grandmother were back from her sister's house. I need her. I need someone. I need Brandon.

*M*ercedes sat on the rocking chair, holding the infant close to her chest. Funny how she remembered this feeling, the placement, the way her arms had to cradle the child to make sure the baby remained content. Only five minutes of holding her and already it came back, as though it were five years ago and Lucy was a newborn in her arms.

"I wanted to name her after you," Geraldine was saying. "After all, if it hadn't been for you . . . but, well, I just couldn't name her after a car." Her worn face scrunched with worry. "I hope I don't offend you by saying that. It's really a pretty name."

Mercedes laughed. "Believe me, I understand. The only reason I have the name is because my father wanted a Mercedes— and got me instead." He'd also dreamed that Texas held a rich future for him, dreaming about it for decades before finally running off to see if it was true. His obsession with cattle and oil was how Austin had received his name.

"Oh, I love my name now," she added, "but I got teased a lot growing up. At least he didn't name me Chevrolet."

"I seem to remember that. The teasing, I mean." Geraldine shifted her position slightly in the other rocking chair, pulling a crocheted blanket further up on her lap to ward off the slight breeze that reached them on the Pinkhams' front porch. In the distance, they could hear the shout of children, who had only recently arrived from school and were taking advantage of the women's visit to play tag around the huge grain storage bins across the road from the house. "Anyway, I was thinking of calling her Mercy instead."

Mercedes smoothed her fingers over the baby's cheek. "Mercy is perfect."

"That's what I think. There was a lot of mercy going on here last week. We are so blessed."

"Mercy Pinkham," experimented Mercedes. "Maybe you ought to give her a very regular middle name, just in case." She herself didn't have a middle name, and she'd always regretted it. Growing up, she'd wanted her mother's name, Lucinda. Then she could at least have carried that little bit of her mother with her always. Instead, Mercedes had given the name to her own daughter: Lucy Marie. Now she had lost both Lucys.

"Good idea," Geraldine said. "How about Suzanne?"

"Now that's pretty." Trying to shake the sudden melancholy that had come over her, Mercedes asked, "So you said you took her to the doctor? I'm assuming he said her heart was fine?"

"I made him check twice. She's perfect. To tell you the truth, it's me he's worried about. He gave me pills to build up my blood, and I pretty much have to stay down for another week." She laughed. "Eleven children—he really doesn't know what he's asking, does he?" She held up a hand before Mercedes could protest. "Believe me, I'm going to milk this for all it's worth. You got the whole county bringing in food, and the older girls are being helpful. Even the little boys cleaned their rooms without being asked. But between you and me, I did sneak in a load of laundry after they were all in bed."

"Well, you shouldn't have to do that for a while. I think we've got it pretty much finished." Mercedes had taken home the Pinkhams' laundry yesterday and brought it back today, neatly folded in baskets.

"I really appreciate everything you've done."

"I'm glad to help out." Unspoken between them but not forgotten was the time when Geraldine had offered a similar service. It had been months before Mercedes had felt up to common tasks after Lucy died, and Geraldine had been a vital part of keeping things together for Mercedes' family.

Mercedes stared out at the grain bins, gleaming bright silver in the afternoon sun. Scott was nowhere in sight, but she spotted Joseph's hair as he squatted behind an old wagon full of last year's straw. After the wheat harvest, straw was aplenty, and what they didn't store to use for their animals, they could sell to other animal owners who didn't raise grain. Squeezing money from every seed was how farmers survived year to year.

The baby in her arms began moving, rooting around for something to suck. She found her fist, but Mercedes knew she wouldn't be content with that for long. "Looks like Mercy here is a bit hungry."

Geraldine laughed. "She was born with an appetite, I tell you."

Giving the baby one last gentle squeeze, Mercedes arose and handed the baby to Geraldine. "I'd best get home. Wayne told me they'd likely finish early today, or at least Darrel will. I'd like to be there when he gets home."

"Wait." Geraldine looked up at her, ignoring the infant's searching mouth. "Is everything okay? Every time I've seen you this week, you've been, well, a little out of it. Is something wrong?"

Mercedes looked away before the tears came, staring out at the grain bins to compose herself. Children ran from one to the next, and she thought she saw Scott with two of Geraldine's boys.

Finally, she looked back at Geraldine, who was nursing the baby now, partially hidden under the crocheted blanket. Mercy's gulps sounded loud in the stillness.

"There is something I'm dealing with, but I'm not sure how to explain it." She crossed back to the empty rocker and sat down. "I feel like I'm two people. One is the person you've always known, and the other is the person I might have become if I had made different choices in my youth." She looked away from Geraldine's concerned stare. "I wouldn't give up what I have now—I'm not so childish as all that. I can see the value of what I have. But there is still this . . . this wondering inside. What if in another life I could have been just as happy, or maybe happier?"

Maybe if she'd told Brandon about Darrel thirteen years ago, things would have worked out between them. Maybe there wouldn't be the hole that had begun to grow in her heart since Brandon's arrival. Maybe Lucy would have had Brandon's help and survived. One choice, so many consequences.

"I sometimes wonder that myself," Geraldine said softly. "But it's madness to think about. The way I see it, we have only one life. You have to live it the best you can. Going back is not an option. Going forward is." She leaned toward Mercedes. "It's never too late to go after what you've dreamed of—to earn a degree, to learn how to sky dive. But sometimes we forget that when we go after our dreams, we have to give up something to get there. If the exchange is good, then fine and dandy. But if the cost is too high . . . well, maybe we need to find another dream that makes us happy." Geraldine sat back in her rocker. "That's why I didn't study to be a lawyer, though I once thought I wanted it more than anything. I realized years ago that I would have to give up having more children—and living here." She motioned to the yard and the surrounding fields. "I decided I didn't want to be a lawyer as much as I wanted what I already had. In the end I was more in love with the idea than with the actual doing."

Mercedes nodded. Maybe, if she thought about it, there was some sense in her friend's words. Though she longed for knowledge of the life she would have had with Brandon, would she want to give up the life she had experienced?

No. That was the only possible answer.

"What do you dream of doing?" Geraldine asked. "You almost became a psychologist, didn't you?"

Dream. Lately she'd been dreaming of Brandon. Of his dragging Darrel away. And, just as painful, of the months together before he'd left her to face the future alone.

"I don't really know," she said. "Maybe that's the problem." Silence fell between them, heavy and uncomfortable. "If you ever want to talk about it, I'm here."

"Thanks." Mercedes rose again. "Do you want me to help you inside before I go?"

"No. The girls are around somewhere if I need them. I want to sit here and enjoy the moment." Geraldine looked down at Mercy, whose forehead was all that could be seen under the blanket.

Mercedes' lips curved into a tender smile. She remembered that feeling of peace, of wishing she could hold that precious moment forever when the miracle of new life was so vivid and immediate. And maybe in a way she had, somewhere inside the heart where memories never die. She could recall each of the boys but more particularly little Lucy in her arms. "You do that. Call if you need something. Otherwise, I'll be out to check on you."

She went to her battered truck and got in, starting the engine and giving a loud honk as a signal to the children. They came running as she began backing out, having learned the hard way to come when called or walk the long miles home.

They were full of talk and laughter, as was always the case when they were allowed something out of their normal routine. "Remember, we still have the chores when we get home," Mercedes cautioned. "I'll do the milking so Darrel won't have to. He'll be tired."

"I can do it, Mom," Joseph said. "I'd rather do that than feed the animals."

Mercedes grinned. "Okay. You do the milking. I'll get you started. But call me when you're finished, so I can see how you've done. And there's still weeding in the garden." There was always weeding, a little each day to keep the task manageable.

The boys were in the barn and Mercedes in her garden when Brandon came striding across the fields. He looked different than he had last week. He wore a wide-brimmed hat to shield his face and neck from the sun. His long-sleeved shirt protected the burn he'd managed to get on his arms the day before despite the sunblock, and they were as dirty as Wayne's were each day. The jeans, once new, were stained and torn in two small spots, one near the knee and another near the hip as though caught on a piece of machinery. Out of a pocket sprouted a pair of Wayne's work gloves. He walked stiffly, painfully, and she stifled a smile. He'd been a good sport about this, but then he always had been willing to try to please others. She'd loved that about him.

He walked along the field of alfalfa that had sprung up tall this past week. Another few weeks, and they'd take the first cutting, leaving it to dry in the sun. First she'd have the boys try to scare out all the wild ducks that might be nesting there to prevent them from being chopped to bits by the mowing machine. A few were always caught each year, despite their efforts, but over the years they'd been successful at moving many nests to safety.

Mercedes looked down at the bowl of peas in her lap. She'd planted them as soon as the soil was workable at the end of March, but the pods weren't fully ready yet. The boys loved them in their salads, as content to munch up the pods as they would have been to eat the fully developed peas. The only way they wouldn't eat peas was cooked, which was probably because she'd never served them that way. Her mother had never bothered to cook anything they could eat raw, and though Mercedes had learned to like some cooked vegetables, peas weren't one of them.

Brandon didn't see her among the plants at first, but when he did, his step faltered. He took a few steps in her direction, altered course and veered toward the house, then finally turned toward her again.

She arose and went to meet him, deciding not to comment on his indecision. "All finished?"

He nodded, his eyes fixed on her face, their green color emphasized by the green of the trees and grass and garden around him. "Just one more field. Darrel wanted to stay to help Wayne."

"I see."

He looked down at the basket in her hands. "Need a hand?"

"No. I'm all right. Just getting some peas for dinner. Pulling a few weeds along the way. You eating with us?"

He shook his head. "I'm expecting a business call. I'll need to clean up first." He gave her a smile that didn't reach his eyes. She knew without knowing how that the business he would be discussing was Darrel. "I'll call tomorrow," he added.

His hand reached out, the fingers dry from the past days of hard work, and touched the skin on the back of her wrist, barely showing beneath the long-sleeved T-shirt. A fluttering touch, unsure, apologetic. Images went through her mind: Darrel catching his first fish, Darrel holding Lucy. Lucy's grave. Wayne's newly red hair. Brandon at the swimming hole. Brandon kissing her so long ago.

Their eyes met and held.

She took a deliberate step backward.

With a nod, he walked away, and she watched him go.

CHAPTER 14

Diary of Mercedes Walker
June 20, 1995

Brandon hasn't called. Is he waiting for me to make the first move? I keep thinking maybe he doesn't know where I am, and that could very well be it. But why doesn't he call our friends and find out? I talked to Sandra last week, and she hasn't heard from him either, though she thought he'd been talking to Chad.

I know Brandon's silence must be partly because of his parents. I always felt there was something about them that he hadn't told me. Or maybe he's just involved in his work. He does get obsessive when he's occupied, and he has a strong desire to prove himself. Maybe he's working so hard he doesn't realize how much time has passed. But that's ridiculous. Surely he misses me as much as I miss him!

I thought by now he'd wake up to how much we belong together. I want to call him so badly, but the memory of Momma

won't let me. Living here with Daddy these past weeks has shown
me how awful her life must have been. I won't live like that. If
Brandon doesn't love me enough, then I don't want him to call.

*E*ach step he took was torture, reminding Brandon
of the other time when he'd felt such heavy despair.
He'd tried to stay away from Mercedes as Wayne
had said, but he found himself helpless to do so. She had stood
there with her basket of peas, looking so much like the woman
he had loved—still loved? No, he couldn't let his mind confuse
the present with the past. She wasn't the same, and neither was
he.

What had possessed him to reach out to her, to touch her?
Did he hope she would fall into his arms? Hardly. He was the
enemy here, for all that Mercedes and Wayne had opened their
home to him. Their intent was clear: to show him what he'd
be taking from Darrel—the security of youth, the farm, his
family. But what about the things Brandon had to offer? Surely
those were worth something.

Where had he gone wrong? But he knew. His efforts thirteen years ago hadn't been enough, though at the time they'd
seemed more than sufficient.

"Is Mercedes there? I'm a friend of hers. Brandon—from the
hospital. We met a few times when she brought me out to your
farm."

"I remember," came the gravelly voice of a man who had
lived too hard and drunk too much.

"Look, I've tried calling her apartment, but she hasn't been
answering the phone, and now the line is disconnected. Is she
okay?"

"My daughter is fine, but she ain't here at the moment."

"Could you give her a message?"

"Yeah. I guess. But don't be surprised if she don't call. She's a purty woman and not one to sit home and mope."

"Tell her I'd like to talk to her. Tell her I miss her."

"Well, then maybe you shouldn'ta left."

Brandon wished he could strangle the man. Only two weeks away from Mercedes, and it felt like a lifetime. "Just tell her, okay?"

Another week passed. Nothing. He called again, but Mercedes wasn't there. Just the old man. The grouchy old man. Another two weeks. Same thing.

"Look, did you give her my messages?"

"What do you think I am, an idiot?" her father growled. "Besides, she lives here. She knows who calls. If she wanted to talk to you, she woulda called ya by now."

"Well, she might have tried. Like I've been doing."

"If you were any kind of a man, you woulda married her months ago when you had the chance. Anyways, you're too late. She's going with someone else now. You had your chance."

Brandon hung up the phone, smarting from the rebuke. He alternated between worrying that Mercedes was in her father's clutches and feeling hurt from her apparent rejection of him. He should have talked things out with her before leaving Wyoming, telling her the truth about what awaited him in Massachusetts, but he'd thought it might turn her away from him. It probably would have. She would have seen through the charade and insisted he be honest with his parents from the beginning.

"I'll write her a letter," he said, his voice sounding loud in the quiet of his new apartment in Boston. Once he explained, he knew her heart would be big enough to forgive him and to help him make things right.

He wrote the letter.

No reply. So he wrote another.

Six months after he'd left Wyoming, he received the envelope. His hands shook as he opened it. She'd finally written!

A wedding announcement fell onto the table, complete with a lovely head shot of Mercedes and some guy he didn't recognize. The man was older but good-looking in a rugged way that Brandon knew he could never emulate. Jealousy formed a tight ball in the pit of his stomach. Apparently her father had been telling the truth about her dating someone else. Six months. Only six months to forget him.

He never learned who had sent the announcement.

Brandon sighed as the memory faded, leaving behind a sharp hurt. At the time he'd been sure of her rejection, but now he knew his perception to be twisted somehow. Mercedes had been expecting his child, had been expecting *him* to return. He hadn't. The words she'd said that first day he'd challenged her about Darrel here on the farm returned to haunt him: *When all was said and done, when you had broken my heart into so many pieces that I thought I'd never be whole again, even then I wanted our child.*

That didn't make sense with how he'd imagined the events after his departure. What about the calls to her house? Was she so hurt that she couldn't just pick up the stupid phone? A wave of bitterness made him feel lightheaded. She'd made no secret about blaming him for leaving, and he admitted fault, but she also had some guilt in the failure.

He reached his rental car and practically fell inside. Blistered palms gripped the steering wheel until the lightheadedness passed. Then he started the car and drove away. He couldn't help glancing out to the side after he passed the house, to see if he could spot Mercedes in the garden. She was still standing there where he left her.

Still standing there. Alone.

He shut his eyes for an instant, feeling the hopelessness of the situation. The best he could hope for was to share Darrel.

That was all. Weariness pressed against his eyelids.

So tired, he thought. *I'm so tired.*

Farming wasn't at all what he'd expected. It wasn't sitting on the tractor all day, though wrestling with the tractor was tough in itself. It was digging with the shovel when something was in the way, it was filling the seed drill or lying under pieces of equipment trying to fix them when they malfunctioned. Feeding the animals, riding out to check on the herd, doctoring those that needed help. Even pulling a calf or two. And so much more. He'd used muscles he'd only learned about in medical school, and every one of them ached.

But the real tiredness came from his emotional state.

Mercedes, he thought. *What have I done?*

There was a loud honk of a horn and then the high-pitched squeal of engine brakes as a semi behind him closed the gap between them on the highway. Brandon moved over a little so the truck had more room to pass.

He thought of his parents. He'd called to get their attorney's contact information so he could request a recommendation of a good custody attorney in San Diego, but he'd told them it was for a friend. It was an unspoken part of the promise he'd made Mercedes when he promised not to tell Darrel until they decided what to do. If he told his parents, they'd be on the first plane here, suitcases full of presents for their grandson and questions about what color he'd want his room at their house so he'd be comfortable when he visited. They'd set up an account for his education and start collecting college brochures.

Yet didn't Darrel deserve that? He had no living grandparents here. Grandparents were one more thing Brandon could give the child. That, and as many space camps as he wanted to attend, the latest computer, and the best schools. Fury built in Brandon's heart, but he didn't know where he should direct the emotion. Though he and Mercedes were guilty, neither had intended things to turn out this way.

So tired.

His phone rang, and after some searching he found it shoved in the pocket of his jeans, remarkably undamaged after his hard day at playing farmer. He checked the caller ID. His new attorney, Miles Graf.

"I think you have a case," Miles said after their initial greeting. "Especially since you were not aware of the boy's existence and immediately sought him out upon learning of his relationship to you. There will be hoops to jump through, and it won't be cheap, but I'm positive I can get you significant access to your son. You'll have to pay child support, of course."

"That's fine," Brandon said quickly. From what he'd learned of the farm, any payments would help Mercedes and Wayne. Maybe money would soften their hearts, though he wouldn't hold his breath on that account.

"I'm not guaranteeing anything, of course, but I'll do my best. The rest will depend upon how good the attorney for the Johnsons is."

Johnsons. For a moment, Brandon had trouble placing the name since he still thought of Mercedes by her maiden name, Walker. But she was Mrs. Wayne Johnson now, though they'd kept the Walker name for the farm.

"Thank you," he said. "I thought I'd have some kind of a chance. It's not my fault she hid him from me all these years."

"Well, it won't be easy. Just possible. We should meet soon to map out a strategy—I have some openings next week if that works for you—and we'll need an attorney there as well to work with us. They'll know all the ins and outs of the state laws and have a pulse on the local judiciary. After I do some checking, I'll be able to recommend someone."

"Sure. Great. I can fly back next week." Brandon felt a thrill ripple through him. Darrel was going to know who he was! He'd be able to take his son to the beach in California, to show him off to his parents in Boston. Maybe Darrel and Hannah would get along—providing she was still interested in meeting him. As long as Brandon didn't think about Mercedes and Wayne, he could be happy with even a little time with Darrel.

Then why did he still feel so much despair?

He drove down the highway. Slowly, as though driving through water. He kept seeing flashes of Darrel's face as he chose to stay with Wayne, of Darrel excitedly discussing nano-technology, and of Wayne reading up on all the latest events solely to help Darrel learn. He thought of the sacrifice Wayne and Mercedes would be making to send him to space camp, to college. And Mercedes . . .

So much time wasted.

He missed her laugh, her unique way of looking at things, her kindness. Her touch. The way she'd loved him. How could he still miss that after so long?

How could he have lived without it?

His phone rang again. Hannah. He was feeling dizzy, so he put on his blinker and pulled off the highway. Besides, Hannah would ask. She hated for him to talk when he drove, saying that too many accidents were caused by inattentive phone users. She was probably right.

"Hello?"

"Hi. You survived."

He grimaced. "Barely."

"Where are you now?"

"On the highway. Don't worry, I pulled over to answer."

Then to assert his independence and pretend he hadn't done it for her, he added, "I was feeling a bit dizzy."

"I bet you haven't eaten yet."

"I ate a big lunch. But farming's hard work."

"So, I guess you're not planning to quit being a doctor." Amusement was thick in her voice.

"Uh, that would be a big no. But there is good news. I talked to my new lawyer. He says I have a chance."

"That's great! So what are Darrel's, uh, parents saying?"

"We haven't discussed it further."

"What about your parents?"

"Not yet. You know them."

She laughed. "Yeah. Good idea to wait. They'll be choosing what college they want him to attend."

"That's not going to happen." Brandon surprised himself at the fierceness of his reaction. He wasn't going to let his parents control Darrel's life as they had his. Mercedes had suffered enough at their hands, though she was unaware of it. They all had.

"I mean, they can make suggestions, but the choice is his."

His head was pounding, and he felt like throwing up. Adjusting his seat as far back as he could, he lay down and closed his eyes. What was wrong with him? He hadn't felt this way in a long time.

Not since the cancer. At the thought, blinding, black fear struck him dumb.

"Brandon, are you okay?"

"Fine," he managed.

"You don't sound fine. You moaned."

"It's this stinking headache."

"All that sun."

"I had a hat."

"You're not used to it." He chuckled.

"What?"

"You sound like you did when we were married. When I worked too many shifts."

She was silent, and he suspected he'd offended her. "Not that I mind," he added. "It's good to have someone to worry."

"I do worry. You need to take better care of yourself. I'm not sure what you were trying to prove with this farm stuff."

"I'm fine." He was feeling better now that the wave of nausea had passed. "I just wanted to spend time with him in his environment. Get a feel for who he is and what he needs."

"And what is that?"

Brandon couldn't answer. The truth was that Darrel seemed to have everything a child could need or want. Except maybe the whole truth, which only Brandon could give him.

Hannah sensed his reluctance. "Look, you should go get something to eat."

"You're right." He sat up, reaching for the seat controls. Blackness appeared at the edges of his vision. "Hannah, I'm going to—"

Everything went dark.

"Dr. Rhodes, can you hear me? Brandon?"

Lights shone in Brandon's eyes, forcing him to leave the soft, comfortable place where he was resting. Reluctantly his eyes blinked opened. Pain sliced through his head as images rushed to greet him: Dr. Peck from the hospital flashing a light in his eyes, concern evident on his narrow face; two nurses standing near the doctor; an IV tube snaking to his wrist; Dustbottom from the morgue leaning against the wall with his arms folded, watching the whole scene.

"Stop that," Brandon told the young doctor.

Dr. Peck straightened and switched off the light. "Welcome back, Dr. Rhodes."

"What happened?"

"You passed out. Hit your head pretty good. We put in some staples." Dr. Peck reached for the chart in one of the nurse's hands and made a notation. His strokes were short, compact, and precise, in contrast to his tall, lanky stature. His balding head shone brightly, unpleasantly, reflecting the lights overhead.

Brandon looked toward old Dustbottom, whose real name he couldn't even recall at the moment. With a lazy smile the short doctor shoved himself off the wall and walked toward the bed. "Your ex-wife called us. I thought you'd left Wyoming after the seminar, but apparently you had other business in town? We tracked you down on the highway."

"Thanks."

"What we don't know," Dustbottom continued, "is what caused the blackout. Hannah says you had stomach cancer, so Dr. Peck and I think you should undergo a few tests. You know the routine."

Brandon shook his head. "I had them all a few months ago. Not a trace of abnormal cells. I'm fine. Have been for a year." He struggled to sit up, but the searing pain shot through his head again. Cursing, he lay down and closed his eyes until the worst of it passed.

"We know that," Dr. Peck said, "but we have too many unanswered questions. Of course, the best thing would be to get you back to California and your regular doctor."

"I can't leave—at least not yet."

Dustbottom regarded him, his eyes behind the glasses without expression. Brandon had never been able to say what color his eyes were—blue, gray, or perhaps even hazel. They seemed to change with his mood and the light. The man had aged in the past thirteen years, though not nearly as much as Brandon had expected. His hair was peppered with gray now, but the cheeks were unlined—probably due to the extra twenty pounds he'd gained. As always, his white coat was sprinkled with tiny dark spots and sat crookedly on his wide shoulders. He seemed the same old Dustbottom who had been willing to answer any question from the residents so they didn't have to look stupid in front of the other doctors. The morgue had always been open to them—for those who could stomach it— and Brandon had spent more than his fair share of time there. He'd learned more from Dustbottom than from any other doctor at this hospital.

"Why can't you leave?" Dustbottom asked. "Your seminar is over. And I know you aren't hanging out here because I'm so good-looking. You've only come down to the morgue twice during your visit. What's up?"

Brandon looked at Dr. Peck and the two nurses. Dr. Peck took the hint. "Let me know if I should order those tests." He motioned to the nurses and together the three left the room.

"Well?" Dustbottom prompted.

"I have a son here. I'm just getting to know him."

"Mercedes' child."

"You knew?"

"Not until this minute. I only met her a few times, and I haven't seen her since you left. But you talked about her nonstop for an entire year, so it's hard not to remember her."

"She remembers you too."

He smiled. "I hope you didn't bore her with too many stories."

"Believe me, we had better things to talk about than your precious morgue."

"Apparently."

Brandon sobered. "I don't know what to do. I didn't know about him all these years, and now I find the day I left here, I made the worst mistake of my life. But there's no going back, and there's no second chance."

"There's always a second chance. But at what, is the question."

Brandon guessed that was true. His second chance could only involve Darrel.

"You should do the tests because I seriously doubt you passed out solely from a little farm work."

"Have you seen what these guys do? It's torture." Brandon tried to move again, and this time the pain wasn't as bad. He lifted a hand and gingerly felt the staples above his right ear. Blood had caked around the wound. He'd have to wash it off well, or when they took out the staples, they'd tear off the scab and reopen it. He'd seen many inexperienced nurses do just that to their helpless victims.

"You may have to face the chance that your cancer is back," Dustbottom said. "The sooner you find out, the better. You know that as well as I do."

Brandon stared at him, his jaw clenched. He wasn't sick—why couldn't they believe that? He'd simply worked too much this week, trying to keep up with Wayne. But he knew Dustbottom well enough to know that he wouldn't let it go. "I've got an appointment with my attorney in San Diego next Wednesday. I'm flying in for a day—two at the most—but I can get the tests done with my regular doctor then. You know as well as I do that a week won't change the outcome this early in the game."

"Just so you do it." His job accomplished, Dustbottom turned without another word and strode to the door.

Brandon stared at the specks of dirt on the back of his white coat, looking exactly as though he'd sat in a sandbox somewhere. Or perhaps they were mold spores. At the door, Dustbottom paused and looked back.

"As for Mercedes and your son, you should make sure you won't regret today as badly as you regret what happened the last time. If I were you, I'd make the best of what time you have, regardless if it's one year or fifty. Got it?"

Brandon nodded. Well, at least he understood the words, if not how they applied to his life. Regretting the past was not something he was sure he could fix. Some consequences he'd never anticipated.

"I'm an idiot," he said to the empty room. "What is it I want?"

But he knew. He wanted his life back the way it had been before leaving Wyoming that first time. He wanted Mercedes in his life. Mercedes and Darrel, the way a family should be. It wasn't fully his fault that things went wrong, though he knew most of the blame rested on his shoulders. Yet surely it wasn't too late to find some way to make the future bearable. Maybe it was time to fight for what should rightfully have been his.

CHAPTER

15

Diary of Mercedes Walker
July 10, 1995

 I saw Brandon on TV at some gala event for a hospital! Caught my eye because it was in Boston. What are the chances I'd be watching the TV right then? Of course, I'm watching way too much TV now. That's practically all I do. He was surrounded by important-looking people, and there was one woman in particular that I noticed. Long hair, dark, though not as dark as mine, and she was movie-star beautiful. She kept a hand possessively on his arm.

 It was a brief clip, so I don't know if it was real or something affected for the taping, but now I have the feeling of being used. Could he have dated this girl before me? Is she the reason he didn't want his parents to meet me or why he didn't ask me to go with him to Boston? Did he have a commitment with her all this time? If so, he isn't the man I thought I loved. And he isn't someone who deserves me.

Unfortunately, that doesn't seem to make these feelings go away, though seeing him on TV with her has ripped out one more piece of my heart. I'm going to add a black heart to the baby quilt. A heart as black as Brandon's betrayal and my despair.

E arly Friday evening, Mercedes reached into her cupboard and drew out a jar of powdered herbs: lobelia for pain, slippery elm for healing flesh and skin, comfrey to heal and remove toxins, goldenseal as a natural antibiotic. She made it by the quart now because the boys were constantly needing the mixture for all their cuts and bruises. It also worked well on the animals. She'd even begun growing some of the herbs herself to save money.

"It's hurts, Momma." Joseph looked up at her, his eyes full of tears. He'd stepped on a nail in the barn somewhere, one she suspected he and Scott had been hammering into boards last week when they were making stilts for Cub Scouts. The nail had gone deep into Joseph's heel, but the nail wasn't rusty and the blood had cleaned out the wound. Using this poultice for the next few days would assure there would be no infection and that it would heal quickly. By tomorrow morning, Joseph would be running around as though nothing had happened, and she'd have to practically hold him down to change the bandage.

"Here, this will help." She cut a piece of fresh apple pie she'd baked that afternoon. Wayne's favorite. He'd been endlessly supportive of her these past three days as they waited to hear from Brandon. He'd rubbed her shoulders at night, taken the boys out with him to check on the cattle to give her time alone to quilt, and hadn't appeared to mind when she hadn't responded readily to his romantic advances. She was so nervous and worried about what Brandon was planning that every task took more effort than it should, and even the easiest chore was a hardship. Most of the day, she walked around in a haze, as though someone had filled her mind and vision with a murky cloud.

The doorbell rang, and Scott jumped up from the floor where he had been sitting to better examine his brother's injury. "I'll get it."

Mercedes measured a small amount of powder into a dish, dribbled a few drops of water on top, and began mixing. "Darrel," she said, "I think you'd better go search for any more nails you boys might have left around."

"Right." He gave her an apologetic glance.

"There weren't any more," Joseph mumbled through his pie.

"Don't talk with your mouth full."

"I'd better check anyway." Darrel started for the door. "Then can I ride out and meet Dad? Dinner's almost ready, isn't it?"

Wayne and the boys had gone fishing after dinner yesterday, and they'd been uncharacteristically lucky to catch several large trout, which she was baking for dinner. Darrel was especially pleased because his fish had been the largest, and now he didn't want Wayne to miss out on one minute of the special dinner. Wayne would be full of praise for Darrel's accomplishment, and that meant a great deal to the boy.

Mercedes watched him with a tender sadness. Her innocent child. Her little boy. In a few days his entire world would change forever. Would he hate her? Would he ever trust her again?

"Are you okay, Momma?" Darrel asked. "I won't go if you don't want me to."

Words so easily spoken. Of course he didn't know what was in store for him or how desperately she didn't want him to leave.

She smoothed the concern from her face. "No, go. That's a good idea. He'll be glad to have you meet him."

He grinned. "Okay. I'll be back."

A promise she knew he'd keep—for now.

"This pie does make my foot feel better," Joseph said as Darrel shut the door behind him.

Mercedes laughed. "I knew it would. But you can't have another piece until after dinner."

"Aw." He faked a sad expression, but she knew it was only an act.

She scooped out the paste onto a bit of plastic wrap and knelt by his foot. "This may sting just a bit."

"Momma," Scott said reappearing in the kitchen doorway, "it's that doctor guy." She looked up to see Brandon entering behind her son. He was tanned from the days of working the farm and his nose was partially peeling, but he appeared weak and tired, his coloring a sickly pale beneath the tan.

"I hear you have an emergency," he said. He smiled, but she didn't smile in return.

"A nail went practically all the way through his foot," Scott said with relish. "He was jumping off the gate into the stall, and boom, he fell right on it."

"It was in a piece of wood we were building with the other day," Joseph added. "There was blood everywhere. *Everywhere.*"

"Yep." Scott looked happy. "It was wicked awesome."

Brandon frowned. "Shouldn't you take him to the doctor?"

"Why?" Mercedes made an effort not to roll her eyes. "So he can ask me if Joseph's tetanus shots are up to date while he's putting on a bandage? Three hours wasted at the least. No thanks. This stuff will make sure there's no infection and have him up and running by morning."

She pressed the herbs over the wound, secured the plastic wrap with tape, and pulled on a clean sock. "There, all done." She leaned over and kissed Joseph on the forehead. "You, my dear, are free to hop around wherever you want, or even walk on it if you can."

"Can I swing?"

"I'll push you!" Scott bounded to the door and waited as Joseph hopped after him. "Don't worry, Momma," Scott said, placing a hand on his brother's back to help him balance. "I'll look after him."

"Of course you will. You're a good brother."

The door banged shut, leaving Mercedes uncomfortably alone with Brandon. "You like fish?" she asked, peering into the oven.

"You know I do."

Her hands froze. She did know that. His favorite was shrimp, a dish her family detested, but Brandon had always devoured any seafood put before him. Next to that he loved pizza, especially cold in the morning for breakfast. He'd lived on the stuff during his residency. It was a miracle he hadn't killed himself with all that cholesterol-filled cheese and pepperoni.

She forced herself to close the oven, turning slowly to meet him. The expression on his face was one she'd recognized from the old days. "Look," she said. "I realize you want to be in Darrel's life, but if you think about it, giving him time—giving all of us time—to adjust to you would be a good thing. I was hoping you could come and visit occasionally, get to know him. And then when he's near graduation, we could sit down and explain. He'd already have a relationship with you, and it'd be less of a surprise that way. And meanwhile, you could email as much as you wanted over the years."

"With you guys reading all the emails."

She blinked at the bitterness in his voice. "Responsible parents do read their kids' emails, don't they?"

"You don't want him to know the truth."

"Not yet." She took a step toward him. "Please. Let him have these few more years. It's not his fault we messed up."

Brandon's face was dark. "More years that I'm not in his life. More years that I have nothing to say about his education."

"But you'll be here, as much as you can be, and I promise, we'll talk about it all . . ." She was starting to feel faint. The set of his jaw told her he'd already made up his mind. Placing a hand behind her back, she felt for the counter to steady herself.

"I'm thinking we should share custody." He said the words with strength, standing boldly in the middle of her kitchen. He wasn't a big man like Wayne, but suddenly the kitchen felt too small and she wanted to escape. "My attorney thinks we have a good case, but I hoped we could work it out between us. I could have him holidays and summers. Maybe a few longer weekends. I'll pay for the flights, of course."

She struggled for breath. "You want to take my son away for the summer, our busiest season? And all the holidays? What kind of holiday do you think we'd have without him? What kind of holiday would he have without us?"

"One with grandparents who adore him." He took two steps toward her, and she pressed against the counter to get away from him. "Or he can stay with me for the school year and you can have summers."

"So he can go home to an empty house while you're at the hospital?" She lifted her chin, glaring at him. "You're crazy! I'll fight you with everything I have before I'd let that happen to my son. No judge would ever approve it. They couldn't!"

"I can give him a lot, Mercedes. I'm his father. I have the right to know my son." His voice had deepened as he talked, as it always did when he was serious.

"You have no rights, none at all! You left. You never called. You turned away and never looked back."

He tilted his head to the right, a line of puzzlement forming between his eyes. "What do you mean I never called? I told you before that I called."

"Not until weeks later after I'd left the apartment and the number had been disconnected. You gave up too easily. You could have called here, you know. Where else would I have gone?"

He gaped at her. "I did call here! I called and called and called. After I realized what a mistake I'd made, I wanted to make it right. I was going to tell you everything about how my parents had put pressure on me to marry this girl and how I had started going along with it before I met you because I wanted the position her father could offer me. I wouldn't have gone through with it—I swear after I met you, I never once considered marrying her. But I still wanted that position at the hospital. Thought I deserved it. I didn't realize what an idiot I was being."

"You called here?" The rest of what he said slid past her.

"Repeatedly. I talked to your dad several times. I even wrote two letters. The only response I got was a wedding announcement—yours and Wayne's."

She held a hand to her pounding heart as she moved away from him, slumping into Joseph's vacated chair. "I never saw any letters. He never told me you'd called."

Who would have taken the letters? Her father? Wayne? No, Wayne would never have lied to her that way. She could believe it of her father, though. He'd never cared for anyone but himself. But why would he have done such a thing?

"I sent them. I promise you that." He sat on a chair and scooted it closer to hers. "Look, I told myself I came back to Wyoming only for Darrel, and I am here for him, but I think, after all this time, I also wanted to know what happened between us. I always thought we were meant to be together. It didn't seem possible things should have gone so wrong. But if you didn't even get my letters, if your dad didn't tell you I called . . ." His green eyes held hers. "That means it was all stolen from us, and I'm not sure what to do with that information."

She couldn't seem to process it either. Surely none of this was real. It was too much like the dreams that had tortured her after he'd left thirteen years ago. Dreams in which he returned and told her it had all been a mistake.

Time ticked away as they sat staring at one another. One second, two . . . more. Just like the ones that had separated them all these years.

"I know you've hated me for a long time because of how I left," he said finally, "but you have to know that I've been angry at you too, for getting married, for replacing me so easily."

"It wasn't easy!" she retorted.

"I realize that now. I'm sorry for everything, and I don't know how any of this will play out, but I still care about you."

An emotion she recognized finally bubbled to the surface: anger. She transformed the anger into words, spitting them at him. "You tell me in one breath that you're going to take away my son—"

"Not take him away—"

"Take my son away, under whatever guise you call it, and then in the next breath you say you care about me. Seriously? You expect me to believe that. What do you want from me?"

"Talk around it all you want, but what it boils down to is that we could have had a future together. Wayne's a good man—I know that. But tell the truth. You don't love him the way you loved me."

She couldn't answer. Maybe it was true, though how he could possibly guess at her inner feelings, she had no idea. A sob escaped her lips, and she clenched them tightly. Why was he doing this? Hadn't he hurt her enough?

He started to reach for her, but she shook her head. "Please," she whispered. But she wasn't sure what she was asking for. To leave her alone? Not to fight for Darrel? To not give up on them?

His hand dropped to his lap. He looked vulnerable, and she averted her gaze.

"Mercedes," he began again, "the other day after I left here, I had an . . . incident. I passed out, ended up in the hospital. They don't know why. It's always possible the cancer's back, but I don't really believe that. I feel well—or as well as a man could be after working in the sun for days and then cracking his head open. Anyway, Dustbottom was at the hospital. He told me that it's never too late for second chances, and I suddenly realized this is the only chance I have to tell you how I feel, to set straight what happened."

She jumped up from her chair, backing away toward the door. "Would you listen to yourself? You come here knowing you might be dead in a year, and you want me to trust my son's happiness to you? That's caring about me? How dare you even consider telling him who you are when you may not be around to finish what you start!" She wiped impatiently at the tears on her cheeks. "But then, you're never around to finish what you start, are you?"

"I want to finish this." He stared at her, his face ashen. "I want you and Darrel in my life."

She gave a derisive laugh. "Tell me this, does cancer give you the right to tear apart a family? To tear me apart again? If you really cared about me like you say you do, maybe you should think about what you're doing. Maybe you'd remember I've made a life without you—a good one." She shook her head, her renewed fury the only thing keeping her upright. "I don't need or want you in my life."

He arose from his chair and took a step toward her, one hand extended. "Mercedes . . ."

"Get out!" She was frantic now. She wasn't strong enough to permit his touch. The memories were too powerful.

"All I'm saying is—"

"Go!"

His shoulders sagged, and his head hung down. "Just think about how unfair it is," he said, his voice scarcely a whisper. "I deserve to know my own son. I will know him! And I really don't want to spend the rest of my life wondering what could have been between us."

She hated him at that moment, hated him with everything that she was. And yet he was right. Hadn't she been doing exactly that these past years—wondering what could have been? Hadn't she been dishonest by not loving Wayne as much as he loved her? Holding a part of herself back was the same thing as not loving enough.

"Please leave." The words were the most difficult she'd ever said.

He turned and walked heavily across the kitchen, apparently intending to leave by the front door. She watched him take three steps, four, and then she went after him. He hesitated in the doorway, his head swinging back toward her, light flaring in his eyes.

She stopped within an arm's length. "When you say I never loved him the way I loved you," she began. She could see he was listening intently, aching to hear more. Hoping.

"Well, you left out another thing, something that thirteen years ago hurt me more than you can ever imagine. You know what that is? It's that Wayne loved me more than you did. More than the man I loved, the father of my child. And how do I know? Because Wayne would never have left me, no matter the excuses. You should have taken me with you."

"I'm here now." So much emotion in his face—it hurt her to see. "Mercedes, you have to believe there was never a time when I didn't want you."

"Now is thirteen years too late."

As he disappeared into the hallway, she collapsed onto a chair, a hand at her mouth to deaden her cries.

CHAPTER 16

Diary of Mercedes Walker
July 17, 1995

 I want to die, just plain die. This baby is growing, I can feel it, but I'm losing weight. I've been horribly sick. Part of me would like to simply lose enough weight to disappear forever, but I know this is a consequence I need to face. How could I have let myself love a man so much that I lost the very essence of myself? Now I understand how my mother was able to endure such treatment from my father.

 Oh, Momma! I'm sorry! I didn't realize before how awful life was for you. Even though I don't agree with what you did, I forgive you. We are alike in this, but I will take your example and learn from it.

 I'm determined to pull out of this and be myself again. But I don't exactly know how to do that. Wayne once said I was stronger than my mother, and I'm trying to live up to his vision of me. I must pray for strength—and for forgiveness.

Daddy is worse each day. Not physically—he's seemed to reach a plateau with his health where he doesn't get worse or better— but he is secretive and verbally abusive. Wayne doesn't even know about the baby, but he said yesterday that I should call or write a letter to Grandmother. He thinks I'd be better off living with her.

I've thought about moving to her house even without her being there, but I would miss my talks with Wayne. We keep each other good company. He rides with me sometimes in the evenings, and I've taken to bringing him lunch. It gives me something to look forward to besides lying here missing Brandon and feeling sorry for myself.

I can't even think about the baby. The baby quilt is about half finished. I work on it very slowly. I want it to be perfect.

*B*randon walked out of the house onto Mercedes' front porch, unsure what to do. He didn't want to hurt Mercedes further, but neither would he give up his son. He had a lot to offer. And what about Mercedes herself? He could tell it made a difference to her knowing about the letters. Somewhere inside, she still cared for him.

It was all so unfair. Everything should have been different.

Does that give you the right to expect something from her now?

It was his own voice in his thoughts, the clinical, professional side of him. No, it didn't give him that right—or any rights at all. But the enormity of losing everything still seemed too much to comprehend.

He couldn't think about Wayne and the other children. He wouldn't think about them. Or Mercedes either. He would focus on Darrel. His son. There seemed to be no way to follow

Dustbottom's advice about not creating more regrets. He already regretted hinting to Mercedes about his continuing feelings for her. Yet he also regretted not declaring the full depths of his emotion. He regretted hurting her about Darrel, but he also regretted that he wasn't leaving here with the boy this very minute.

He walked blindly down the steps, stopping to kick at a rock, sending it shooting over the gravel drive.

"Brandon!" Darrel was coming toward him from the side of the house.

Warmth filled the emptiness in Brandon's chest. "Hey, how are you?"

The boy's chin lifted in much the same way Mercedes' had. "Why is my Momma crying?" His tone was protective, and in it Brandon glimpsed the man he would become—fiercely loyal and ready to defend those he loved. "I heard her through the back door."

"We had a disagreement, that's all."

Darrel's face was shuttered. He stared down at his hand that held two half-rusted nails. "She disagrees with me and my dad all the time, and she doesn't cry then."

Brandon knew he had to proceed with caution. If Darrel started hating him, it would make becoming a part of his life more difficult. "You're right," he conceded. "Will you tell her I'm sorry? I didn't mean to make her upset."

Darrel relaxed. "I'll tell her you're a stubborn old fool. That works for my dad."

"I thought you said he didn't make her cry."

"He doesn't, but when they disagree, that makes her laugh." Darrel smiled at him, but the smile wasn't as genuine as it had been days earlier. He put his hands in his pockets. "I was going to ride out and get my dad."

"Sounds fun."

Darrel walked to the porch and sat down on the steps. "I changed my mind. He'll be back soon anyway. We're going to eat my fish."

Brandon understood that Darrel was putting himself as a barrier between him and Mercedes. Tears stung Brandon's eyes. He was a good kid—more than he could have hoped for. He only wished the boy didn't feel he had to protect his mother from him. Would he if he knew the truth?

"Well, enjoy yourselves." Brandon headed for his rental car, not looking forward to the long drive back to Riverton.

He'd done the right thing demanding his rights. Hadn't he? When he glanced in the rearview mirror, Darrel was standing on the porch watching him go.

An hour later, Brandon went up the walkway of the Alpine House. He stopped briefly in the doorway to stretch his back, his thoughts returning to Walker Farm. Were the Johnsons sitting down to dinner even now? Was Mercedes telling Wayne about his visit? Shame washed over him at the thought.

But what else could I do? Maybe she wouldn't tell him.

"Brandon?"

He looked for the voice and saw Hannah in the sitting room across the entryway. Arising from a love seat, she walked toward him. He was so surprised to see her that his mouth wouldn't work. She looked great. Her blond hair was still cropped around her head and face but styled differently, with soft feathering that flattered her rounded cheeks. Her blue eyes were large in her face, clearly her best feature. The fitted yellow blouse and cropped pants showed her slender figure to best advantage, a figure that often had men stopping to stare. She looked incredible, much as she had on the day he'd married her.

"I've been waiting for you. I went to the hospital first, but they told me you'd been released." She stretched to give him a soft kiss on the cheek and a token hug. She smelled of something sweet, perhaps flowers with a touch of honey. A new perfume?

"They let me go this morning. Would have been yesterday, but they seemed to like holding me prisoner." He wanted to ask why she was here, but phrasing the words so they didn't sound ungrateful and rude was an effort he wasn't up to at the moment. "It's nice to see you," he said instead, something that wasn't exactly untrue.

"I bet you're wondering why I'm here."

"Kind of. It is a surprise—a good one, of course."

"Well, I was worried."

"You could have called."

"It's not the same thing." Her eyes fell to the carpeted floor, and he knew there was more. How long it might take her to tell him was something he couldn't predict.

It was just as well she wasn't ready to talk. He was tired and wanted to lie down, yet he was also afraid to be alone, and her company would distract him. Until he had new tests and the results came back, he feared his mind would stray to the negative. What if, after he'd finally learned about his son, he became too ill to be a real father?

"Well, uh, since you're here, would you like to have dinner? They have a nice little place nearby that sells seafood."

She grinned. "Shrimp, I bet."

"Among other things." He offered his arm as he had in the old days.

"Do they have takeout?"

"I think so."

"Then let's get it to go and come back here."

"Why?"

"You look pale."

"I'm tanner than I've been in years."

She came to a stop and studied him. "Well, you are tan, that's true, but you don't look right."

"You wouldn't say that to me if I were a woman."

She smiled. "You know what I mean. You've been in the hospital."

"Okay, we'll get takeout." Truthfully, he was feeling nauseated, but that was likely due to the hospital food he'd been forced to ingest. Or he'd picked up a sickness there. It happened often enough.

"My room has a nice table and a view," she said as he opened the passenger door of his car for her.

"Are you staying here?" At her nod, he added, "How long?"

"Until Sunday night. I flew up after lunch—that was as early as I could leave, but I have to be back by Monday morning."

"I see."

"Your parents sent you a care package."

He grimaced. "Why am I not surprised?" "They miss you."

He had no reply for that. They'd been helpful during his illness, but he simply couldn't face their constant hovering after everything was finished. Moving to California had been his way of starting over. Only it hadn't really worked that way. He'd been there more than a year and most of his belongings remained in boxes in his new garage.

Less than thirty minutes later, they were back at the Alpine House, and Brandon relaxed at the table while Hannah set out the meal. Not having to think for the moment, to see her eating across from him as they had so many times before, comforted him.

"So how's it going on the custody front?" she asked when he'd retrieved a stack of photographs he'd taken Monday at the farm.

"I told Mercedes today I wanted Darrel for holidays and the summers."

Her fork hesitated over her plate. "And?"

"She turned me down flat."

"What would he do at your house all day in the summer? You'd be working."

Did all women think alike? "I hadn't thought of that. Well, maybe not the whole summer then. I'd take my vacation and we'd spend that time together. If I went on another charity mission, he could go. He'd learn a lot. Might even want to go into medicine."

Her right eyebrow quirked. "And if he doesn't?"

"He can be anything he wants. I won't force him."

"I meant, and if he doesn't want to go with you? Even to visit?"

"I'm his father. Why wouldn't he want to know me? I'd make it fun." He stared down at the remaining four shrimp on his plate, his appetite completely gone. "Unfortunately, Mercedes doesn't see it that way."

"She was mad?"

He nodded. "To put it mildly."

"She's the one who kept the secret all these years."

"Not her fault, not really." He pushed the plate away and leaned back in the chair, which was surprisingly comfortable.

Again the eyebrow quirk. He'd forgotten how often she'd done that and how it fascinated him. "You're defending her?" she asked. She took a last bite of shrimp and sat back.

"It's complicated." He found himself telling her the story of Mercedes' father and her quick marriage.

Hannah had a soft smile on her lips, one that seemed more regretful than happy. "You still love her."

"I still love you," he countered. "Feelings like that don't disappear."

She looked away. He'd surprised her. He hadn't meant to say it exactly that way. What he meant was she'd been someone special in his life and that hadn't changed with the divorce. Perhaps it would have if they had parted under worse conditions.

Worse? That almost made him laugh. What could be worse than cancer? But he knew that for a marriage there were a lot worse things.

"I think it's going to be okay," he said quickly to cover the awkwardness. "She'll come around. I'm flying home next week for a day to meet with my attorney and have a few tests done at my doctor's, and then I'll fly back and see where I stand. Maybe Merce—the Johnsons will have softened. Still, I expect I'll eventually have to get a court order for a paternity test and go from there."

"Tests?"

"Yeah, you know. The test that'll prove I'm Darrel's father."

"No, I meant the other ones. You said you were going home to get tests. Plural. Are those because of your collapse? I thought they decided it was because of stress and exhaustion."

"No, *I* said that. They wanted to fool with some tests. I agreed to do them at home to get them off my back."

She was shaking her head. "You're afraid it's back, aren't you?"

The knot in his stomach wouldn't go away. He fought to keep down the shrimp. At this rate he'd begin to hate seafood. "Yes," he finally admitted.

Hannah stared at him without speaking for a long moment.

Her blue eyes were like the sky he'd worked under at the farm. Quite a contrast to Mercedes, whose eyes were as dark and rich as the freshly plowed soil. But both had looked at him in the same way, a mix of pity and horror—and anger. The anger from Mercedes he understood but not from Hannah. Unless she still cared for him in a way that expected more. A future.

"You don't know about the results, and you want to fight for custody of your son? Brandon, he's only a child. What's it going to do to him if he learns to love you and then you get sick?" She tapped a picture of Darrel laughing with his brothers.

"That's exactly why I have to tell him. This might be my only chance to know my son."

"Then this is for you, not him." She folded her hands quietly in her lap.

He didn't reply. She had it all wrong, but how to explain so she'd understand? Darrel deserved to know him, whatever his health status.

"Look," she said into the silence. "I work with children every day, and I've seen what parents and other relatives do to kids in the name of what's good for them. Many times it ends up being better only for the parents. My job as an administrator has always been to protect the children and help the parents understand the child's needs. Have you thought about Darrel's needs? What *he* wants?"

"He'd want to know the truth."

"Perhaps. But is the truth best for him? At least until you know what's going on with your tests?"

He crossed an arm over his stomach, feeling her words as an attack. "Hannah, I'd like to say I know what's best for my son, but I don't. I'm working on instinct here." He paused and then added in a rush, "But I'm not totally without a plan. I don't expect to take him away from his mother."

"And what does that mean?" Her eyes narrowed, but he shook his head, unwilling to explain how strongly he hoped that given time Mercedes would come to understand they shouldn't have to live without each other.

Yet Hannah could always see right through him. "Brandon, suing for custody is not going to make a good impression on Mercedes. If you think she's angry now, that won't be anything compared to how she's going to feel later. She'll wish she'd never met you."

"Is that how you feel?" The words tumbled out before he could stop them.

She shook her head slowly. "There are things I would have done differently, but I've never regretted knowing you. I loved our life together." She leaned forward, her eyes earnest. "Didn't you? Weren't we happy?"

"Yes." He let his gaze drop from hers.

"I'm glad to hear that because lately I've been wondering if it was all a lie."

"It wasn't." The realization made him feel slow, as though he were slogging through a river of mud. "If it hadn't been for the cancer . . ." The mood swings, pushing her away. His fault, all of it.

Their eyes met again, but this time she broke contact first. "And now it might be back."

"No." His fingers tightened on the stack of photographs. "And even if it is, I'll beat it. Whatever the tests say, I'm going to be fine."

"And if you're not? Do you remember why we got divorced? You didn't handle the whole cancer thing well. You took your frustration out on everyone around you, especially me. Would it be different with Darrel?"

"Of course it would. He's a child. I'd be responsible for him."

"I was your wife. You were responsible for me." The sorrow in her face was unmistakable.

"What do you want me to do? Give up on my son?" He sat up and leaned his arms on the table. "I can't do that. I feel a connection with him. I want to be a part of his life. I know I have something to offer him."

She picked up another photograph, this one of Brandon and Darrel playing with the dogs. The evening light angled in through the sheer curtains covering the window, and now that he was leaning forward, he could see tiny particles of dust dancing in the air between them. Fairy dust, Mercedes had once called it years ago.

"I'm not saying you should give up any idea of a relationship," Hannah said finally, tossing the picture onto the stack. "I'm only saying perhaps you should wait and see what the tests say. Or maybe even wait until you've passed the five-year mark. He'd be older, and surely then his mother wouldn't object to a relationship."

"I'd have lost four more years."

"And he'd have lived a happy, normal childhood without worrying about losing a parent from cancer."

"That's not fair."

"None of it is." She reached across the table and took his hand. The light caressed her face, tracing the familiar lines as he had once done with his fingertips. "But you're the one here with the responsibility. You've seen children lose their parents. You've seen their suffering, their heartache. What do you want for your son?"

"If I'm well, waiting would all be for nothing."

She nodded. "Maybe so. Or maybe it would be a base for your future relationship. If you upset his whole family, there might be resentment there that would prevent you from ever having a real relationship."

"It's not my fault she hid him from me!" Brandon pulled his hand from hers and slapped the open palm on the table. The skin on his hand felt abruptly cold where her hand had been.

Hannah was unmoved at the display of emotion. "It's not his fault, either."

She was right about that, at least. And it wasn't really Mercedes' fault. Both of them had made serious mistakes, but none had been deliberate.

"So what exactly did his mother say?" Hannah asked. "Does she want you out of his life completely?"

"She says I should visit, email. Until after high school."

Hannah heaved a sigh that visibly made her chest move. "Brandon, I sympathize with you, I really do. You know I've been supportive since I heard about your son. But now that I'm here, I'm suddenly seeing this child"—she nodded toward the pictures—"as if he were one of the many children who come through my office. I can't tell you what's right, but if he were my son, and if I were in Mercedes' position, I think I'd feel the same way she does. When all is said and done, he's a little boy who needs his mother."

Brandon shook his head and leaned back in his chair, as far away from her words as possible. "I won't give up."

"I'm not telling you to give up. Just think about it. You'll figure out the right thing to do. You don't want to have any regrets."

Brandon drew in a swift but silent breath. Dustbottom had said nearly the same thing to him, though Brandon felt he'd been encouraging him in the opposite direction as Hannah seemed to be. Why was it all so convoluted? In the end was he trying to avoid regrets or to avoid only the greater of the many possible regrets?

"I'll think about it." He waved his hands in the light, sending the dust particles dancing.

For some reason he was reminded of the river on Walker Farm—the first time when he'd been there, his head in her lap, the sun warming his face, her breath against his cheek as she leaned down to kiss him.

So many memories, he thought. *So many regrets.* Why didn't youth understand that tomorrow was almost here? Too late he'd realized that you had to grab onto true love when you had the chance, or the memories of what you had let slip through your hands would haunt you for a lifetime.

Hannah smiled and began clearing the table, stuffing everything back into the takeout bag. "This is a first. You leaving shrimp."

"I'm maturing, that's all."

"Oh, I see." She chuckled and added, "I'd ask you to go dancing, but I think maybe that's not a good idea. So how about a movie?"

"I could dance." He jumped to his feet to show her. His head was clear now, and his stomach upset had passed. "I feel good."

"You look better. Must be the food."

"Could be you. It's good to talk to someone." He closed the gap between them and pulled her from the chair. "Thank you for coming. I needed a friend, even if you didn't say exactly what I wanted to hear."

"We were always friends, even before we got married. And you know I always say what I think." She moved away from him, suddenly acting nervous.

"So what aren't you telling me? There's something more to your coming here, isn't there?" Did she want to try again? At one time he'd wanted that more than anything, but now with Darrel and Mercedes back in his life, he didn't want anything to mess that up.

She made a sound in the back of her throat, a mixture of amusement and dismay. "You know me too well." One eyebrow rose, and he stifled an urge to touch the spot. "Well, it's like this." She went to the garbage and deposited the takeout bag. "I wanted to talk to you about . . . Well, I've been dating someone." Her face flushed. "He's a teacher. A very good one. And he's asked me to marry him. I'm not rushing into anything, but I really care for him. I think it could work."

Brandon reeled with shock. Whatever reason she'd come, he hadn't expected this. "You came all this way to tell me you're getting married?"

She stepped toward him, stopping uncomfortably close. "No, I came mostly because my ex-husband, my friend, has been sick alone in another state while he's trying to work out a way to get to know his son. I thought you might need a friend. Though I guess in a way, I do want your blessing."

"My parents are going to hate this." Never mind them. *He* hated this.

"I'll keep in touch, of course." Her hand brushed his in a fluttering movement. "I worry about you . . ." She trailed off, but he knew what she'd been going to say. She worried about him being alone, about his cancer returning. Like Mercedes, she was a nurturer; perhaps they were more alike than he'd realized.

"He's a lucky man."

"Thanks. It'll mean no more alimony, so you'll have more money for Darrel." Her smile was wide and open, and yet he felt a disappointment there. Or was that his own? But that was crazy. What he felt now for Hannah was friendship and remorse that he hadn't been a better husband to her. Wasn't it?

"So, are we going to the movies?"

"Sure." He took her arm and steered her toward the door. "But I'm paying. It's the least I can do after you came all the way out here."

"Don't flatter yourself. I had frequent flyer miles. It was completely free."

"I didn't know frequent flyer miles paid for hotel rooms."

"Oh, shut up." She slapped his arm with her free hand. They walked from the room, laughing, the tension and sadness draining away.

It was only much later, when he was in bed that night, having kissed Hannah on the cheek and left her at her door, that he realized she hadn't mentioned a thing about loving the man she planned to marry.

Maybe it wasn't love she was looking for this time around. As for him, love was all he wanted.

CHAPTER 17

Diary of Mercedes Walker
August 4, 1995

    Still no word from Brandon. I was in the barn today, crying and upset. I haven't been feeling as sick lately, but all the worrying got to me and I began throwing up. Wayne found me there. He helped me clean it up so Daddy wouldn't see, and then he asked me to marry him. I was so shocked I didn't know what to say. I felt grateful he was willing to sacrifice himself that way, but it didn't feel right for him to throw away his life for a woman he didn't love.

    Then a miracle happened! He said he loves me, that he has for some time. I don't know how I didn't see it before. We've been good friends for so long, and I thought that was all we'd ever be, but when he kissed me after asking me to marry him, things changed between us. I know I can trust him. He'll make sure both

me and my child are safe—from Daddy and the world. I'll do my
best to make him happy too.
    I told him yes.

M ercedes let habit take over. She set the table, finished the dinner, and had everything prepared by the time Wayne returned to the house. The boys were excited to eat the fish they'd caught. It was only the third time they'd been fishing this season, and the other times hadn't yielded nearly as great a catch. They were giggling and poking each other, asking Mercedes questions she didn't hear.

He's robbed me, she thought. *Brandon has robbed me of this night with my family.* She tried hating him, but it wasn't in her. She'd seen the longing in his eyes for Darrel, for what he saw as his family. Or what could have been if her father hadn't . . .

No. She didn't want to go there.

"Right, Momma?" Joseph asked her. "Isn't that the best place?"

Mercedes blinked. "What?"

"To go camping."

She knew instantly what he was talking about. Joseph loved a remote place up in the hills where they sometimes went during the summer, but the other boys preferred any place with a lake. "Yes, you're right, honey. That's my favorite place too."

She wished she could go there now and take all her children to safety. And Wayne. Yes, Wayne had to be with them to make their family complete.

He was watching her, and without his saying anything, she knew he wondered what had happened that day. She'd tell him as soon as the boys were in bed, though since it was a Friday, that might take a while. On Wayne's face was the uncertain smile she remembered well from that day in the barn, the day he'd asked her to marry him. The newly vibrant red hair added to the impression.

While she washed out her mouth with the water in the bottle he always carried, he scooped up the soiled straw and removed it from the barn in an old bucket. Then he sloshed water over the rubber flooring in the horse stall, cleaning away the last bit of vomit.

Mercedes watched silently, her hand on her throat, but the urge to be sick had passed as suddenly as it had come.

"Are you okay?" he asked.

She started to nod and then shook her head. "No." Her voice was small and weak.

"Do you need a doctor?"

"I'm pregnant."

Tears began again, and her face felt hot and sticky. If only she could simply disappear. She didn't want to see the disappointment in his eyes. She didn't want her father to know. Why had she been so stupid?

Wayne took her hand and led her out into the walkway between the stalls. He put both hands on her shoulders and stared down into her face. "Mercedes, I'd be honored if you would marry me."

She blinked, so shocked that her tears stopped. He looked terribly vulnerable standing there—and ruggedly handsome in a way that made her breath catch in her throat. There wasn't a mocking line in his face.

"This isn't your problem," she whispered.

"It's not a problem. Leastwise, it won't be if you marry me."

Her head swung back and forth, almost of its own accord. "I appreciate what you're trying to do, but I know you've been making plans to leave."

"That was before, when I thought you were marrying that doctor."

"*What?*"

He smiled his slightly crooked smile. "*You heard me.*" He was still holding her shoulders, and she was grateful for the support. "*I've only stayed because of you.*"

"*That's not true. There's a million ladies around here who would make you a better wife.*"

The next words shocked her. "*You don't know this, but I was married before. Just out of high school. I loved her very much.*"

An unreasoning jealousy pulsed through her. She felt anger at this woman she'd never known. How could Wayne have loved someone who hadn't been a part of their life on the farm? It seemed he'd always been there, though he hadn't come to the farm until she was eight. That would have made him twenty-one at the time. But who lived an entire life before the age of twenty-one?

"*She died giving birth to our son.*" Tears glittered in his eyes, and his voice was hoarse with emotion. "*I lost them both. People said it was a blessing about the baby because what would I do with a child? But I didn't see it that way. For a year I wandered around, working odd jobs, and finally ended up here. Your momma, she took me in and convinced your daddy to give me a job. He was drinking pretty heavily by then, and they needed help.*"

"*I'm sorry. I'm so sorry.*" Mercedes' hand went to her stomach. She'd not given much thought to the life inside her, except as a source of guilt and pain and hurt, but suddenly it seemed infinitely precious.

"*Don't be.*" Wayne wiped the tears from her face with a warm, callused hand.

"*I don't want you to marry me because you feel sorry for me.*"

"*Oh, sweetheart*"—his voice was as powerful as a physical caress—"*I've dated a lot of women. I've tried to find a better life, but these past few years . . .*" He paused, swallowed hard, his face earnest. *"I wouldn't be marrying you because I feel sorry for you. I'd be marrying you because you're the only woman who makes me forget her face. I know you don't love me yet, but I think you will. Surely you've seen how well we've got on these past months. I think we could make a great life together. I promise, I'll do everything I can to make you happy, and I'd be proud to raise your baby as my own. I give you my word."*

She looked into his face and saw the love, the willingness to be there for her. A great weight lifted from her shoulders. Wayne was a good man, and he would never, ever leave her.

"Yes," she whispered. "I'll marry you. Thank you."

"Don't thank me, Mercedes. It's me who will be thanking God for every day we spend together." He kissed her on the lips, a gentle, chaste kiss that nonetheless shot fire through her veins.

I can love you, *she thought, amazed at her feelings.* I promise to learn. *Her arms went up around his neck, and he pulled her into his embrace. Their kiss deepened. As if he didn't care that she'd been throwing up. As if all of her was cherished.*

Mercedes was no longer alone.

After dinner, the boys spread their sleeping bags on the deck, checked the batteries in their flashlights, and began playing board games. Though they'd just eaten, the ever-starving Joseph had gathered a mound of food to tide them over until morning—popcorn, chips, dried bananas and apricots, the remains of an apple pie, oranges, beef jerky, pretzels, and the chocolate bars they'd bought at school that day with their own money.

Wayne got his own bag and set the rolled bundle in a corner, signaling his plan to sleep near them, though usually when the boys slept on the deck, she and Wayne would stay in their own bedroom with the window open to keep an ear out for them. Mercedes started to ask him why, but the question died on her lips. They might never again be able to leave the boys on their own without fear of Darrel coming up missing.

"He wouldn't take him," she said to Wayne softly. "Would he?"

Wayne shrugged. "I don't know how many more times I'll have the chance to sleep out with all the boys together."

Her thoughts had been so far from his that she wondered at her own morals. Would she resort to kidnapping if she were in Brandon's place?

Wayne took her hand. "Come on. Let's go for a walk."

She nodded and slipped her feet into her shoes, sticking a finger in the back to ease in her heels.

"We'll be back in a while, boys," Wayne said.

"Can we come?" Scott jumped to his feet.

"Not tonight."

"Pleeeassse?" Scott blinked his eyes and jutted his lower lip.

Wayne was unmoved. "No." Then he grinned. "I plan to kiss your momma—a lot."

"Ew, gross!"

"Besides, you'll miss all the food," Joseph said, throwing a piece of popcorn at his brother.

Scott's face brightened. "Try to get it in my mouth."

Wayne and Mercedes left them, tossing popcorn into the air.

Their feet instinctively followed the path out beyond the garden, past the orchard to the grove of trees that marked the family cemetery.

"So what happened today?" Wayne asked.

"Brandon stopped by."

The muscles in Wayne's jaw clenched, and when he spoke, his voice was a growl. "That boy needs a collar. I told him not to come around when I wasn't here."

"He had a collapse of some kind and was in the hospital. That's why he hasn't been back before." She looked down at her mother's grave as they passed and added softly. "He's been in touch with a lawyer and says he wants to share custody. He wants Darrel for holidays and summers."

Wayne rolled his head with the same frustration Mercedes had felt. "He can't be serious. Darrel doesn't even know him."

"According to Brandon, that's my fault."

"He's the one who put you in an impossible situation."

"I'm at fault here too. There hasn't been a day gone by that I haven't wished you were Darrel's father."

"I *am* his father."

That was true. In any way that counted, Wayne was Darrel's father. "You know what I mean."

"The point is, Brandon left and never looked back until it was in his interest to do so."

With the new information of the phone calls and letters, Mercedes wasn't so sure, but she didn't want to defend Brandon to Wayne. Besides, if she did, she'd have to tell him about the letters and what Brandon had said about still caring for her.

I can't hurt Wayne that way, she thought. Or was she only protecting herself?

They continued a few steps in silence, and then Wayne asked, "What did you say to him?"

"I tried to talk him out of it, of course, but he wouldn't listen. He told me his cancer might be back—that might have been the reason for his collapse. He hasn't done the tests yet, and he claims he's fine. I think the fear of the cancer returning is what made him come over so . . . so boldly, I guess."

Wayne scrubbed a hand through his hair. In the quickly fading light he seemed much younger, more like the man who had proposed to her in the barn thirteen years ago. She felt a rush of emotion that she couldn't quite identify as love. Gratitude? Companionship?

"He might have cancer again?" Wayne kicked at a half-buried rock, wincing at the impact. The rock didn't budge.

"More likely he was exhausted from all the work here. I told him we'd fight. I begged him to wait until Darrel was older." She looked over the grass that covered the peaceful graves. The air was perfectly still, almost supernaturally so, as though she and Wayne were in another world entirely. The world where the dead slept, unconcerned about mortal affairs. But Mercedes didn't quite believe that her grandmother would rest peacefully when she was so troubled.

"I'm so sorry, dear." Grandmother set down the clothes she was unpacking from her suitcase and hugged Mercedes. "I should have been here for you. I wish you'd written sooner. Or that Wayne had."

"I was too miserable." Mercedes still couldn't look her in the eye. Her grandmother was deeply religious and would not be happy that her unmarried granddaughter was pregnant. "I've been so stupid, and I feel so—so used. I'm sorry, Grandmother. I know I let you down. I let everybody down, including myself."

Grandmother put a finger under her chin, guiding her face until Mercedes had no choice but to look into her blue eyes. "Everyone makes mistakes, Mercedes. Some big, some small. It's unavoidable. The real test is what we do next. Do we let it beat us? Do we commit the same mistake again? Or do we learn and grow from it? Right now you have to decide what's best for you and that baby. Have you thought about that? Are you going to be able to raise a child alone?"

She knew her grandmother was thinking of adoption. "I won't be alone. I'm getting married."

"I thought the doctor left."

"I'm marrying Wayne."

Grandmother took her hands. "Honey, are you sure? Isn't he a little old for you?"

Something inside Mercedes rebelled at her words. Wayne was exactly what she needed. "He loves me, and he's willing to raise my child. I couldn't imagine a better father. Can you?"

"No, I can't. But you shouldn't marry him just for the baby."

"I'm not. Grandma, I—when he kisses me, I just know it'll be okay." Mercedes blushed, like a young teen with her first crush, though Wayne had been a complete gentleman, and for the first time in a long time, she felt valued as a woman and a person. He cared about her future.

Grandmother studied her for several long moments and then nodded once. "He'll make you a fine husband, child, no doubt about that. Let's get started planning a wedding. You can't hide that baby any longer."

Mercedes smiled at the memories. At this moment her grandmother would be watching them from wherever she had gone, her heart full with their challenges. *Help me, Grandmother,* Mercedes thought. *I need to get through this . . . somehow.*

"But he won't wait, will he?"

Mercedes looked at Wayne blankly, pulling her mind back to the present. "What?"

His thumb rubbed the palm of her hand. They'd stopped walking now and were several paces from Lucy's grave. "You told him to wait. What did he say?"

Mercedes swallowed with difficulty. She couldn't look Wayne in the face. "I told him it wasn't fair to tell Darrel, at least until he knew for sure about his cancer, but he kept saying it was his right." She clenched her free hand, remembering the longing way Brandon had stared at her when he'd tried to explain about the letters.

"I told him to go," she added. "And he did."

Wayne drew her into his arms, but she couldn't find the usual comfort there. "Is that all? Did he say anything more?"

"No." It was the first time she hadn't been completely honest with Wayne. She lifted her face and kissed him with an urgency she hadn't known since they'd been trying to have a baby before Lucy was conceived, as though kissing would make a difference in their lives. As if it might be the last time.

"Come on," he said, his voice low with desire. "Let's get back to the house."

She went willingly and spent the night enfolded in his arms, comforted by their intimacy. Long after the children's excited voices had faded into sleep, she lay awake, her cheek on his shoulder, her forehead pressed into his neck, his arm underneath her. Her body moved slightly in time to his breathing as he slept.

She could smell the clean shirt he'd pulled on earlier when he had gone to spend a short time on the deck with the boys. She loved the fresh scent of clothes dried on the line, but even more she loved the underlying smell of Wayne, his skin—him.

Arching her neck, she lifted her lips to the curve underneath his jaw, kissed him softly, tasted his skin with her tongue. Her husband. Hers. And she was safe in his arms.

Closing her eyes, she finally slept.

CHAPTER 18

Diary of Mercedes Walker Johnson
September 15, 1995

Wayne and I were married yesterday. Grandmother, Daddy, and a few of our friends were present. Only those who know about the baby. I'm getting bigger now—finally. The doctor says I still need to gain more weight. I already feel huge, but Wayne laughs at me and tells me I'm beautiful. He picked me up and carried me to the car as if I were a child.

We went to a place in Green River for our honeymoon. It was beautiful, and we had every comfort. I worried about the cost, but Wayne said he'd wanted to take me to Paris. I asked him why would I want to go to Idaho, and we laughed ourselves silly. He has a friend who lives in Paris, Idaho.

Wayne has been so tender and gentle and loving. I love to sit and look at him watch me because nothing is hidden. His emotions are plain to see, and I know he loves me. I've grown to care about him too. I don't know if it's love yet—I feel so bruised even thinking about love and how Brandon hurt me—but I'm willing to believe it is.

When Wayne kisses me, I'm certainly not thinking of anyone but him. We are going to make this work.

When Mercedes awoke early Saturday morning to drive to Rock Springs to see her father, Wayne was already out checking on the cattle. After making sure Darrel was up to milk the cow, she scribbled a quick note and left in the old truck. Usually, she'd take the boys along for the visit, but she needed to see her father alone today. She hadn't even told Wayne because with the planting finished and the cattle taken care of, he'd have the day to spend with the family—and usually he only wanted to be somewhere that included her.

The thought made her feel even more guilty.

The drive always took nearly four hours one way, and she had to fight not to go faster. She was already pushing the speed limit. For long stretches there was nothing but flat land and sagebrush, as though this part of Wyoming had forgotten how to bloom. Then the highway would snake around a city where trees emerged stubbornly from the ground, strangely haunting and inspiring, proof that life fought to survive wherever it could.

When she arrived in the city, there was too much traffic, and Mercedes felt anxious, her empty stomach acidic and hurting by the time she walked into the assisted-living facility. She smiled at the receptionist, took the stairs to her father's floor instead of the elevator—she hated closed-in spaces—and walked until she stood in front of room 214.

At her knock, her father, Jed Walker, opened the door so quickly she wondered if he'd been waiting, hoping this week she would finally show up. She was his only visitor besides Austin, who had come twice in the past year, though she knew her father had made friends among the other residents.

Her father's smile creased his face into a myriad of wrinkles. Not a few wide furrows like Wayne's, but small, numerous dry fans, like toothpicks under the skin, lining his fathomless black eyes, forehead, and mouth, making her feel as if she were looking at death itself. He grew weaker every month, and she believed he wouldn't be around to see another spring.

"Mercedes." He fell on her in a hug, eager for human touch. She made an effort not to recoil—an effort not previously necessary on other visits. What had changed? Could the knowledge of his duplicity so long ago have an impact on their present? She'd forgiven him for the past. Yet how could she forgive something of which she had no knowledge?

"Where is your momma?" he asked. "I need to see her. Tell her I'm back."

Mercedes stared at him, her amazement at his sudden appearance in the barn turning into anger. "You don't know?" she said. "You didn't hear?"

"Where is she?" His face flushed. "Spit it out, girl! I don't got all day. She didn't go and get herself married again, did she? 'Cuz I ain't dead."

"No, but she is."

He blinked, whatever evil words he'd planned to say next dying on his lips. Mercedes felt a sliver of satisfaction, followed closely by remorse that she could experience this bit of satisfaction only because her mother was gone. She'd trade that feeling and more to have her back again.

"Dead?" he asked dumbly.

She hated the way he stood there, all innocence and questions. "It was you!" she said in a voice like ice. Then she was crying, sobbing without control. "You killed her! You killed her! And I hate you!"

Her father lifted his hand, aiming a blow, but Wayne grabbed his arm. "Lucinda's gone," he said calmly. "Come on back to the house, and I'll tell you what happened."

Mercedes watched them go, her chest hurting. "I'll never forgive you, Daddy," she whispered. "Never."

Yet she had.

He was so frail that she feared to squeeze him too tightly lest his bones break. Had he been taking his supplements? The question died on her tongue. She didn't really care about his supplements today. Maybe she would never care again.

"I wondered when you'd come." Even his voice was raspy and ancient, a life used up by abuse. "I missed you the last time."

She disconnected herself and walked to the brown couch. "I'm sorry." The words were mechanical. She wasn't sorry; she was furious. Heat rose in her face, but she clenched her mouth shut. Not yet. She had to decide how to begin.

"What about the boys? Couldn't they come?" He slowly lowered himself onto the easy chair, pulling out the footrest for his slippered feet. "You should have brought them. Or maybe you've come to take me to the farm for a visit?" He looked at her, his dark eyes hopeful.

"We're planning a dinner for Father's Day. Austin and Liana are coming. Oh, I don't know if you heard. She's pregnant."

"It's about time. I thought that boy would never get married. He never comes to see me, you know."

"He has good reason." She wouldn't let him pretend to be innocent. "You were a terrible father."

His jaw twitched. "Are we back there again? I thought you forgave me."

"So did I."

His eyes narrowed, and the gray head angled back to look at her. "Are you gonna tell me what this is about? Or should I guess? We have no secrets between us now. I know I was a lousy father—no father at all—and it's a miracle you and your brother survived. But you did survive, and you're strong. Maybe you have me to thank for that."

Mercedes' stomach lurched at this glimpse of the man he'd been. "Brandon's back."

He frowned. "Brandon?"

"Darrel's father."

"Wayne's Darrel's father."

"You know that's not true. He said he wrote me."

"That's what this is about?" His voice was flat, as though drained of all life.

"Did he?"

Her father cursed. "Why'd you want to go into that after all these years? It don't make sense. You got a good life. What you want to mess with that for?"

"He wants to share custody of Darrel. Says I should have told him."

"Maybe he's right."

Mercedes rose, barely able to stop from launching herself at him. "You're such a hypocrite! If I'd known he cared, I *would* have told him. He called, didn't he? But you didn't tell me. And what about the letters? Was that you? Or was it Wayne? Or was it both of you?"

"Wayne's a good man."

Mercedes' short fingernails dug into her palms. "Did you see the letters? I want the truth."

He sighed, a long drawn-out breath that rattled in his throat. He twisted the knob to put down the footrest and came slowly to his feet.

"Wait." His shoulders were slumped as he shuffled down the hall.

Mercedes paced as she waited. She passed the family picture she'd taken at Easter; the books she'd bought him for Christmas tucked in a corner of a bookshelf, still untouched; a picture Scott had drawn on the small refrigerator in the adjoining kitchen; a half-finished puzzle on the tiny round table, his eyeglasses nearby.

He returned with two envelopes, the edges jagged where he'd opened them, the paper slightly yellow but otherwise looking like letters he might have received yesterday. "Don't know what good this'll do." He thrust them at her. "I only saved them for Darrel. I thought his dad might help him in college when he's older. I know the farm's struggling."

She ran her fingers over her name, read the return address. Brandon had written! She suddenly had to sit before she collapsed. There, the kitchen chair. There were two, but her father didn't sit with her. He stood watching. His turn to wait.

She didn't want to read the letters in front of him. She wanted to do it in a private place. Or maybe she shouldn't read them at all. For an instant, she almost ripped them up into tiny pieces, knowing what was inside would only hurt her further. But she had to know. Now.

Her hand drew out the first letter.

Dear Mercedes,

You were right, as usual. You said I'd miss you, and I do—more than I ever imagined possible. I've tried calling you to beg you to come here, but I just get your father. (He sure is grumpy—you're right about that as well.) I wanted to make sure you got my messages, so I'm writing. I've been a stupid fool to think I could last any time without you. The months we've been apart already seem like years. I need to hear your voice. See your face. Hold you. Call me as soon as you get this. You do still love me, don't you? Did I say I've been a fool? That doesn't even touch how stupid I've been, but I know with your help I can make it all right. None of my life means anything without you.

I've been working so much overtime that I fall asleep whenever I'm not moving, and when I do sleep, I see your face. Every time the nurse shakes me awake, I'm so disappointed to learn she's not you and that we're not in Wyoming anymore. What I seem to remember most is that first time at the river, holding you in the water when your hired man stumbled on us. You flushed clear down your neck—probably to the tips of your toes—and sprang away from me as if the guy were your father and you an underaged girl. I felt jealous you even cared that he saw us there together. Stupid, huh?

I can imagine us growing old together. Maybe have a child or two in five or six years. Mercedes, please forgive me for the way I left. I will never be happy until I can right things between us. I love you—and will love you until the day I die. No, even after that. This kind of emotion doesn't die. I've seen enough of death here to know that. Love endures forever.

Yours, Brandon

The words blurred under Mercedes' eyes. She was shaking so badly that she wondered if she was experiencing some kind of attack. Once again her father had stolen something infinitely precious from her. First her mother and her childhood, and then the man she'd loved. Had she read that letter any time before marrying Wayne, she would have been on the first plane to Boston. She would have married Brandon and pursued another life. But Jed Walker had let her suffer, had let her son grow up without his father. No matter that Wayne had given her a better life than she had ever thought possible—it could have so easily gone wrong. She believed all these years that Brandon had abandoned her, and her heart had never fully healed. But it was all lies. Her entire life was based on a lie.

Her eyes lifted to meet her father's. She wanted to rage and cry, but the shock had numbed her so only one word escaped her frozen lips. "Why?"

He had his hands in the pockets of his overalls, looking as much the farmer as he ever had. "He wasn't no good for you. He proved that by what he did."

"It's all a lie." Tears came now, flooding her eyes, wetting her face. The futility of discovering this now when it could no longer make a difference was overpowering.

Her father took a step toward her, his face drawn. "You have a good life."

"It's a lie!" That tortured scream, could it be hers?

"Mercedes. Please. I was scared. I lost everything. Lucinda, Austin. You was all that was left. I didn't want you to go."

"This was for you?" She shook the letter at him. "For you? You have no idea what you've done. No idea at all."

She started for the door, but he reached out, stopped her

with his gnarled hand. "I knew I shouldn'ta given you those letters. I should have burned them."

"What you should have done was give them to me when they arrived." She flung off his hand and reached for the door.

"It wasn't just for me."

She hesitated but didn't look in his direction.

"I saw where you and Wayne was headed. He was a steady man, and you belonged on the farm as much as he did. You wouldn't be happy nowhere else. You still wouldn't."

She turned her head toward him. "Tell me one thing. Did Wayne know?"

Jed snorted. "He'd have made me give them to you."

Her anger wilted marginally with that information, though she'd known it all along. Wayne was not a man to hide things.

Without another word, she left her father standing there. She heard him move to the door, imagined him gazing after her, his shoulders slumped in defeat, black eyes begging. Usually when he was irritable—which was often—compassion would compel her to return, to assure him it would be all right and that she'd be back. But this time was different. She hated him more than she had on the day her mother had taken those pills.

She drove from the town, letting tears fall unchecked from her eyes. Try as she might, she still couldn't wrap her mind around the enormity of what she'd learned, how her father had altered her life so irrevocably.

Irrevocably?

The tears slowed and stopped, leaving her face feeling tight and sticky. Outside the truck the landscape changed to empty land with scatterings of sagebrush—grays and browns smearing along the edges of her vision.

Next to her on the seat sat the letters, the one she'd read

sticking out slightly. Pulling off to the edge of the road, she picked up the other letter, opened it. Her eyes devoured the words.

Dear Mercedes,

Why haven't you written? Or called? I've been the biggest idiot ever, but I know you will forgive me and that we can go on from there. I keep worrying that you've met someone else, but knowing what we are to each other, I can't imagine such a thing ever happening. My heart is with you, and I have to believe you feel the same.

But maybe I'm wrong. Maybe I don't know us at all. I miss you. I miss you. I miss you. And did I say that I miss you?

Brandon

The words hurt. Little slivers of pain that pierced deeply, taking her back to a time when she thought she would die without him.

It was all a lie.

She read both letters again, seeing Brandon's face. Not as it was then but as it had been in her kitchen the day before—vulnerable.

Eventually, she put the letters neatly back in their envelopes and set them deliberately down, the corners touching her leg. It was impossible to feel them through her flowered dress, but she imagined a heat that seared her.

She put the truck in gear and steered onto the road. Minutes slid into hours. She had no idea how much time had passed. The dash in the old truck didn't have a clock, and she wasn't wearing a watch. More blurred scenery streamed past the truck, mixing with images from the past that she made no effort to restrain. Some part of her craved this torture, the rehashing of the past. The past that could have absolutely no connection to her future. She wouldn't let it. *Couldn't* let it.

By the time she arrived at the farm hours later, she had placed the letters in her purse and the memories back in the dark, hurtful place in her heart where they had lain for thirteen years. The kids came running out as she drove up. Joseph was last, one hand stuffing a hotdog into his mouth.

A wave of guilt surged through Mercedes. She hadn't remembered to leave a lunch for them, and though both Wayne and Darrel were perfectly capable of fixing everyone something to eat, it wasn't like her to be so careless.

I'm back now, she thought. *That's all that matters.* This too was a lie. She'd returned, but she wasn't the same. Something had changed within her.

"Momma, we've been waiting for you!" Scott yelled as she climbed from the truck. "We want to go to the river. Can we? Can we? Daddy wanted to wait for you."

"He was worried that the truck broke down." Darrel's gaze wandered over the length of the truck.

"Did it?" Joseph asked, crumbs dropping from his mouth.

"No, it was fine." How long had she sat on the side of the road? "It's a long drive, that's all." She slammed the truck door shut.

"I hate going to see Grandpa," Scott added. "It's boring to drive that long."

"Well, he missed you." Mercedes pulled her purse over her shoulder.

"He's a grouch." Scott folded his arms, his mouth in a thin line.

"He's old, that's all," Darrel said.

Joseph nodded emphatically. "So can we go to the river? Darrel will watch us if you and Dad don't want to go."

"What about your foot?"

"It's perfect. See?" Joseph hopped up and down on his injured foot to prove his words.

Wayne emerged from the house, but he didn't come down to the truck. He stood on the porch, watching her. Mercedes knew she had to give him an explanation.

"Go get your suits on," she told the boys, "and I'll go with you in a while."

"Our suits *are* on," Scott protested.

"Then wait out back for me. I'll be there in a minute."

"Awwww," Joseph and Scott began, but their cries faded as Wayne walked toward them, his face serious and unsmiling.

"Come on," Darrel urged. Tugging on his brothers' shirts, he headed around the house. "I'll race you!"

Mercedes' eyes followed Wayne. His steps slowed and stopped several feet away from her. *No kiss,* Mercedes thought. *No hug.*

"I would have gone with you," he said. "Or the boys could have."

Her hand gripped the strap on her purse. "I needed to talk to my father without the boys." She didn't say without him as well, but the implication was clear.

"Why?"

Mercedes stared into his face, every line and furrow as familiar—no, more familiar than her own. The bright hair looked suddenly out of place on his head, as though he was trying to be something he was not. For her.

Her eyes dropped to the gravel beneath her feet. They'd discussed putting in a driveway of concrete up next to the house and maybe even building a garage. There just never seemed to be enough money or time.

"Mercedes." His voice pleaded for her attention.

She lifted her eyes. "Brandon told me he sent letters after he left. I never got them. I thought it was a part of his . . . trying to get Darrel. I had to know."

"And did he?"

She nodded. A burning rose behind her eyes, but she held them open, willing the tears away.

"I would have gone with you," he repeated.

"I didn't want to hurt you."

"It wouldn't have hurt at all if you'd told me. Then I'd know it didn't mean anything."

"I had to know."

"It makes a difference?"

She hesitated. "Of course not." How could she tell him she'd been living a lie?

Wayne smiled, but no joy reflected in his eyes. "You're an incredible woman, Mercedes, and any man would be out of his mind not to want you. So I guess I'm not surprised he wanted you back. But what he wanted then doesn't really matter now—unless it means something to you now."

"It doesn't." Even to her own ears, her words sounded false.

Wayne let his gaze drop to the ground. "I always knew that—" He stopped and shook his head. "The boys are waiting." Turning, he strode away.

She hurried to catch up with him, her hand grasping at his sleeve. "You always knew what? That I didn't love you enough? That I'm a self-centered idiot? Wayne, please." Please what? She didn't know.

He turned and gazed at her steadily. "I always knew there would come a time when you'd have to choose."

She felt stung by the words. "I did choose. In the barn that day."

"Did you?" One quirk of his gray-streaked eyebrows emphasized his question. "You drove eight hours today, a drive you hate to make, to visit your father, a man you never like to see alone. To me, that says a lot."

The energy drained from her. He was right. Her decision in the barn that day had been made because she'd seen no other choice. The adult in her knew she had used Wayne, which wasn't right, even though it had been exactly what he'd wanted.

No, not exactly what he'd wanted. He'd wanted her to love him as she'd promised on their wedding day. But if she were to admit the truth, a part of her had been in limbo for thirteen years. Waiting. Waiting.

I don't deserve Wayne. I never have.

She felt smaller than a grain of wheat, as insignificant as the kernels of corn the animals chewed up in their feed. All these years she'd been doing so well, and now she realized she'd been pretending. She'd grown so good at it that she'd even fooled herself.

So what did that mean for her future? Panic spread through her chest, reaching to the tips of her fingers and toes, very like the fear she'd felt the first time Darrel fell out of the oak tree by the river and lay unconscious. At first she'd thought he'd broken his neck, but in the end it had only been his arm.

Wayne made a sound in the back of his throat, calling her back from the panic. She focused on his face. His fingers brushed her cheeks with gentleness, the way the wind caressed her when she stood near Lucy's grave.

"I love you, Mercedes. Don't forget that. I love you with

everything I am and all that I will ever be. I need you. The boys need you. We have a good life. But it has to be the life you want. I want you to be happy."

His thumb ran over her lip. She could feel the roughness of his skin, and she felt a desire to kiss it, to fall into his arms and be safe. But she didn't do any of those things.

Still smiling sadly, Wayne dropped his hand and walked away. She stared after him, not knowing what she would do but so very, very afraid.

CHAPTER

19

Diary of Mercedes Walker Johnson
October 18, 1995

Wayne talks to the baby in my tummy. He is, well, adorable—if you can call a rough, full-grown man adorable. I'm beginning to feel excited to see my child where before I wondered only what would happen to us. I hope the baby doesn't look too much like Brandon. That would be hard. I've almost stopped dreaming about him, and when I do dream, I wake up and I'm in Wayne's arms, protected and loved. I never felt this way before, not even when I was with Brandon. I'm safe. Maybe I'd have felt that way with Brandon if he'd loved me enough to marry me, but I can't think that way. Wayne and this baby are my life right now. No, wrong again. They are my life for all the time I have left here on this earth. I promised, and I will keep that promise. Wayne loves me so much that I don't think it'll be too difficult.

The baby blanket is three-fourths finished. I've taken care with every single stitch, and it is a thing of beauty. My best work. Only another two months, and my baby will be here. Will Brandon feel anything that day? No, and I don't care. He gave up any right he had to our child when he left.

Wayne went around to the back of the house where the boys waited, trying not to drag his feet over the grass they'd worked so hard on in the past years to rid of alfalfa, which sometimes sent roots eight feet deep and was almost impossible to kill. He was like the alfalfa. His roots were sunk deep in Mercedes and in this farm where he'd given nearly a lifetime of work, love, and devotion. And in the boys, of course.

"Let's go," he said.

"Ain't Momma coming?" Scott asked.

"Maybe later. She had a long drive."

Joseph looked hopefully toward the house. "She could bring a picnic."

At the rate he was eating, he would probably grow as tall as Darrel by the end of summer, which wasn't saying much, of course, but Wayne hoped Darrel wouldn't mind. Wayne had no personal experience to draw on, because he'd never had siblings, but he figured it might bother Darrel at least a bit.

"Let's race!" Scott said. The boys ran ahead, beating Wayne to the river by several yards.

He came to a stop on the bank as the two younger boys scurried up the big oak, as sure-footed as little squirrels. Darrel hung back with him, glancing over his shoulder as though expecting to see Mercedes coming at any moment. Wayne brought a hand to his heart, kneading the hurt there. What would happen to his family?

He hadn't much luck in the family department. His father

dead in an accident with the farm equipment before Wayne really knew him, his mother dying when he was in high school, leaving him to finish up the last two years living with an aunt, now also long dead. His first wife and son. Mercedes and the children were his only family now.

But what about the future?

He couldn't believe this was happening. He knew Mercedes, and he knew the time they'd spent together. That was real. Even if all these years she'd been holding a part of herself back from him, they'd still been happy. But did she see that? The fear inside grew worse, the fear that had tightened his chest from the day he'd first seen Brandon on the deck with Mercedes. The time had come. He'd always known it would.

If he were any kind of man, he'd have to tell her that he'd known about the letters.

"Go get in the truck," he told Jed in the kitchen where he sat staring at a magazine.

"I don't want to go nowhere."

"You're going. There's a place I want you to see."

"What's this about?"

Wayne's anger raged through him, but he struggled to hold it in. "Yesterday I came home and found my pregnant wife crying on the floor as she cleaned up a plate of food you'd thrown there. This can't continue. I won't let it. You can't stay here anymore."

"This is my farm," Jed said with a sneer. "You can't kick me out."

"It hasn't been your farm since you drank away all your interest in it. You know that as well as I do."

"The old lady won't kick me out."

Wayne snorted. "She thinks you killed her daughter. The only reason she hasn't kicked you out already is because I asked her not to. But I can see it's not going to work. I promised Mercedes I'd

make her happy, and that means you're out of here. Come on."
He put a hand on the old man's arm and half dragged him to the
front door. "We'll come back for your things later."

"Mercedes!" Jed shouted. "Your husband's hurting me!"

"She's not here. This is between you and me." Wayne had
picked Mercedes up from the floor, helped her pack a bag, and
taken her to stay with her grandmother for a few days while he
dealt with her father.

Jed sagged, letting his full weight press against Wayne's hand.
"I'm sick. I can't work."

"I found a place. You don't deserve it, but you're Mercedes'
father, and I'll take care of you."

"You'd better. If it wasn't for me, she never woulda married
you." He was walking again, and Wayne was able to get him out
of the house and halfway to the truck.

"What do you mean? You haven't had a good thing to say
about our marriage. You told me the other day I only married
her for the farm."

"Well, you did it for that too. Of course, Mercedes is a fine-
looking woman."

"I love Mercedes. That's the reason I married her. And why
you're leaving. It's too much stress with the baby coming." Wayne
opened the passenger door and hefted Jed inside.

Jed slapped his hands away. "If I'd given her his letters, she
wouldn't have married you. You have me to thank for that."

Wayne froze. "What are you saying?"

"I'm saying that doctor wrote her. Wanted to marry her."

Wayne shook his head. "We've been married more'n three
months now. It's too late. It'd never work between them. Mercedes
wouldn't leave."

"Maybe not. But I got those letters before you got married,
and you'd better be good to me or I can show 'em to her any time."

"Where are they?" Wayne demanded.

"I ain't saying." Jed folded his arms and pressed his lips tightly together.

"Stay here." Wayne slammed the door and stomped to the house.

Frantically he searched Jed's room. Was the old man telling the truth? He could tell Mercedes was beginning to love him. She already trusted him. But if those letters existed—could that kill their future? Didn't he have the obligation to tell her? Or was it better to burn them? He searched every place he could think of, including under the mattress, before sitting back on his heels in frustration.

"Are you quite done?" Jed asked from the doorway, a smirk on his weathered face. "You ain't gonna find them."

"They don't exist, do they?" Wayne stumbled to his feet. "This was all just another one of your tricks."

"You're so stupid that if they did exist, you'd probably show them to her."

"You're lying. One more lie."

Jed gave him a disgusted look. "When you're finished with this, I'll be in the truck."

So was Jed lying, trying to use imaginary letters as blackmail, or was there something to the claim?

Wayne thought of Mercedes and how broken she'd been after Brandon left, how worried he'd been she might lose so much weight that she'd die herself. She was a different person now. Different because of his love and care. Her confidence was returning.

"He had his chance," Wayne muttered. If that doctor had cared about her, he would have taken Mercedes with him in the first place. Or he would have come to see her. He wouldn't have sent a letter, not when he'd known Mercedes was living with a controlling, abusive father.

The tenseness eased from his muscles. This was all another

of Jed's manipulations. There were no letters. If there had been, the doctor would have had the guts to show up by now. That's what Wayne would have done in his place. He shut his eyes in relief, unwilling to imagine how such a visit now would affect Mercedes' budding self-esteem. No, the man was out of their lives. He had to be, for Mercedes' sake.

Wayne drove Jed to Rock Springs and signed him up at the assisted-living facility he'd researched. Two days later Jed was completely moved out, and Mercedes came home to a house that for the first time was truly a home.

"You don't even have to go see him, if you don't want to," he told her. "But if you do, I'll go with you."

"I don't want to."

And they didn't see Jed again—until after the baby came and changed them both.

He should have told her about the possibility of the letters. If she'd made her decision then, to stay or leave, they wouldn't be facing such turmoil now. Of course, that might also mean he wouldn't have had these years with her and the boys. The thought was unbearable.

"Daddy, watch me!" Scott was on the tree branch, holding onto the rope. When Wayne looked up, he jumped outward, hooking his toes over the bottom knot. "Yeaaaaaaaaaaah!" he screamed. After only one arc, he let go of the rope and splashed into the water. Wayne peered into the water to be sure he was all right.

"He's getting to be a good swimmer," Darrel said.

"Yep, you all are."

"Dad?"

"Yes?"

"What's wrong with Momma? She's acting really strange." Darrel's eyebrows scrunched together, making his thin face look older. Then, as though realizing his comment needed an explanation, he added, "Well, I mean she's kinda acting like she did when Lucy died. She's working on that quilt all the time, and she stares funny, like sometimes she sees right through me. Does it have something to do with that doctor? He came here yesterday, and they were fighting. I didn't hear what they said, but he made her cry."

Wayne had forgotten how sensitive children were to the emotions surrounding them. Every day they brought him surprises—it was one of the things he loved best about being a father—but he too had been wrapped up in the events and hadn't noticed how closely Darrel watched them. For a moment Wayne was tempted to tell him the truth. Darrel was his best friend after Mercedes, and it'd be a relief to get it all out. Except it wasn't exactly his decision to make, nor perhaps in Darrel's best interest. If Brandon proceeded with his plan, Darrel would have to know soon enough. For now, Wayne had better choose his words carefully.

"Your momma is dealing with a few things right now. Sometimes it takes a little time to work things out. But she loves you boys—that isn't a part of the problem."

"I don't like seeing her this way. I wish she could have another baby."

Wayne had to smile at Darrel's simple solution. After Lucy died, Mercedes had tried to have another baby to dull the ache, but as time passed, she'd told him she'd accepted God's will. Of course, that didn't mean they stopped missing Lucy.

Above them, Joseph, his hands on the rope, was jumping from the branch, howling like an Indian. His feet missed the knot at the end, and he slipped from the rope and into the water before he could take advantage of the full ride.

Wayne knuckled his chest. "Don't worry about your mom.

She'll be all right. Now why don't you go show your brothers how that's done?"

"They are pretty bad at it." With a grin, Darrel shot toward the tree.

Wayne watched them play, feeling suddenly old and worn. So many regrets, and yet, he'd do it all again for them and for Mercedes. He sat down on the grassy bank and took off his shoes, letting his toes press into a bare patch of packed earth.

He felt her presence before her hand touched his shoulder. Closing his eyes, he dared to believe in what they'd built together all these years. Dared to believe that somewhere in her heart, she loved him enough.

She knelt next to him, her dress and hair spilling onto his shirt and jeans as she pressed herself against his side. Her hand rested on his thigh, suffusing him with heat.

"I believe in our promise," she said quietly. "You kept your word when you said you'd make me happy."

She hadn't said "I love you," though happiness was a form of love. Was it enough? The ache within Wayne said it was, but his mind rebelled. All these years of love and sacrifice and companionship. All he ever lived for was her touch, her smile, and her words of love. But even when she said the words, he couldn't help but think of an invisible barrier between them, as though a part of her couldn't love.

Or belonged to someone else.

What about Brandon? He wanted to ask but didn't. He was too afraid that saying the words aloud would open an unwanted door. She was here, and he would make that be enough.

He placed his hand over hers, pressing it firmly, a stray tear slipping from the corner of his eye. With a soft sigh, Mercedes laid her head on his shoulder, her hair wiping away the tear.

Hope filled Wayne's heart.

CHAPTER
20

Diary of Mercedes Walker Johnson
December 16, 1995

My baby is here! A week early, according to the doctor. We've named him Darrel Austin Johnson. Darrel is Wayne's middle name, and Austin is, of course, the proud uncle, or will be once he gets here to see the baby.

Darrel is so tiny and so perfect, and I have never felt such love in my entire life. Never. Or at least never this kind of love. It is so miraculous. The labor went on forever, and I thought I'd die, but every single bit of the pain was worth it when they put him in my arms. I couldn't stop crying. I KNEW him. Words cannot express the . . . well, the majesty I feel. It's more than the farm, all the fields, the sky, the universe.

Wayne goes around with a silly smile on his face and tears in his eyes. He strokes Darrell's cheeks so gently and looks at me like I've given him the world. But it's him who has given me the *world. He has made all this possible, and I can never repay him except with the thing he wants most—my love. He has that. Now and forever.*

The only problem is the baby quilt I made so carefully. It's exquisite, I must say, but I see it now for what it contains: all the bitterness and anger and pain in my life associated with both Daddy and Brandon, the two men who should have been the ones to have given me joy. But I won't give that burden to Darrel.

Instead, I'll use the quilt Geraldine made for him. It's a mixture of lovely blues—the color of a summer sky, the bluebells in my flowerbed, the shallow water in the trough, the hint of blue in the lilac bushes by the river, the deeper blue of the berries I use for my pies. Memories of the farm will cradle my child as we take him home.

*O*n the surface everything was the same, and yet it was not. For the next few days Mercedes washed dishes, made meals, took the children to activities, visited Geraldine and the new baby, and worked on the quilt that had once been destined for Brandon. Wayne played with the boys, read to them, rode out to check on the cattle, and talked about the growth of the crops. They didn't talk about Brandon or the past.

On Tuesday morning, Mercedes saw the boys off to school and then busied herself in the kitchen. Wayne was in the fields, having gone off before she woke up to make him breakfast. Almost as though he didn't want to face her. Yet each of the past nights he had clung to her in the dark with so much force that she found it difficult to sleep. Sometimes she thought she heard him crying, but the sounds would stop when she tilted her head to listen. She wanted to ease the tension between them, but she didn't know how.

I've made my choice! she cried silently. *Please forgive me.* Would Wayne believe her if she said the words? Did she believe them herself?

They waited.

She tried hard to put the words of the letters from her mind. They made no difference at all because her place was here now. Her girlish dreams meant nothing. Still, knowing Brandon hadn't left her, not really, softened her feelings toward him until she feared she might not have the strength to win the upcoming custody battle. Darrel was the only biological child Brandon would ever have, and she'd kept him a secret. If she hadn't, things might have ended up differently. So differently.

There had been many turns of the road where one minor occurrence could have meant a different world entirely. A world where Mercedes wouldn't have grieved so deeply, one where her daughter might have survived. One where Wayne might have found a woman worthy of him, able to fully return his love.

Not that it mattered. Not one little bit. She'd once told her sister-in-law, Liana, that past relationships were like cattail fluff on the wind, blown about at the whim of nature and never to be recaptured.

She still believed that. And yet . . .

When the phone rang, she stared at it with mistrust. They didn't own a mobile phone, so it couldn't be Wayne, and the boys rarely called from school. That left her brother, a neighbor, or Brandon. Or his lawyer. But she knew it was Brandon himself. She felt it with every part of her that had ever known him.

"Hello?" She tried to mask her sudden breathlessness.

"Did you talk to your dad?"

"Yes."

"And?"

"It makes no difference." She wouldn't tell him she'd read the letters, nor would she think of the life that had been stolen from her.

"It does to me."

"Please leave Darrel alone until after high school." She sat down at the kitchen table and cradled her head on her arm.

"I can't."

"You would if you cared about him."

His voice hardened. "I do care, and that's exactly why I won't give up."

"What about the cancer?"

"I'm not sick, and I'm not going anywhere. There's no reason to wait."

Tears dripped from her eyes and slid down her arm. Her grasp on the phone was painfully tight. "Then do it for me. Please. I promise you'll get to know him. Please, Brandon."

"I let go once before, and I've always regretted it."

"Please." She was sobbing openly now. "I can't lose another child."

"You won't lose him." Was that a softening in his voice? "Mercedes, I'm not trying to take him away from you. I just want—" He broke off.

She knew what he wanted was impossible. "We don't have to wait clear until after high school. We can see how things go in a year or so. You could consider moving closer to visit more."

He snorted. "As a friend?"

"He doesn't need another father right now. But he could use a friend. And once you have that relationship, learning the truth will be easier."

"On who? Him? Or you?"

"I don't care about me." *I deserve to suffer. I'm the reason for this mess.* But she wouldn't share that with him.

"Children are resilient. The younger the better. He'll be fine."

Mercedes' mind searched desperately for something to sway him. "You say you still care about me, but that's just one more lie, isn't it? If you did, you wouldn't take me to court to try to steal away my son."

"I told you I'm not—"

"We don't have much, but I swear I'll sell the farm if I have to and go to work as a waitress or whatever. I won't lose my family that way!"

Even as she spoke, she knew selling the farm would mean risking her other children's future. Would she really do it? What choice would she have? She knew enough about the world to know money was everything in court. Money—something Brandon had plenty of.

"Think about Darrel," she continued. "Please, Brandon. We can't put him through that. This is his home. How is he going to feel about you after it's all over? After you've stolen the farm from him? Please, wait. If you ever cared anything for me, don't do this! If you do, I'll know you never, ever loved me."

"That's not fair." He was silent a moment, with only her tears between them. "There's another choice," he added softly. "Our future was stolen—you don't have to be a martyr."

His words cut deeply. Cut because a part of her could also see the options so clearly—but none of them ended well. Leaving Wayne would only further tear apart her family. "I see you still don't know anything about commitment." She put all the bitterness she felt into those few words.

"I wrote you!"

"You weren't willing to make a commitment to me then, and you left. If you changed your mind, you should have come back, not sent a stupid letter!"

"So I was an idiot. Do I have to pay for that for the rest of my life?"

"Apparently we both do." She hung up, feeling hopeless and sad, a prisoner in her own nightmare. Leaving the dishes half finished, she left the house, heading for the barn and Windwalker.

Moments later the wind rushed into Mercedes' face, slapping it with a force she welcomed. She headed for the hills beyond their property—hills she knew as well as her own farm. There was a comfort in the movement of her horse, in the green growing things surrounding her.

If only Brandon had never returned. Yet she felt different now somehow, different from the woman who'd once thought herself abandoned. Brandon had loved her, had valued the girl she'd been.

How long she rode, she didn't know, but Windwalker was drenched with sweat and the sun had moved higher in the sky. She felt a sense of freedom she hadn't experienced in years. She came to a hill, higher than the rest, that looked down on part of her farm. Everywhere she looked, she saw Wayne—in the green alfalfa fields, the even stalks of winter wheat, the neat tending of her trees in the graveyard.

Wayne would never abandon me. He would have come back for me. The thought came with a rush of love. And she would never abandon him.

The desire to see her husband, if only from a distance, spurred her toward the north fields, where she knew Wayne would be checking on the cattle.

She found him on a small rise, standing by his horse as he stared down over the cattle. He made a noble figure, as much a part of the land as the grasses that grew from the dirt and so peaceful that she meant to slip away before he saw her.

Yet something in his stance, in the tilt of his head, the set of his jaw, chilled her.

"Wayne!" she called.

He didn't move, though he must have heard her.

Urging Windwalker up the rise, she came to a stop and slid off beside him. He didn't glance toward her but stood transfixed, staring at the cattle below, tears wetting his face.

Mercedes experienced a sudden fear. "What is it?"

His face was haggard, and the dark half circles under his eyes told her he wasn't sleeping nearly enough. Her fault, she knew. He lifted his chin slightly toward the cattle. At first she could see nothing wrong, but then she saw two—no, five of the cattle lying on their sides.

"What's wrong with them? They're not breathing!" She started forward, but his hand grabbed her.

"I don't know what it is yet. I saw one dead last week, but it looked pretty decomposed—wasn't even sure if it was one of ours. But this is definitely a problem. I've got to get Duane out here. He'll know what it is or how to find out. It could be dangerous."

With a sinking feeling Mercedes replayed all the information she knew about cattle diseases in her mind. "It could take out half the herd," she whispered, barely breathing. That meant no calves to sell. There went the money to pay for the new tractor, the new well they'd planned, the storage bin that needed to be replaced, and the bit they'd put away for Darrel's education. Raising cattle had been so promising, but in a moment, it could all be wiped out.

She turned to Wayne, clung to him, finally one as they hadn't been in weeks. "What are we going to do?"

Wayne shook his head, red hair shining in the sun. "I don't know."

He sounded defeated, more than she'd ever seen him in all the years since he'd come to the farm. Even more than when she'd told him about the letters, though she knew that had hurt him in a way that this never could. She tightened her grasp around his middle and lifted her chin.

"We'll get through this, Wayne, just the way we have everything else. That's what farmers do—and cattle ranchers. We won't give up. It might not be as bad as we think, but even if it is, in a few years it'll make no difference. Not really. We'll make it . . . together."

He buried his face in her neck, and she felt the wetness of his tears. Wordlessly, his lips found hers, and they stood locked together. His hands untied her braid, and his fingers ran down the length of her black hair.

She tasted tears—but whether they were his or hers, she couldn't say. Didn't care to say. She kissed her husband and forced all other thoughts from her mind. This life of hers was real and urgent. Brandon had no place here.

"Come on," he said when they finally broke apart. "Let's get back to the house."

Mounting their horses, they galloped in the direction of the farm. In the barn, they unsaddled the horses. "Let's do that later," Wayne said, when she started to rub Windwalker down. "The sun's warm, and we'll need to ride out there again when Duane comes to check on the cattle."

They let the horses into the small corral in back of the barn, their hands doing the work of habit that their minds were too stunned to consider. Halfway to the back deck, Brandon came from the side of the house, and Mercedes felt a shock ripple through her like a spasm of pain. Her hand reached for Wayne's.

"What now?" Wayne growled under his breath. His face

was ashen, and his hand tightened on hers. As one, they stopped and watched Brandon approach.

Brandon's strides were purposeful, and Mercedes wondered what hurtful thing he had planned now. *Haven't you done enough?* she wanted to scream. She stepped closer to Wayne, his bulk giving her comfort. Her husband, her chosen life. She wouldn't let Brandon separate them.

Brandon's eyes went to their linked hands and then slowly to Mercedes' face. There was a tautness about him, a rubber band stretched to breaking. At last his gaze rested on Wayne.

"I've been doing a lot of thinking in the past few hours, and I've decided to honor Mercedes' wishes regarding Darrel. But I want it on the record that I'm doing this only because I owe her. I still think I have a lot to offer my son. You've been good parents—I won't deny that—but that doesn't mean what I offer is worthless. I love Darrel, and like it or not, he's a part of me."

His eyes drifted back to Mercedes with an intensity she could feel. "Here's the deal. I'm going to let things stand for a year and see how it goes. But I'm not disappearing. I need to be a part of his life. That means I'll be visiting—a lot."

Relief swept through Mercedes. Brandon was backing down! He wasn't going to take Darrel! And he might say he was going to be around, but the truth was his career was in California and that couldn't be changed overnight. He might let years go by, enough time for Darrel to enjoy an unfettered childhood. Time for him to mature enough to understand how young and stupid and vulnerable she had been. Maybe he would be able to forgive her.

"I have only one stipulation," Brandon continued. "I want to pay for anything extra he might need. I want him to have every advantage money can buy, and if that means footing the bill for activities for your other boys to keep things looking fair in Darrel's eyes, so be it. I know you'll be reluctant, but I don't want pride to stand in the way of my son's learning. It goes without saying that I'll set aside money for college, so he can have his choice of education. I don't want you to fight me on the money issue. I have to be involved in some real way, and money is at least real. Something I can point to after he learns the truth. That's my offer. Take it or leave it." He watched them steadily, hands fisted at his side.

Mercedes closed her eyes, a tear seeping under her lashes. When she opened them, both men were watching her. "Thank you," she said. "Thank you."

Wayne released Mercedes' hand, stepping forward to offer his own to Brandon. The men shook solemnly, not speaking a word. Then Brandon turned and strode away.

"Wait!" Mercedes called after him. "Would you like to eat dinner with us tonight?"

Brandon turned, his face a mask without emotion. "I don't think so, but I'd like to come over a bit later. I could take the boys to the river. If that would be okay."

Mercedes looked at Wayne before nodding. "Okay."

"Thank you." Brandon resumed his path around the house.

"This isn't going to be easy," Wayne said, his brow furrowed. "He wants more—a lot more. He could change his mind. I don't trust his intentions."

Mercedes shrugged, too happy about Brandon's capitulation to feel anything but relief. Even if Brandon had ulterior motives, she could deal with that later.

"And the suggestion that he has to pay for our other sons' activities so Darrel won't be singled out—I would never accept his money."

Mercedes had no such qualms if it kept Darrel safe. "I'm sure it won't come to that."

Wayne started for the house. "Well, I'd better call Duane. I hope he's not out."

"He has a mobile phone."

"I'm starting to consider getting one of those myself."

Mercedes made herself busy in the kitchen as Wayne, phone pressed to his ear, explained the problem to Duane, their veterinarian. It was still too early for lunch, but they might as well eat something—it looked as if they'd have a full day ahead.

Wayne was pacing near the doorway to the hall, still talking, when his face abruptly paled. His words died in mid sentence, and the phone dropped to the linoleum. He brought a hand to his chest, massaging fiercely.

"Wayne!" She was at his side in an instant, helping him to a chair. His breath came in ragged gasps.

"Hello? Hello?" came a tinny voice on the other end of the phone line.

Mercedes grabbed it. "Duane, get an ambulance out here—quick! I think it's a heart attack."

Dropping the phone, Mercedes took her husband's pulse. Still there, though erratic, but his head was wet with sweat, and he was struggling to breathe.

"Lie down on the floor." She helped him stretch out and began to knead his chest, checking his pulse every few minutes and praying for all she was worth.

"It's feeling better," he said after a while, giving her his crooked smile. "I guess I'm just tired." He tried to sit up, but she pushed him back down with one hand.

"Don't move." Scooping up the phone, she dialed quickly. "I had a friend call emergency. I think my husband's having a heart attack. Is someone on the way?"

"Is it for Wayne Johnson?" asked a woman.

"Yes."

"We're on the way. You live so far out that it will be some time before they can get there. But I can help you until they get there. Is he breathing?"

"Yes. But he doesn't look good."

"Is he conscious?"

"Yes."

"Does he have a pain in his chest? A tightening? Or numbness in his arm?" The woman on the other end of the phone sounded calm and reasonable, but Mercedes wanted to yell at her for asking so many stupid questions.

"He did have something in his chest, but it seems better now. I don't know about numbness in the arm." Mercedes looked at Wayne, who shook his head. "No. I don't think he had numbness. But please hurry. Please." Wayne was far too pale.

"Don't worry. They're on their way. Just keep him lying down. If he starts having problems breathing again, I want you to have him cough and then try to breathe deeply, repeating until he can breathe. That sometimes helps."

"Cough. Breathe. I got it."

"Now I'm going to ask you a few more questions." Her voice droned on, and Mercedes answered without really thinking about what she said. She had a vision of Wayne dying in front of her eyes before the ambulance arrived.

The minutes ticked by: five, ten, twenty. How fast could they make the drive that usually took her an hour? *Drive faster,* she told them silently. The woman on the phone was talking to her about CPR. Mercedes was only half listening, her eyes fixed on Wayne, feeling if she looked away, even for a moment, she might lose him.

"I'm fine, really." Wayne reached up and wiped a tear from her cheek.

She covered the receiver. "You'd better be."

But the next minute, his eyes fluttered closed.

"He's shutting his eyes," she said to the woman on the phone. "I think he passed out."

"Ma'am, they should be there in five minutes. Where are you in the house? Should they come in the front door?"

"Yes, please."

"Can you feel a pulse?"

She checked his heartbeat and couldn't find it. "Oh, no!" She started to sob. "I can't find it!" Her breath came fast and sounds emerged from her mouth that she didn't recognize. Desperate, strangled cries.

"Calm down, ma'am. We just talked about CPR, remember? It's time to do that. Put the phone down and start now."

Mercedes dropped the phone and began pushing on Wayne's chest. She felt an odd sense of déjà vu, though doing CPR on him was far different than on Geraldine's baby. Or on her own little Lucy. Wayne was so large, she hardly made any impression on him. Were her efforts useless? She wished someone were here to help share this burden. If the attack had happened even thirty minutes ago, Brandon would have been there. As a heart surgeon, he would have known what to do.

But Brandon was never around when she needed him.

"Please, Wayne!" Tears wet her face and blurred her vision, dripping onto Wayne's inert form. Her arms began to ache, but she'd die before she'd give up. She was grateful now for the hours of hard work on the farm, for the many times she'd milked the cow. All this helped her endure the fire burning up her arms.

I can't lose him!

Endless minutes passed before the ambulance workers raced into the house and took over. An older, dark-haired man began compressions, while the other strapped an oxygen mask over Wayne's face. The second man was hardly more than a boy, his thin face as pale as his blond hair. After the mask was in place, he gave Wayne a shot in the chest. Mercedes huddled on the floor some distance away, feeling weak and useless as the adrenaline rush faded.

Unreal. Everything was completely unreal.

"Mr. Johnson, can you hear me?" This from the man doing compressions. His build and dark hair reminded her of Austin, but his face was pockmarked, as though he'd suffered terrible acne as a teen.

"Should we use the defib?" asked the younger man.

"No. I think I have a pulse. Mr. Johnson?"

A moan came from Wayne's throat. Giving a sob, Mercedes scooted closer, and the men parted to let her in. "Wayne?"

His eyes moved in her direction. "I'm okay." He didn't look okay.

"We have to take him now," the boy-man said. He'd been scared, and only now was the color returning to his face.

He'd thought Wayne was going to die, she realized.

"You can meet us at the hospital," he added.

"But—"

"If you follow us, I bet you won't get a ticket," the dark-haired man offered.

"Okay."

She left the house open, knowing the boys would be home later and would need to get in. Besides, no one would steal anything here, even if she had something in the house worth stealing. Once at the hospital, she'd call Geraldine and have one of her sons drive the boys into town. Or maybe she could arrange to have them picked up before they left school. It all depended upon what happened next.

How odd that her mind was able to contemplate such things when her heart was filled with terror. What if Wayne died in the ambulance? What if she never had the chance to tell him she loved him? Really, really loved him.

Please, God, she prayed.

The ride to Riverton went more quickly than she expected, though it was all Mercedes' old truck could do to keep the ambulance in sight. At the hospital, Wayne was whisked behind closed doors. Hands shaking, she made a few phone calls. Her tears for the moment had ceased, replaced by a surreal numbness.

To her relief, the physician appeared after only forty minutes. "I'm Dr. Peck," he said, offering his hand. He was a lanky, thirty-something man who was going prematurely bald. As he explained his findings, he spoke in concise medical terms, as if sensing Mercedes would know what the words meant. As if understanding she'd been through something like this before.

"So it's definitely a heart attack," he finished, "though he seems to be remarkably fit. Has he been under a lot of stress lately?"

Guilt grew in Mercedes' heart. Brandon, the planting, and the cattle had given Wayne stress, but she most of all.

"Yes, a lot of stress. Our cattle—" Oh, that was one more phone call she'd have to make. She must try to limit their losses. The thought put her over the edge, and she started weeping again.

Dr. Peck stood by helplessly. With a jerky movement, he reached out a hand to pat her back and then pulled it away again. "I've contacted your regular physician, and he'll be in shortly."

Mercedes wondered who he'd called. She couldn't remember a time when Wayne had visited a doctor, though she must have put someone's name down on the papers.

"What he really needs is a heart specialist," the doctor added, "and soon."

The "soon" made Mercedes' legs weak. "Can I see him?"

"Yes. But he isn't conscious."

She went in Wayne's room, her hand going to her mouth to stifle a gasp at his appearance. He was almost unrecognizable under all the wires and monitors. His eyes were closed, and his face was gray. The bright red hair contrasted starkly, ridiculously, with the white sheets. He looked horribly old.

"We do have several heart specialists here." Dr. Peck didn't meet her eyes. "This is a teaching hospital, so we have the staff. But you are certainly free to choose an outside physician or facility."

They'd told her that with Lucy too, and she'd tried, but in the end it had made no difference. "I'd like the names, please."

"I'll get them for you." He started to leave, but her fingers clutched at his sleeve.

"I also want recommendations for the best physicians for his condition, regardless of where they work. My brother from Nevada will be here soon—I left a message for him—and he'll help me decide what to do."

Dr. Peck nodded. "Look, truthfully speaking, I think the doctor we have here over cardiology is really good. Name's Dr. Shubacker. I've put out a call to him already, and he'll be in to consult with you as soon as possible. But there are a couple of doctors out of California that were here a week ago. They're top in the field, and I was really impressed with their methods. Last I heard, one of them might still be in town."

Mercedes' mind reeled as she struggled to hold onto his words. "You're talking about Brandon Rhodes."

Dr. Peck arched a brow. "You know him?"

What to answer? She had thought she knew Brandon at different times in her life, but every single time he'd turned out to be something other than what she'd expected. How cruel that fate would put Wayne's life in Brandon's hands. "I—I tried to get him to operate on my daughter once," she said in a near whisper. "He was out of the country."

"Well, he's not now. Or at least I don't think so. I can get you his contact information." He leaned forward. "Frankly, and this is between you and me, if I were in your shoes, I'd really think about contacting him. His reputation is brilliant, and you don't come by that easily in this field."

"I know where to find him."

Dr. Peck drew away. He was even taller than she'd first noticed, and his manner of speech and the tight way he walked seemed unnatural to his height, as though his nervousness alone decided who he was. "You can stay with him."

She took a step toward the chair by the bed. "Will he wake up?"

"I don't think so." Dr. Peck's thin face was grave. "We've got him on a lot of medication. He'll need a few additional tests, but my opinion is that he needs surgery right away. Dr. Shubacker will, of course, confirm that."

Mercedes nodded and blinked, trying to stop new tears. The numbness she'd known too intimately when Lucy was dying had slowly spread throughout her entire body. The day when her precious little one had taken her last breath, Mercedes had been holding her. She'd thought no pain or loss could ever equal that moment, but she'd been wrong.

"Wayne, I'm here." She said the words quickly so that if he

could hear her on some level, he wouldn't notice the shakiness or her obvious fear. She sat down, took his hand, and held it to her lips for a long moment, unheeding of the tears that washed down her face and onto his skin. "It's going to be all right," she whispered. "I'm here. We're together. We'll face this together. Don't give up."

He didn't open his eyes or stir in any way, yet Mercedes felt hope. He was alive, and the hospital had doctors here to help him.

Doctors like Brandon? Could she trust him with Wayne's life? No. Better to trust the others.

She'd been sitting with Wayne only an hour when a nurse came to get her. "Your children are here, and a friend."

"Thank you." To Wayne, Mercedes added, "I'll be right back."

"Dr. Shubacker is also here," the nurse added. "He's going through the test results now and will meet with you shortly."

"Thank you." With a fleeting touch to Wayne's cheek, Mercedes left the room.

Geraldine was in the waiting room with the boys, who immediately converged upon her. Mercedes couldn't believe how wonderfully alive her sons felt in her arms.

"Is he going to be okay?" Darrel's face was streaked with tears.

"I hope so, honey. The doctors are helping him."

"Can we see him?" Joseph's eyes were red and puffy, and for once he wasn't eating.

"Not right now, I don't think. But maybe before he goes into surgery."

"When's that?"

"Soon. I don't know exactly. They have a doctor here who specializes in the heart. He's looking at your dad's test right now, and then we'll know more." The boys all nodded, their faces somber.

"Momma," Scott said, sucking in a sobbing breath, "I'm scared."

She sat down and pulled him onto her lap. "I know. Me too. It's okay to be scared. But we're together, and no matter what happens, we're a family."

Scott nodded and pressed his face into her shoulder, sobs shaking his thin frame. Joseph sat on the next chair and leaned against her side. Darrel stood with his legs touching hers. Each seemed intent on feeling her closeness, and Mercedes was happy to give them what comfort she could.

Geraldine approached hesitantly, baby Mercy in her arms. "I came as quick as I could. I picked the boys up at school and sent my Jimmy over to look after your animals. Jacob went with the vet to see to the cattle. You don't need to worry about anything. Your friends will help. There'll be more here soon. We're all praying." Her chin wobbled, and she clamped her mouth shut to still it.

Mercedes bit her lip hard for a few moments in an effort to maintain her own composure. "Thank you," she managed finally. "I never imagined . . ."

"We all love you." Geraldine nodded vigorously, tears welling in her eyes. "We'll help you through this."

Mercedes reached up and squeezed her hand, eyes drifting to the bundle in the crook of Geraldine's arm. By the look of her chubby face, little Mercy was healthy and content. Her button mouth worked in her sleep as though she were nursing.

"I'll stay until the boys need to go home," Geraldine said. "Then I'll take them back with me. They'll have a campout with my boys, and I'll bring them by again tomorrow."

"Thanks so much. But it might not be necessary. I'm sure Austin will fly here tonight, if he gets his messages in time. Probably his wife too."

Geraldine smiled. "That's good. He'll be company for you. But still don't hesitate to ask for anything."

"You should be home resting."

"Nonsense." Geraldine flicked her hand as though pushing the idea aside. "I've had plenty of days to rest. I feel great now, thanks to you. Besides, all I'm going to do is sit right here and take it easy."

The clearing of a throat caught their attention. "Mercedes Johnson?" The man's eyes went between the two women for an instant before settling on Mercedes. His gaze was questioning, the tiny lines around his eyes belying the smooth cheeks.

Was this the cardiologist? He seemed somehow familiar. Then she remembered him. Though his hair was graying and he'd gained weight, Mercedes couldn't mistake the ink-sprinkled coat that sat crookedly on his wide shoulders.

"Dustbottom?"

He grinned a wide smile. "You remember."

"Yes." She tried to stand, but Scott clung to her.

"Don't bother." Dustbottom was short for a man, about as tall as Geraldine. Mercedes hadn't remembered that about him. She did remember the way he moved, like a cat that had just drunk a bowl of cream. "I heard you were here and came from the morgue to see if there was anything I could do."

"Word travels fast, huh?"

"Only when a woman is as pretty as you."

Mercedes gave him a genuine smile, feeling as far from pretty as she ever had in her life but grateful he would say so anyway. "Who really told you?"

"Dr. Peck's a friend of mine."

"I see." She couldn't imagine that. Surely Dr. Peck was too high-strung to be friends with the languorous Dustbottom.

"So, what's going on?"

Mercedes' smile faded. She looked pointedly at Geraldine and then at the boys. Dustbottom was a part of her past with Brandon, and she worried what he might say in front of the boys.

"Come on, kids," Geraldine said, picking up the hint. "I saw a vending machine down the hall. Darrel, if you'll help your brother, we'll go get some candy bars. I'm sure I have enough change. Scott, do you want to push the buttons?" Scott was gradually enticed away, and Mercedes felt grateful for Geraldine's efforts.

"My husband had a heart attack," she told Dustbottom as he sat beside her. "Dr. Peck thinks he'll need an operation by tomorrow."

She had the feeling she wasn't telling him anything he didn't already know, but he shook his head and said, "I'm so sorry."

"Thanks." She smiled again, but it was forced. "Dr. Peck says you have a great cardiologist who works here, a Dr. Shooo-something."

"Shubacker?" Dustbottom shook his head. "No, I'll give you a list of names. In fact, I have it right here."

"But Dr. Peck—"

"I have the utmost respect for Dr. Peck, but he's a company man."

"Well, he was complimentary about Dr. Shubacker, but he actually recommended that I contact someone else."

"He did? Well, good for him. I must be rubbing off on the man. Look, Mercedes, you know as well as I do if you want your husband to have every chance of recovery, you must choose the right physician. One who's willing to come here, and soon, because by the looks of your husband's chart, he can't be moved."

"You saw his chart?"

Dustbottom shrugged. "So sue me." He fished in his pocket and drew out a handwritten list of names and phone numbers.

Mercedes tried to scan them, but her eyes stopped at the first name on the list.

"I've written them in order of preference."

"No."

"Yes. And the second name is the man Brandon works with. Brandon could get him back here, if he thinks there's enough time."

Mercedes was shaking her head. "You don't know what you're asking."

Dustbottom's brow creased. "You aren't giving him enough credit. He's a doctor first. I know that about him."

"He was," she agreed bitterly. After all, he'd tossed out their future for his career.

"Truthfully, I don't think you have a choice. He's the only one you're going to get at such short notice. It's him or Shubacker."

Mercedes nodded. "Thanks for your advice." She pressed her fingers against her temples. "I need to think."

Dustbottom hugged her, as though they had been friends for years, instead of people who'd met only because of a shared acquaintance. Mercedes felt a sudden regret that she hadn't known the man better. His hug filled her with the warmth of friendship and gave her new strength.

"We all do what we have to," Dustbottom said in her ear. "Now go talk to Brandon. I'll keep watch over your husband while you're gone."

She blinked back more tears. "Brandon said you knew more than any of the doctors here."

"He always was a smart boy." He gave her a lazy smile.

"Not always."

Dustbottom's brow creased again. "Not about some things, no. But I'm right about this. Now go."

Mercedes nodded and went to find Geraldine and the boys. As Dustbottom said, she knew what she had to do.

CHAPTER 21

Diary of Mercedes Walker Johnson
January 16, 1996

Darrel is a month old now. I never knew life could be so wonderful. Darrel is with me constantly, and I can barely stand for Wayne to go away to the fields. I want both my men here every moment. Did Momma feel this kind of love when she had me? Did having me bind her just that much more to Daddy? Why, then, didn't I feel a part of that love? I think it's because Daddy took and took and never gave back.

Poor Momma. I really feel sorry for her. I don't feel sad or angry when I think about her anymore, or what she did. I have it easy compared to what she endured. Wayne gives everything back and more, and Darrel won't ever have to wonder about our love for him. I can sit and watch both him and Wayne for hours—at night while I'm quilting and they are together on the couch snuggling, or at mealtimes when we trade off holding him because we can't bear to put him down.

I am happy. I am new. I am loved. My wish now is that I can make Wayne feel the same.

"*I* can't come for a visit now, Mom," Brandon said, tilting his head to hold the phone against his shoulder as he opened the window in his room. A bit of breeze signaled the approaching evening. "I'm really busy."

"But Hannah said you were in Wyoming."

"I am in Wyoming. I came here to teach at a seminar. You know, giving back to the old alma mater."

"When Hannah told me she'd been to visit you, I'd hoped maybe you two would work things out."

So that's what the call was about. Well, at least Hannah hadn't told her about his collapse.

"Actually, Hannah came to tell me she's seeing someone. She's going to marry him." How odd to say that. Brandon walked to the window and looked out at the few people strolling by. One of them was a mother pushing a stroller. Would Hannah be a mother soon? She sounded like she was ready.

His mother's silence dragged on. Finally, she spoke. "I know about him. But I also know she doesn't care about him the way she does about you."

"Did care, Mom. *Did* being the operative word. Past tense."

"She still cares. If you'd just make an effort, you might be able to salvage your relationship."

"We're divorced." He ran a finger along the white-painted windowsill.

"I almost divorced your father once."

His finger stopped. "You did?"

"It was a long time ago."

He could imagine her shrugging, a sure indication that she wanted no more questions. His mother always glossed over the bad in her life; he was surprised she'd admitted this much.

"The point is you have to figure out what you want before it's too late."

"I know what I want."

"She went all that way."

"She had frequent flyer miles. Wyoming's closer than California."

"She loves you."

Brandon stifled a sigh. "Look, Mom, there's someone else. It's complicated, and I'm not going into detail just yet, but I promise you'll be really happy once I can tell you more." His mother would love having a grandson.

As the thought came, the desire to tell her about his son was overwhelming. But he'd promised Mercedes he'd wait, and he had to keep his word. He'd already said far too much. Keeping Darrel a secret from his parents would be the hardest part of this deception, but he was determined to keep his promise.

He'd been so sure things would change for the better between him and Mercedes after she discovered the truth about the letters, but now she acted as if the very sight of him hurt her. Was that because she honestly hated him? Why should he continue paying for Mercedes' father's deception? He deserved a second chance.

Things should have been different. The hopelessness of the situation made him ill with regret.

"Brandon, are you there?"

He forced his mind back to the conversation. "I'm here."

"I was saying you could be happy with Hannah if you tried."

There was a brisk knock on his door, which seemed to verge on the frantic.

"I'm sorry, Mom, but I've got to go," he said with relief. "Someone's here."

"Fine. But call me as soon as you can. Your father will want to talk with you as well."

Brandon figured that, which was why he'd made sure to call her when he knew his father would be away brokering yet another multimillion-dollar real estate deal. He wasn't sure of his ability to keep anything from his father.

"I will. Bye, Mom." He pocketed the phone as he opened the door.

Mercedes stood in the hallway. Her face was rigid and composed, but her dark eyes were wild and full of emotion.

"Mercedes!" He didn't know what her appearance could mean, but he was unable to stop his smile of triumph.

She stepped inside the room, smelling of horse and sweat and something more he couldn't identify. He reached out to touch her, but she pulled away, her body stiff and unyielding. Why was she here? The more he learned about Mercedes, the less he understood.

"Mercedes?" He made it a question this time, wondering how he should act.

She took a deep, shuddering breath, her shoulders shaking. Tears fell glistening onto her cheeks that were a sickly pale beneath her tan.

"Are you okay?" He stepped closer and abruptly she went limp against him, as if her knees had given way. He put a supporting arm around her. "It's okay," he murmured into her hair. "Whatever it is, we'll make it okay."

She was already drawing away, shaking her head. "You don't understand." A sob burst from her throat. "I didn't know what else to do. Dustbottom said you were the only one who could help. I don't want to ask, but I have to. I can't lose him! Please." She gripped his hand tightly, her face pleading, her hair fanning over her shoulders in disarray.

Belated fear gripped him. "What happened? Is it Darrel?"

"No. It's Wayne. He had a heart attack. They say he needs an operation. I don't understand it all, but he could die. I'm so scared! He was just standing in the kitchen when he started rubbing his chest. I got him to the floor, and then his heart stopped." Her breath was quick, shallow. She looked close to passing out.

"Come over here. Sit down." He led her to a chair next to the small round table. "Easy. Take a deep breath."

"It's like Lucy," she keened. "Oh, like my little girl!" She sobbed in earnest, and a thousand emotions flooded him. He'd never seen her feelings so completely bare, not even when she'd fought with her father years ago or when she was challenging him about Darrel over the past weeks. During their relationship they'd never faced anything remotely like this— except when she became pregnant, and thanks to him she'd endured that alone.

He wanted to comfort her, but how? And what kind of person was he to feel the slightest bit of satisfaction that Wayne might cease to be a concern to their future? Revulsion filled him at the thought, and he knelt by Mercedes' chair, patting her back ineffectually.

"He's at the hospital, right?"

She nodded. "They're doing tests and more tests."

"Then he's in good hands."

"Dustbottom says you need to look at him." She bit her lip to stop another sob, and he could see a drop of blood seep from under her teeth. "Please." Her eyes begged more than the simple word. "Please help him. If there's anyone who can, you can. Please, Brandon. Please. I know I've asked a lot of you lately, but I need you now more than I ever have."

He knew what she was saying. He'd failed her once with Darrel and again when her daughter was ill. He owed her.

Before he could answer, she gave a tiny jerk of her head and swiped her hands firmly over the tears on her cheeks. He felt he was watching her pull down a mask, as though this naked suffering was too private to share with him.

"Please, will you help Wayne?" Her voice was more controlled now, but her eyes were still wild, desperate. A strand of her hair caught on the edge of her lip.

He reached for it but stopped short, feeling out of place as reality sank in. She hadn't come here to say she loved him. She was here only for Wayne. *Of course,* he thought bitterly. *Wayne.* At least she had been honest about her commitment to her husband from the beginning.

He stood up, paced to the wall and back again, hands shoved deep in his pockets. He came to a rapid stop before her. "I'm the wrong person for this, Mercedes. The wrong person."

"I know." Her reply was less than a whisper.

She closed her eyes, her jaw clenched. When she opened them again, the black was washed with new tears, reminding him of rocks at the seashore. "There's no one else. If I ever needed you, Brandon, I need you now. Please, don't let me down. Please. I'll do anything."

He paced the room again, whirling on her when he reached the wall. "Anything?"

They stared at each other for a long moment. His eyes challenging, hers shocked and pleading. Then her eyes dropped in defeat.

"I'll tell Darrel," she said, her voice a harsh whisper. "We'll work out visits. I promise I'll be happy about it and supportive.

Whatever you want. Just please help us." Her hands gripped the edge of the table.

He could tell how much it cost her to say the words. "Please," she added again as he slowly walked toward her.

Guilt rose like bile in his throat. He had loved this woman, and she shouldn't have to beg him to help her. She shouldn't feel she needed to sacrifice her son to save her husband. The fact that Brandon should have been her husband meant nothing here. He'd made a terrible decision long ago, and he had to live with the consequences. His foot shot out and kicked the chair as he passed the table. It tumbled across the carpet and slammed into the wall.

Mercedes gasped and leapt to her feet, one hand clutching her purse, eyes darting between him and the door as if contemplating her chance of escape.

Brandon hated the fear in those black eyes.

"No," he said, holding up his hands. "Don't go. I'm sorry. It's just all so . . ." He shook his head. "Of course, I'll look at him. Come on. I'll drive you back to the hospital."

"I have my car."

"You're in no condition to drive."

Her eyes drifted to the chair. "Neither are you."

"But I'm okay to operate?"

She saw at once how ludicrous it was. Her mouth wavered and then curved in a slight smile. "Okay, you drive."

On the way to the hospital, he asked her questions about Wayne's attack and what the doctors had said. He gleaned very little except the attack had caused lasting damage that couldn't be controlled by medication. This could mean numerous things, from certain death to minor surgery. That Wayne was in the hospital but not in surgery was a good sign—someone obviously thought he could wait for a specialist. Of course, he'd seen too many patients die while doctors or families made decisions. Only by seeing Wayne himself could he determine what kind of danger he was in and whether or not his research into heart valves and arteries would be useful.

What if he was unable to save Wayne? Would Mercedes hate him forever? Or would Wayne's death free them for the life they should have had all along?

In the waiting room of the hospital, Darrel and the other children were waiting for Mercedes. Darrel came running to them, his dark eyes searching Brandon's. "Momma says you can fix Daddy's heart."

"I hope so. I'll do my best."

Darrel's brow furrowed, his eyes luminous with unshed tears. "I can't believe this is happening. Just this morning we were planning to go fishing after school." His jaw jutted out as though he was determined not to cave into emotion. He gave his mother a curt nod. "He's going to be okay, Momma. He has to be."

Mercedes nodded, trying to smile but failing. The younger boys clung to her, one on each side, their young faces directed toward him hopefully. He looked away at the blatant need in their eyes. If Wayne died, their entire lives would change.

"I guess I'll go see Wayne," he said, turning as a tall man strode into the room. He had short, black, slightly receding hair, dark eyes, and a face that was handsome despite the hard angles. On the left arch of his forehead, a long scar disappeared into his hair. Brandon knew him at once, not for the boy he'd been but because he was the man responsible for his finding out about Darrel.

"Uncle Austin!" Darrel ran toward him, hurtling his thin body at the newcomer.

Without a word, Austin Walker gathered the boy into his arms, and Darrel promptly burst into tears. "It's going to be all right," Austin murmured. "I promise. No matter what happens, we're a family, and it's going to be okay. I'm here."

"I know," sobbed Darrel. His face was broken, and his grief was painful for Brandon to see.

Mercedes' reaction at seeing her brother was similar to Darrel's, as though she had carried her burden as far as she could and was now giving it to Austin because he was strong enough to take it.

"I knew you'd come," she murmured tearfully as Austin enfolded her with one arm.

"Caught the first flight the minute I heard. Liana's here too. She's parking the rental car."

Brandon edged toward the door. He wasn't needed here. Darrel obviously felt his uncle's presence gave him permission to be a child again instead of the man of the family he was supposed to be in Wayne's absence. He hadn't cried or allowed himself that liberty with Brandon, and that told him a lot. No matter how much the child might like him, Brandon wasn't necessary to Darrel's happiness. Austin was. Wayne was.

What was Brandon supposed to do with that knowledge? Even with the promise Mercedes had made to him, he couldn't exactly walk over and say, "Hey, I'm your real father. Do you want to come and live with me? I'll take care of you."

Besides, who was to say if he took Darrel away from here that he would even be the same child. Darrel might hate him forever.

Brandon walked blindly down the hall, finding his way more from memory than from sight. At the nurses station, he gave his name and asked to talk to the attending physician.

In minutes he was up to his elbows in papers and reports, but he'd barely had time to digest any of it before Dr. Shubacker himself appeared, his round belly sticking out like an expectant woman's. Brandon knew him from the seminar, and they had passed several hours in conversation about Brandon's techniques, but he knew little about the man himself. He was younger than many of the veteran doctors, and he still sported a full head of thick brown hair, though his weight aged him considerably.

His chubby fingers handed over a new report. "They told me you were here. It doesn't look good."

"He'll need surgery?"

"Yes. But come see him for yourself." Dr. Shubacker led him down the hall into Wayne's room.

Brandon was surprised at how still Wayne looked and how large his presence, though most patients seemed smaller in their beds. He appeared helpless with the oxygen and heart monitors—far different from the strong farmer with whom he'd worked side by side the previous week. His face was a sickly color, his eyes were closed, and the red hair stood out like blood on the stark sheets.

Dr. Shubacker made a slight adjustment to a knob on a monitor. "Seems to have been caused by a severe spasm in one of the coronary arteries."

"No plaque blockage?" Brandon thumbed through the papers, mostly to mask his racing thoughts.

"Not big enough to cause something like this. Definitely stress related. Apparently, he's been having symptoms for a while. At least that's what he told the ambulance personnel."

"I'm assuming he's been medicated to prevent a relapse."

"The medication has worked well enough for now.

Unfortunately, we can't risk a repeat of another spasm. The damage from the myocardial infarction is serious. Probably fatal." Dr. Shubacker pulled out the new report from the papers in Brandon's hands. "These tests are just in. If there were any more complications, I wouldn't even want to risk surgery."

Myocardial infarction. The medical name for a heart attack.

Not the first stress-related attack Brandon had seen by a long shot, but the first he'd been partly responsible for. He focused on the report. One of the valves was leaking, and the coronary artery was not opening as it should, even with the help of medication. All the tests pointed to damage they couldn't repair with measures less invasive than surgery.

"He'll need a bypass."

Dr. Shubacker nodded vigorously, his jowls wobbling as he moved. "I concur. First thing in the morning."

Brandon shook his head as he checked the numbers on the charts and the readouts on the machines monitoring Wayne's vitals. "His heart is under too much stress to wait. He can't be getting enough flow right now. He's likely to have another attack before morning."

"I think he'll be okay."

"I've seen patients better off than this die because doctors waited too long," Brandon snapped.

Dr. Shubacker bristled. "I've seen patients die because doctors were in a hurry."

Stifling his irritation, Brandon forced a conciliatory note into his voice. "Look, I know this man, and his family has asked me to do the surgery, so I feel responsible. I don't have time to fly my partner in to help me with this. You're obviously the best heart doctor here, and I'd like your support." Involuntarily, his eyes went to Dr. Shubacker's fingers. They were not the fine hands of a surgeon, but he was a conscientious doctor who would make a fine assistant. Better than waiting until morning.

Dr. Shubacker's lips pressed together briefly before giving a quick nod of assent. "I'd be honored." A sardonic grin spread over his face. "Guess I'll have to tell my wife I'm not taking her out tonight."

"Sorry."

Dr. Shubacker said something more, but Brandon was already elsewhere in his mind and barely noticed when the other doctor left the room. Brandon studied Wayne's face. He was a good man and had been a great husband and father. If it had been anyone else, Brandon would have felt the sorrow he normally worked so hard to keep at bay. But this situation was impossible. If he was honest, he'd have to admit he wanted Wayne out of the way. Saving Wayne would ultimately mean pushing Mercedes away permanently.

But was there any other choice?

"I wish it could be different," he said aloud in the quiet of the room.

Wayne lay there silent and motionless. With a sigh, Brandon went to tell Mercedes the bad news.

Mercedes eyes went to his eagerly as he entered the waiting room. He understood that she wanted desperately for him to tell her everything would be all right, but such a guarantee wasn't within his control. She started to stand, but Brandon shook his head and slid into the metal-framed chair next to her. The cushion was stiff, made of a glossy, impenetrable green material.

Austin took one look at Brandon's face and rounded up the boys, distracting them with promises of food if they'd help him find their aunt, who must have taken a wrong turn in the hallways.

When Brandon and Mercedes were alone, she said, "Tell me."

"He must have surgery—tonight. I believe tomorrow will be too late."

For a moment, he pondered that if he'd gone home last week directly after his hospital stay, he wouldn't be here now to attempt saving Wayne. Why hadn't he gone? Then Mercedes wouldn't be looking at him right now with a world of expectation in her face.

"But you can save him?" The hope in her voice stung.

"I can't promise anything. The truth is, I may not be successful. It was a bad attack."

She was quiet a moment as she considered this. "You're his best chance, aren't you?"

He nodded. "If you wait until tomorrow, he'll die for sure." He wanted to add "I'm sorry" but couldn't.

She closed her eyes, her face drooping toward her chest, tears leaking from under her already swollen lids. Had she cried for him that way? Her bottom lip was bruised and swollen, but her teeth bit into the same spot again and again.

He ignored the urge to free her lip. "I'd better get ready." Her eyes opened and looked in his direction. "Thank you." He nodded, not trusting his voice, knowing he still had a choice before him.

A choice between life and death.

In Brandon's hands lay the power over Mercedes' future—and his son's. One slip, one subtle movement that would go undetected by his fellow doctors or the nurses, and he'd be free to love them both. Or he wouldn't have to do even that. Just work a little slowly, perhaps without his usual brilliant skill. No one would fault him, and Wayne would be gone. No pain, never waking. Mercedes would be free, and Brandon believed he could convince her—eventually—to let him back into her life. Not soon, but sometime, and he would take her and their son away to the life they should have had. No one would know. Except himself. He would feel guilty for a time, but what was that to being with Mercedes?

Yet what of the love and care Wayne had given to Mercedes over the years, the deeply devoted way he'd raised Darrel as his own? What about the other two boys? Brandon certainly wouldn't choose to leave them fatherless.

There was also another issue at stake. In all the years Brandon had worked as a surgeon, he'd always given his best, continually pushing himself beyond all limits to save lives. He couldn't give any less to the man who had done for Mercedes what he himself should have done thirteen years ago.

Swallowing hard, Brandon lowered the scalpel until it pressed into Wayne's chest, leaving a fine line of blood. *Hold on, Wayne,* he told his patient silently. *I'll do my best. I promised Darrel I'd try to make his daddy well.*

What he couldn't promise was that his best would be good enough. It would be in God's hands after that. Or in Wayne's and the will he had to live. If Brandon were in Wayne's place, he would fight with every bit of strength in his body to remain with Mercedes. At least he would now. He wouldn't throw away his chance as he had when he was young and stupid.

The heart was partially exposed, and almost immediately Brandon could see the damage was even more severe than the tests had shown. It would be a miracle if Wayne survived the surgery, regardless of Brandon's skills. He would definitely have to separate the breastbone to get the access he needed to the damaged valve, and for the bypass he wouldn't be able to use the mammary artery, which had a tendency to stay open for more years than the saphenous vein from the leg.

Still, the vein would work well enough to connect the heart to the damaged artery, bypassing the part that was no longer working. What concerned him more was that he wouldn't be able to do the operation with Wayne's heart beating. Brandon was one of a growing number of doctors that believed a patient had a much better recovery if surgery could be accomplished without the heart-lung machine. Though it had saved countless lives, the machine simply couldn't circulate the blood nearly as well as the human heart. The only good news was that Wayne needed a single bypass and not two or three.

Reluctantly, Brandon nodded toward the heart-lung machine and motioned for Dr. Shubacker to begin removing the vein in Wayne's leg. Blotting out everything but the task before him, Brandon went to work. As he stopped Wayne's heart, his own pounded in his chest, as if beating enough for both of them.

Five hours later, Brandon left the operating room. The valve was repaired, and the bypass complete. Brandon didn't feel the mixture of elation and exhaustion that he normally felt when finishing an operation. He felt drained of emotions, energy—everything.

"Good work, doctor." Shubacker nodded at him as they shed their masks and gloves.

Brandon acknowledged the compliment. He hadn't used any new techniques, but he had no false modesty where his skill was concerned. He was simply the best, using his innate sense to perform tasks on a level that most doctors worked a lifetime to attain. It was what had drawn him to medicine in the first place. And eventually away from Mercedes.

"We'll know more in the morning," he said to Shubacker. "You go on home. I'll stay for a bit, just in case."

Brandon found Mercedes alone in the deserted waiting room. She was curled up on a sofa, with an arm on the armrest and her head on top of it. Her knees were pulled to her chest and her feet hung slightly off the edge, unsupported. Black hair spread around her face and over the sofa.

She awoke instantly as he touched her shoulder, sitting up and dropping her feet to the carpet. Her eyes were muddied with sleep, and a mark on her face showed a red pattern where her cheek had pressed into the pink fabric of her sleeve. He noticed now, as he hadn't earlier, that she was dressed in jeans and a long-sleeved T-shirt—her uniform for spending time in the sun. Had she been planning to work in her garden when the attack happened? Or had she intended to be in the fields with Wayne? He bet she was glad for the long sleeves in the slightly chilly waiting room. Or was the cold imaginary, coming only from his heart?

She looked around for a moment, as if digesting her surroundings. He wondered why she was alone, even while being grateful for the opportunity to talk to her without watchful eyes.

"Everyone went home?" he asked.

"I made my brother take the boys. Darrel was having a really hard time. I don't know what I'd have done if Austin hadn't been able to fly in so soon. They'll be back in the morning when Wayne's awake."

He sat next to her and took her hand. "He might never

wake up, Mercedes. There was a lot of damage, and I'm worried that you and the EMTs had to work as long as you did to get his heart started in the first place. If blood isn't being pumped through the body, a lot of damage occurs."

She blinked and swallowed noticeably, her eyes dark and unreadable. "But he's alive now, right? That means he made it through the operation."

"His heart is beating right this minute without help, but we won't know the extent of the damage until he wakes. If he wakes." He spoke as gently as he could.

She blinked again, and this time the lid forced out a tear that wove slowly down her face. "Thank you," she whispered. "Thank you, so much." She sagged against him, and his arm went briefly around her, squeezing gently.

The tightness in his heart diminished, and for a moment he was simply a friend comforting someone over the serious illness of a husband.

"Can I sit with him?"

"Mercedes, I—" He broke off and looked at her hand, which he still held in his. He'd meant it as a comfort to her, but he found he didn't want to let go. "You can sit with him. I'll walk you there—make sure they let you in. He won't be anywhere near awake, but that doesn't mean he won't be able to hear what you say."

She pulled her hand from his and stood. He arose with her, feeling heavy and awkward. "I'm grateful for what you did tonight," she said. "I can never repay you. I—I will keep my promise about Darrel."

He hoped she'd still feel that way in the morning. If so, within a few days his son would finally know who he was.

They walked down the hall together, and Brandon left her in the recovery room with Wayne, ignoring the attending nurse's protest. He knew he was doing the right thing by the gratitude in Mercedes' eyes.

He found Dustbottom waiting for him outside the door. His white coat sat askew on his shoulders, and his graying hair stood on end in the front, as though he'd been pulling on it. Brandon was glad to see his old friend, though he wasn't ready to talk about what had happened, how he'd saved his rival's life, at least temporarily.

"Hey."

"Hey yourself." Brandon indicated the door behind him with his head. "Guess you heard I operated."

Dustbottom smirked. "I know everything that goes on here."

"I wish you hadn't told her to ask me." Brandon felt a sudden, crushing exhaustion.

"My job is to save lives, and you were his only chance. So, how'd it go?"

"Pretty well, actually, considering the damage. Hardly any blockage at all—just one of those freak things."

"Stress."

Brandon looked away. "We won't know if we were successful until tomorrow."

"How do you feel about it?"

"I don't know. It's out of my hands now."

"You did the right thing."

"I did the only thing I could." Brandon started down the corridor, but Dustbottom stopped him with a hand on his arm.

"You're still flying back to San Diego tomorrow?"

"No. I canceled the appointment with my attorney. Mercedes and I have come to another arrangement."

"I was talking about your tests."

Brandon rubbed his eyes. "I forgot. But it doesn't matter.

I can't leave my patient yet." Leave his patient—or Mercedes and his son?

"We'll do them here then. Tomorrow." Dustbottom's face brooked no argument.

"I'm fine."

"In a few days you'll know that for sure."

Brandon sighed. "Fine. Test me all you want. But I'm not coming in early. I've been in surgery for over five hours, and I'm sleeping in."

"I'll schedule the tests." With a flat smile, Dustbottom patted his arm and strode down the hall.

CHAPTER 22

Diary of Mercedes Walker Johnson
December 10, 1996

Darrel is almost a year old. He is so smart and wonderful and makes me love being a mother. But I had an odd experience with him yesterday. He was toddling across the yard to the barn with me to gather the eggs. He'd insisted on walking with his new boots through the mud left by the last snowstorm, and suddenly he looked up at me with his head tilted just so. For an instant, he was Brandon—the smile, the set of the eyes, the shape of his face.

I was startled and nearly dropped the egg basket in the mud. A powerful sense of something missing hit me, and I started to cry.

I feel both mad and sad all at once. It seems no matter how hard I try, there is a piece of me that will always ache for Brandon and feel regret for losing him. Yet how can that be so when I feel truly happy? I love my life with Wayne and Darrel. I wouldn't change it for anything. Not even for Brandon.

I wonder if all abandoned women feel this way—a dark longing and hurt—and if the feeling ever leaves. I don't think it will. But I'll hide it deep inside. No one has to know it exists. No one but me.

*M*ercedes sat by Wayne's bedside, waiting for a response. He looked terrible. He had a tube down his throat to help him breathe, another smaller tube down his nose, three tubes connected to his body to drain off fluid in the heart area, an IV, a bladder tube, and wires that hooked to several different monitors that beeped or buzzed periodically, causing nurses to come into the room and adjust them. Under the two drainage tubes below his chest, other tiny wires that connected his heart to a pacemaker emerged from his stomach. She'd learned all these wires and tubes were normal after heart surgery, but seeing her husband lying there seemingly so lifeless and confined kept reducing her to tears.

Any minute he would open those blue eyes and search for her. "Please wake up," she whispered, rubbing his hand. Bending, she kissed his cheek, and one of her tears fell onto his face. She wiped it away gently.

Her greatest fear was that Wayne wouldn't fight, that he'd let himself succumb in order to free her, knowing she would never leave him while he lived. But she didn't want to be free. "I love you," she whispered.

Dr. Shubacker had been in to check on Wayne already this morning, as had the nurses. Brandon had been strangely absent, but one of the nurses assured her that he'd be called if he was needed.

"Excuse me, ma'am."

Mercedes looked up to see a new nurse standing in the doorway. She was young, with long blond hair and a cheerful face that made Mercedes want to smile. "Yes?"

"Your brother and son are here asking for you."

"Only one of my sons?"

The nurse nodded as her eyes went to Wayne on the bed. "I'll keep an eye on him for you, if you'd like to talk to them."

"They can't come in here?"

"We'd prefer to keep it just to you until he wakes."

"Shouldn't he be awake by now?"

The young nurse faltered a moment, her face revealing a seriousness underneath the happy exterior. "It sometimes takes a while."

"He's going to wake up. He has to."

The nurse nodded, but Mercedes wondered if she knew something more than what everyone had told her. "Would you like me to give your brother a message?" the girl asked.

"No, I'll go out. I need to stretch my legs anyway." Mercedes leaned close to Wayne, caressing his cheek with her hand. "I'll be back in a minute, honey. Austin's here with one of the boys. Probably Darrel. I know he wants to see you. As soon as you're awake, they said I could bring him in." Her voice broke on the last word, and Mercedes had to bite her already swollen lip to keep from crying. The lip throbbed.

In the waiting room, Darrel popped up from his seat when he saw her, running into her arms. "How is he?"

"His heart's working, but he's still unconscious."

Austin met her eyes over Darrel's head, stifling a yawn. "He didn't go to sleep last night until you called after the surgery, and he was up with the roosters this morning."

"I thought I had to do the milking, but Jimmy Pinkham

was already out there." Darrel glanced behind her. "Can I see Dad?"

"I'm afraid not until he wakes up."

Darrel's forehead wrinkled. "Shouldn't that be soon? On the Internet, it said they should wake up after a few hours. Or maybe five."

Mercedes met Austin's eyes, communicating as they'd always been able to do as children. When their father was on a drunken rampage, she'd needed only to widen her eyes for him to understand that he shouldn't go into the house. Or to slightly move her head for him to know he was wanted in the barn. His face paled at the knowledge of what she couldn't say in front of Darrel: Wayne might never awaken.

"I'm sure it'll be soon," he said, a hand on Darrel's shoulder. "Your father's a strong man. But remember, he's been through a lot. He deserves a little shuteye."

Mercedes smiled at him gratefully. "Where are the other boys?"

"Liana took them out to get something to eat. You know how she is with cooking. And I didn't have time."

Mercedes permitted herself a small smile. One of the greatest pleasures of having a new sister-in-law was cooking for her. Liana was always so appreciative.

"Look, I know this isn't a good time," Austin said. "But you should know the problem with the cattle is serious. We're going to lose a lot. With treatment, the vet thinks we can limit it to a third, and we won't be permitted to sell any next year unless we have them tested."

A third. Mercedes felt sick. There went any profit they'd hoped to make on the calves this year, and they'd be further behind on the new tractor payments. And then there were the hospital bills. Her mind dizzied with all the implications. At least it wasn't half the cattle. And Darrel would have his space camp, thanks to Brandon.

That reminded her—she still had to tell Darrel the truth.

"I need to sit down," she said faintly.

Austin made a sympathetic noise in his throat and led her to a seat. "I'm such an idiot. You didn't need to hear that now. But you do need to hear that I'm going to help out. I've arranged with work to do some Internet commuting so I can be here. I'll still have to travel a lot, like I always do, but it won't make too much difference, me leaving from here instead of Las Vegas. The important thing is, I know how much you love having Liana here, and she'll be around even when I can't be. She's good at coordinating things."

Relief flooded through Mercedes. Her brother had always been a constant in her life, and she should have known he wouldn't desert her now. "You'll lose your job."

"I don't think so. As long as I'm at the important meetings. They'd have a hard time replacing me on such short notice, but you know what? I don't care if they do. We've been thinking about moving into Grandmother's house when the baby's born, anyway. We might as well begin working out how that might be possible. For now, it's just a few weeks or months of extra flights. It'll be okay. Family comes first."

She hugged him. "Thank you."

He returned the hug, holding her so tightly she almost lost her breath. His touch reminded her of Wayne and how safe she'd always felt in his arms. "I love him so much," she whispered. "I never knew how much."

"I did. I always wanted to have what you two have."

"And now you do." She pulled away, trying to compose herself for Darrel's sake.

Austin gave her a boyish grin. "Liana is everything I ever wanted. Except Liana—well, let's just say, I'm not holding my breath for apple pie."

"You'd be surprised what women will do for love."

"I don't even care about apple pie anymore. I want her exactly the way she is."

"Mom will make you an apple pie," Darrel said. "It's Dad's favorite." His smile faded as he thought about what he'd said.

"He'll be all right!" Mercedes said fiercely. "We won't give up hope." She reached for his hand. "Come on, I'm going to talk to someone about getting you in there to see him."

Austin nodded. "Good idea. I'll wait here for Liana and the boys."

"Thanks." Mercedes forced a smile and walked out of the room, Darrel in tow. Maybe if Wayne could hear his voice, it would help him fight. He and Darrel had an undeniable connection. Dr. Shubacker, if she could find him, would have to understand.

Two days went by, and Mercedes was still waiting for Wayne to open his eyes. They'd replaced the oxygen tube with a mask, and some of the drainage tubes had been removed, but he showed no signs of waking. She'd been home only once to shower since the operation, but she realized she couldn't go on this way. Either Wayne would have to wake up, or she would have to return to the farm. The boys needed her. The farm needed her.

What if Wayne never woke?

Now that the possibility was upon her, she found she couldn't comprehend a life without him. She lay back in the easy chair next to the bed, her face searching the ceiling. Why had she understood this too late? Being with Wayne wasn't only about fulfilling a promise; it was about love.

For so many years, even through the happiness and passion, she'd imagined a hole in her heart where Brandon had once been. Now she saw this was fatalism she had nurtured, cheating both herself and Wayne from becoming everything they could be. She yearned for the chance to repair the damage because now she understood there would never be anyone for her except Wayne. The knowledge had been in the life they'd lived, if she'd only opened her eyes to see.

There was a sound at the door, and she turned to find Brandon standing there. He glanced toward the bed and then at her. "Could I talk to you a moment?"

She nodded, touching Wayne briefly on the arm as she stood and walked to the door.

"Have you eaten?" Brandon asked as they walked.

"Yes." If she counted an apple from the vending machine as eating.

He waited until they'd reached an area of the hospital she didn't recognize. No one was in sight. "Look," he said. "About Wayne."

"He still has brain activity." "Minimal."

"It's early yet. Darrel's been bringing me stories of people waking up who were in far worse condition. They're on the Internet."

"I'm not saying to give up. I'm just saying it might be time to start preparing yourself for the worst. You have to consider that he might never wake up."

Mercedes looked at her hands. "I have."

He was quiet a long moment and then, "Come on, I'm

buying you breakfast—or brunch, I guess, since it's nearly eleven. The vending machine doesn't count as real food."

"Are you spying on me?"

"I asked the nurses to keep an eye on you, that's all. They like me. I won't take no for an answer. Come on."

"Fine." Mercedes did feel faint, and it was good to let someone take over for a change.

Diary of Mercedes Walker Johnson
May 5, 2000

I can't believe we have three sons now! My life grows fuller and happier each day. I love life and my family. I wouldn't change a thing, not even the mud in the yard during the spring. Well, maybe I'd like a daughter someday, but if that's not the Lord's will, I'll still be grateful for the great blessings I have.

My path hasn't always been straight, but there is only promise in the future if I look ahead and not behind. I'm grateful for a husband who is also my best friend, for a brother who loves me and is close to my children. Even Daddy has asked forgiveness. I think maybe there is enough joy in me to make his life easier in his last years. I think Momma would want us to be friends. In his own crooked way, I think he loves me. Beneath the selfishness he always has.

*B*randon took East Sunset Drive to North Federal Boulevard and then drove south to the Golden Corral. Not exactly his current choice of hangout, but he'd loved coming here with his buddies in the old days. They'd often eaten themselves sick, staying until the staff kicked them out far after closing—which wasn't saying much since the restaurant usually closed at ten—and tipping the waitresses with more money than they could afford.

The restaurant was busy, but the staff was efficient, and they were soon seated near a window that looked out over the street, their plates piled with food. He looked around the crowded room. "Riverton's grown."

"It's Friday. Everyone's getting a start on an early weekend. I'm glad I live so far out of town. I mean, the growth is nice in some ways—we have more shopping—but I like things the way they were." She flushed, as though realizing he might misconstrue her words.

"It's still not very big. I mean, not compared to Boston or San Diego."

"No." Mercedes forked up a huge mouthful, eating the way a woman did when she was really hungry. Still polite and with grace but with an unconcealed urgency. "This is good," she said after swallowing a couple of bites.

"Either that or we're starving. I missed breakfast today too—Dustbottom made me come in early." For an additional test, but she didn't need to know that. A barium swallow on an empty stomach, followed by an upper GI series—X-rays. Even now Dustbottom would be consulting with Dr. Peck and the radiologist. Though he'd be glad when it was all behind him, he wasn't worried. He was no longer nauseated, and after two nights of good sleep, he felt strong. Still, sometimes friends had to be humored.

"You're right—anything tastes good when you're hungry." He'd expected her to be unsmiling and morose, but she was holding up well—unless it was a facade, and the sad thing was he really didn't know her well enough to say.

They talked about inconsequential things until their plates were nearly clean. "About Darrel," she said at last, sitting back in her seat. "I still plan on telling him, but I haven't found the opportunity yet."

She thought this meal was his way of trying to push things, but Brandon had been thinking that if Wayne died, it would be better to wait some time before talking to Darrel.

"No," he said. "I'd rather . . ." There was no kind way to say it.

Her eyes widened. "I have to be the one, Brandon. Surely you see that—"

"I don't want anyone to tell him."

"But we agreed—"

"I'm not saying I don't want to be a part of his life, because I do. But I don't want him to hate me for hurting you right now. And I don't want to make his life any less certain with what he's going through. Let's wait and see what happens with Wayne before we decide how to tell Darrel."

The tears gathering in his eyes made it difficult to see her face. He pretended to take something from the corner of his eye, blinking until the tears vanished. "I've seen how hard this has been on him these past few days," he added. "He's got a huge load on his shoulders right now trying to be the man of the family, and he doesn't need anything else to think about."

"Thank you." Mercedes gazed at him in wonder, reminding him of how she used to look at him, except that it was gratitude, not love, that shone in her eyes. "Thank you so much. You can't know what that means to me right now."

"I think I do." He felt both uncomfortable and jubilant under her gaze. "Hey, you ought to try this cantaloupe. It's really good."

She took the ripe bit he offered with her fingers, laughing as the juice sluiced down her chin. "Mmm, it is good."

More comments about the food and the weather. Her sick cattle. Then silence. Apparently, they'd run out of conversation, or at least the things they could address, but Brandon wanted more.

"Mercedes." Something must have changed in his tone because she looked at him, her face abruptly wary.

"Yes?"

"About Wayne."

She looked down at her hands. "He's going to make it."

"I don't think so."

A swift intake of breath, her teeth biting down on her lower lip.

"I did everything I could to save him, I swear it, but at this point I honestly don't think he'll ever wake up."

She didn't reply or raise her eyes. Brandon recognized shock and knew he had to give her something else to think about. He leaned toward her. "This isn't the right time to talk about it, and I know I'm a selfish idiot for bringing it up right now, but maybe you'll understand it's because I've given up a lot myself recently. All because of how I feel about you. But what we had thirteen years ago was real, and I think we can have a future again. I'm willing to wait for as long as you need. I'm not Wayne, but you loved me once. I think you can again. Am I wrong?"

For a long moment she stared at him intently. He tried not to squirm under her gaze. Then a tender smile formed on her lips, and he dared to hope. She placed her hand over his.

"I will always have a special place in my heart for you, Brandon. You were my first love. I believe if things had worked out for us back then, we would have had a good life together. We were young and adaptable. But things have changed. We aren't the same people we used to be."

"That doesn't mean we couldn't make it work."

"I admit your coming here really confused things for a while"—her voice became momentarily unsteady—"but the moment I saw Wayne lying on the floor of our kitchen, I suddenly realized what is important in my life. These days, just about any movie you see or novel you read talks about self-fulfillment—and forget about anyone else. People have affairs; they betray those they've made promises to. They chase after every fad that offers a new life. But it's all a lie. And it's not right. Too many people give up relationships they have because they think something else is better. But in the end it never is better. It's only trading one set of problems for another. Or one set of good things for another. It has to stop somewhere. The beauty and satisfaction in life is building long relationships that last."

"You love him." The words were like ash on his tongue.

"More than that." She lifted her hand from his and covered her mouth, furiously blinking back tears. When she spoke again, her voice was strong and sure. "Wayne's my best friend—he's always been that—but I didn't see it until now. I know where I belong, Brandon, and I'm happy here with my family. Last week you said I've never loved Wayne the way I did you, and you know what? You were right. I was a girl when I knew you, and that's how I loved you. But now I'm a woman, and I know what it is to love as a woman."

The words didn't surprise him as much as he thought they should. *I knew,* he thought. *I knew all along.*

"But he's dying." Brandon's voice was hardly more than a rasp. He wanted to say more, but he could see she understood what he meant, that he'd be willing to be her second choice—the backup. Was he really that desperate? Did he even deserve that much after ruining their chances so completely?

She gave a shake of her head that was neither graceful nor yielding. "Whether Wayne makes it or not won't change anything. I can't go with you to San Diego or Boston—or any place. I'm as much a part of the farm as Wayne is. I belong here. My father was right about that. I want to raise my children here. I want to live to be an old lady and be buried next to my baby—and Wayne, if he goes before me. I need to be on the farm to be close to him, even if he's no longer there in person." Tears again were falling in rivulets down her face.

"I could stay." He was unable to comprehend the idea of losing her again.

Her eyes were wistful. One corner of her mouth twitched, as though she might have smiled had the situation been less serious. "You don't belong here any more than Darrel does. The past is in the past, Brandon. I have to believe Wayne's going to make it. I can't imagine my life without him—but if he does die, I won't be alone. Wayne is in every field and rock and animal on our land. I'll never leave him. In fact"—she fumbled through her purse—"I need you to take back these letters. I can't keep them."

He knew what more she wasn't saying—more perhaps than she recognized herself. If Wayne died, it wouldn't be Brandon who would dry her tears on some future day. No, it would be a neighboring farmer or someone new to the area who had come to stay for good. She would either live and laugh and recover and raise her sons with Wayne or eventually find someone else like him. Someone that wasn't Brandon.

The realization shocked him, and for a moment he sat dazed, searching for what to say. Then he knew there was only one thing he could say that she'd want to hear.

"I'd better get you back to the hospital."

"Thank you." She stood gracefully, regally, and together they walked to his car.

Brandon watched Mercedes disappear down the hall, knowing she was forever out of reach. Moreover, he'd agreed to wait longer to tell Darrel the truth, which went against all his instincts. So why didn't he feel more upset?

It was the right thing to do. He'd experienced a similar emotion when he was in Guatemala and Brazil operating on patients too poor to pay their bills. Doing good changed a person.

Or maybe he was in shock. Who could blame him, after Mercedes' complete and utter rejection?

Still, he would have a relationship with his son in the end, and that was the bright spot in the whole mess. Soon enough Darrel would know Brandon was his father. If Wayne died, as Brandon expected, Darrel would eventually need him more and more.

He'd have to call Hannah tonight to tell her what he'd done. She'd be happy for Darrel and proud of Brandon's patience.

"Brandon!"

He turned to see Dustbottom approaching from the other direction. From radiology. The doctor glided toward Brandon with his customary gracefulness that contrasted so with his disheveled appearance.

"You talked with Mercedes?"

"I told her I didn't think he'd make it."

"And?"

A strange fury rose inside Brandon, slicing through his former complacency, and he had to force himself not to grab Dustbottom and shove him against the wall. "Even when Wayne dies, she still won't be a part of my life."

"At least now you know."

Dustbottom was right. Yet Brandon should have known all this from the moment he'd first seen Wayne and Mercedes together. From the uncanny connection between them that was so strong it would call Wayne from the fields when Mercedes needed him. From how utterly committed they both were to their family.

Brandon's anger drained away as suddenly as it had come. That was when he noticed Dustbottom's eyes. Behind the glasses, the eyes that never seemed to have a color were the exact shade of tears. Their usual distracted aspect had been replaced by a heavy sadness. Brandon felt as though someone had pushed him off a cliff.

"You know my results."

Dustbottom rotated his shoulders, causing his jacket to fall partially off one shoulder. Brandon had seen him go around like that all day, unnoticing or uncaring. He reached out and pulled it back into place. His friend didn't acknowledge the effort.

"Everyone I consulted with is unanimous. There's no doubt."

Brandon felt his whole body slump. "It's back."

"Yeah."

"I'll fight it."

"It's beatable, if you go at it aggressively. Everyone agrees on that too. We caught it early, so it hasn't spread. Still, you know as well as I do that recurrence is not good news."

An understatement if he'd ever heard one. Too often recurrence was a death sentence. Brandon felt a desperate, sweeping despair. It came to him with startling clarity that he'd wasted most of his adult life mourning losing Mercedes. Why hadn't he lived and enjoyed the life he'd had? Why hadn't he held onto Hannah? Hannah with her beautiful blond hair and wry sense of humor. He'd been like a dog biting the hand of the person who fed him. All because of some vision of how his life was supposed to have been.

What was it Mercedes said? That too many people gave up the good life they had for the false dream of something better. He was glad at least she had the sense to recognize where her path lay.

He walked blindly to the exit, barely noticing that Dustbottom was still with him, until he felt the hand on his shoulder. "You shouldn't be alone."

Just in time Brandon bit back the sharp retort that threatened to burst from him. The last time, his anger and frustration had driven Hannah away, but he was finished acting as if his emotions were the only valid ones.

"Thank you," he said, forcing his voice to be steady. "I could use a little company."

As they walked to Brandon's rental car—neither trusted Dustbottom's heap of junk—Brandon thought about his son with a mixture of despair and satisfaction. The only thing, apparently, that he'd done right was to tell Mercedes to hold off telling Darrel. Now his son wouldn't have to endure the same pain he'd already experienced this week, watching Wayne lie in that bed.

Well, not exactly the same. Darrel didn't love him like he loved Wayne. But he might have, given the chance.

Now Darrel would never know.

It was the right thing to do.

Maybe, but it left Brandon without hope. Darrel was better off without him, without the pain cancer would bring to his life. Spying a garbage bin near the parking lot, Brandon tossed in the crumpled letters Mercedes had returned to him. No one needed them now.

CHAPTER
24

Diary of Mercedes Walker Johnson
March 24, 2007

Wayne surprised me today with flowers. Lucy would have been four. I took some of the buds, and we walked out to the graveyard to sit with her. I know she's not really there. I imagine her in heaven playing with my grandmother and other little angels, but it comforts me to have some place to sit and imagine. The pain isn't gone, but it's different now. My belief that I will see and hold her again softens the emotions. She will always be mine. I feel such a love for Wayne. Many couples drift apart after the death of a child, but our experience has made us stronger. We are united in our goal to live the best lives we can to prove ourselves worthy of being with our little angel girl in heaven . . . someday.

"*H*e's going to wake up, Momma, I know it." Darrel was staring at Wayne intently. The nurses had begun letting the boys visit Wayne one at a time, though Darrel always stayed longer than the others.

"Hey, I think his eyes moved." Darrel's hair fell into his eyes as he leaned forward to study Wayne's face.

Time for another haircut, but Mercedes didn't know when she'd be able to do it. If Wayne didn't come out of the coma soon, she'd have to begin thinking about a long-term strategy for taking care of the boys and the farm—and Wayne as well. She didn't want to leave him here alone, but there would be no choice.

"See, Momma? Did you see that?"

"He does that sometimes," she said gently, so his hopes wouldn't fly too high. She knew only too intimately the depths he would plunge afterward when there were no signs of life for hours except the rise and fall of Wayne's stomach as he breathed. She'd experience those depths herself.

At least he was breathing. She'd heard repeatedly that falling into a coma was the way the body recovered from trauma, especially brain trauma. According to Darrel, who'd been spending way too much time on the Internet, Wayne's brain had been cut off from circulation for less time than hundreds of other people who woke up and were all right in the end. She clung to this hope without letting any of her sons know how desperately she prayed for it to be true. If they knew the extent of her hope, they might realize how serious her fear. She was beginning to wonder if Brandon was right, that Wayne would never awake. Instinctively, she was preparing herself for the worst.

Mercedes placed a hand on Darrel's shoulder. "Will you

be okay alone for a few minutes? I need to walk a bit. I have a cramp in my leg."

"Yeah, I'm fine. I have a book." He lifted it, and she saw a human heart on the cover. How like Darrel to research what he didn't know. This tragedy might make him more like his biological father than anyone had anticipated.

Mercedes rifled through the bag of clothes and goodies one of her friends had brought. She'd been visited almost constantly by friends over the past few days, though none were permitted in to see Wayne. She had been warmed by their love and offers of help. Austin had sat with Wayne last night so she could go home for a few hours, but she'd ended up back here before midnight, unable to be away so long.

Austin arrived again half an hour ago, bringing Darrel. He was still in the hospital somewhere. Mercedes should find him and thank him.

Her hand closed over an orange. That would calm the hunger in her stomach. She couldn't remember eating since the meal Brandon had bought her the day before, though she knew she likely had. She was forgetting a lot of things lately.

"See you in a minute," she told Darrel. "Call the nurse if you need anything. She can page me." Darrel nodded.

Outside the ICU everything was awash with sound and color. Visitors carrying bright flowers, nurses laughing together in the hall. A man carrying a little girl who clapped her hands and sang a nursery song. Mercedes watched the child, smiling. Her daughter would have been just that age. There was no bitterness at the thought.

She walked the halls, peeling and eating her orange, not knowing where she was going until she saw the sign: MORGUE. She walked up to the door but didn't enter. She didn't want to go inside. What was she doing here? She turned around and had gone only a few steps when Dustbottom emerged from the morgue doors.

Mercedes waited for him to reach her. She didn't have anything to say to the man, so why was she here? But she knew. Brandon had been unhappy when she'd refused to give him any hope yesterday, and the eccentric doctor was his friend and could look out for him.

"I was hoping I would run into you today," Dustbottom said to her, absently rubbing the stubble on his chin. If possible, his white jacket looked more disheveled and stained than usual.

"I'm glad to see you too. I wanted to know if you'd do something for me. It's not something really big, and you'd probably do it anyway, but I have to be sure."

He looked at her blankly before shaking his head. "I'm sorry, would you say that again? I'm afraid I'm a little tired. Been up all night."

"They kept you here all night?" She shivered at the vision of him working on a patient who might have died during the night.

"No, I was with Brandon. He had some bad news."

Guilt ate at Mercedes' heart. "That's sort of what I want to talk to you about. I know you're friends, and I hoped you'd keep an eye out for him while he's in Wyoming. He'll realize eventually that it's for the best, but I worry . . . I don't know, that maybe he'd do something rash."

Dustbottom's eyes behind the glasses remained placid. "What are you talking about?"

"What are *you* talking about?" She felt suddenly embarrassed. She rubbed her fingers, sticky from the orange, on her jeans.

"His test results came in yesterday."

"What?" But she understood instinctively what the words meant, and the knowledge made it hard for her to breathe. "His cancer's back, isn't it?"

"Officially, I can't tell you anything more, but as his friend, I can say that you might want to talk with him."

"When did he find out?"

"Yesterday afternoon."

"What did he—he shouldn't have been alone."

"I was with him all night. I finally convinced him to call his parents. He won't leave here, so they're flying out later today. He's sleeping now. At least that's where I left him. We were up pretty much all night. I came back here this morning because I had a few things I needed to finish up."

Mercedes' strength failed her, and she leaned against the wall for support. She thought of Brandon working in the fields with Wayne and Darrel, of Brandon agreeing not to seek custody, of Brandon and Darrel together at some vague time in the future after Darrel learned the truth. Would it even happen?

"How bad is it?"

"Hard to say. He needs to get back to his regular doctor. The good news is we've caught it early. If he'd waited until his next checkup, his outlook could be a lot worse." He let the words trail off, and Mercedes was grateful to latch onto the hope they offered.

Yes, if Brandon died, her secret would die with him and Darrel would forever be safe. Yet she found that wasn't exactly what she wanted. As much as she needed to protect Darrel, there would come a time when he could learn from Brandon. Especially if Wayne didn't . . . That was a thought she wasn't willing to finish.

"I'll go see him later. I can't leave my husband now." Almost to herself, she added, "I was wondering why Brandon hadn't come to check up on him today."

"Shubacker can do that well enough." Dustbottom shrugged one shoulder, causing his jacket to fall partially open.

"I hope he doesn't change his mind about waiting to tell Darrel." She hadn't meant to say the words aloud and hoped Dustbottom hadn't heard.

Dustbottom studied her, his graying eyebrows like caterpillars peering over his glasses. "I know about your son, and you don't have to worry. Brandon thinks that boy is all he has left in the world, and he's willing to suffer alone to protect him. He's wrong, of course. He's not alone. He just doesn't know it yet. His ex-wife is still in love with him, you know. Hannah. But he will never forgive himself for their breakup."

The doctor turned to go, saying over his shoulder, "It's really too bad. This battle would go so much better if he felt he had something more to live for. But from what he said to me last night, he doesn't plan to tell your son anything until he's cured. Or dead. And dead men don't talk."

Mercedes watched him leave, feeling heavy and sad. There was nothing she could do for Brandon. Slowly, she retraced her steps in the direction of Wayne's room.

"Mercedes!" Austin came toward her, the young nurse from Wayne's room at his side.

Trepidation made the hair on her neck rise. "What's wrong?"

"Don't worry. It's good news. We've been looking all over for you."

"Your husband's awake," the nurse added. "He's alert enough that they're changing the oxygen mask to nasal prongs so he'll be able to talk."

Mercedes clutched a fist to her heart. "Is he okay? I mean, they said there might be brain damage."

"We don't know yet, but he was able to ask for you first thing."

Mercedes hurried in the direction of the intensive care unit, Austin and the blonde nurse struggling to keep pace behind her.

Wayne was relieved to have the oxygen mask removed from his face, as well as the feeding tube that had been down his nose. The latter especially was uncomfortable to the verge of pain. His whole body ached, and when he moved, cautiously to avoid the hurt, the remaining tubes pulled uncomfortably at the tape that attached them to his body. The nurse told him he'd had heart surgery. From how bad he felt, he had to believe her. He had fought to come awake, and now that he was, he almost wished he was still unconscious.

But Mercedes had been calling to him, seemingly from far away. And Darrel—had he heard him crying? He had to help his son.

His son. If only.

Darrel was beside him now, beaming through the tears on his thin face. "I knew you'd wake up! Momma did too. We just knew it!" He squeezed Wayne's hand, and Wayne tried to squeeze back, but his fingers had little strength. So much effort.

"Just needed a little rest," he assured Darrel.

Mercedes rushed into the room, looking slightly wild-eyed and with her hair hanging loose and her blue shirt—one of his, from the way it drowned her—decidedly wrinkled. He had a brief memory of her and Austin playing in the alfalfa fields as children. She'd looked much the same in those days. How uncomplicated their relationship had been then.

"Wayne!" She placed her hand over his and Darrel's,

pressing her cheek to his forehead. For a long moment they stayed that way, neither moving nor trying to speak. He was content to have her there, touching him.

"I'll be right outside at the desk if you need me." The mousy nurse who was checking his vital signs on the monitors smiled widely at them and left the room, followed by the younger nurse who had appeared with Mercedes.

"I love you," Mercedes said with a new fierceness he'd never heard directed toward him before. To the children, yes, but never at him. "I love you so much."

He swallowed with difficulty. "I love you too." It hurt to speak, his throat raw from whatever they'd had to do to him when he'd been out. "Now when can I go home?"

She lifted her head and smiled. "Not quite yet."

"The little boys?"

"They're fine. And don't you dare ask about the cattle. It's all under control. You just worry about getting better. Austin and Liana are going to stay with us for a while to help out. Everything will work out fine."

Darrel made a face. "Good thing the neighbors are bringing food, though. Aunt Liana burns practically everything."

"Honey," Mercedes said to Darrel, "Uncle Austin is outside. Could you have him call Liana and have her bring in the boys? If he hasn't already?"

"Sure." Darrel let go of Wayne's hand and sprinted for the door. "I'll be right back."

"I'm not going anywhere," Wayne called after him, but his voice didn't carry far enough for Darrel to hear.

Mercedes was staring at him as if she couldn't believe he was alive. Wayne took her hand, glad to see that his movements were more sure. Her hand felt small in his, and a desire to protect her washed over him.

"I had a dream," he said. "A dream that Brandon was here."

"It wasn't a dream. He did your surgery."

"And I'm still here?" He arched a brow and smiled to show that it was a joke, while at the same time a cold sweat washed over him. Brandon had operated? That didn't make sense, not with the way the man felt about Mercedes. No wonder Mercedes looked at him as if he'd returned from the grave.

She bent and kissed his lips where his mouth curved up to create what she called his crooked smile. "Yes." A tear dropped from her cheek, and he could taste the salt.

"Don't cry." His hand went to her face.

"I will if I want. I deserve a good cry—after all I've been through."

Her voice sounded odd, but he chuckled, hoping to soothe her. "Well, then, I guess I shouldn't stand in your way." Instantly, he regretted his choice of words, but he didn't retract them. Because he wouldn't stand in her way, not even if she chose to leave him. His sore throat felt tight.

"I love you. That's all that matters."

The tightness relaxed as he saw her love, the same love that had been in her eyes all these years. Except now it was different somehow. Dared he hope they would emerge from this crisis stronger and better? Was she finally all his?

"I knew about the letters." Again his words surprised him. Why couldn't he leave well enough alone? The pain of losing his first wife had been terrible, but he knew it would be much worse if he lost Mercedes. She was his entire life, meaning more to him than even the boys and the farm.

Her mouth parted—in shock or surprise, he couldn't tell. "You knew?"

"That day I took your father to the retirement center. He told me about them. I searched everywhere, but I didn't find them. I assumed it was another of his lies." He frowned. "I should have told you. It might have made a difference."

She shook her head and said very slowly, "It doesn't matter, not in the slightest bit. I am where I belong, Wayne. With you and the boys on our farm."

The meaning of her words shook him. She didn't care about the letters. She was choosing him and the boys over Brandon and the past. *She loves me.* The emotion was almost too much to contain in this body that couldn't jump up and hug and kiss her.

"If I could go back and change the past so I knew about the letters," Mercedes continued, "I swear I wouldn't do it. The only thing I would change is that I would want you to be Darrel's biological father." A worry line appeared between her eyes. "Except, then, of course, Brandon wouldn't have been here to save your life."

He contemplated that reality for a few minutes. The nurse had told him a part of his heart had been permanently damaged, but he was alive. Brandon, his wife's first love, had saved his life. What did a man do with that kind of knowledge? Wayne was grateful, but he still wished Brandon had never returned to Wyoming.

"I'll have to thank him. Is he here?"

She didn't respond right away. Her eyes slid away from his in a way that told him there was more. He turned his hand, tightening his grip. The attempt was pitiful but enough to get her attention.

What? he asked. Not with words but with his eyes.

She brought her other hand to cradle his bigger one, rubbing it gently. "I promised him if he helped you, I'd tell Darrel everything right away, but after the operation, Brandon wanted to wait to see what happened with you. He worried it would all be too much for Darrel, especially if . . . if you didn't pull through. Then he learned his cancer is back. Brandon could die."

Wayne's first reaction was shock, followed closely by relief. Even if Brandon beat the cancer again, he wouldn't be able to take his place in Darrel's life. At least not any time soon. Shame washed over him at these thoughts, and for a long while he couldn't meet Mercedes' gaze. But sorrow for Brandon was quick on the heels of the relief.

Poor man, Wayne thought. And he *was* poor. Wayne had Mercedes and the boys, and Brandon was alone.

"I'm sorry," he said, meaning it.

"Me too. I haven't seen him since I heard. I don't know how he's taking it. I was worried he'd want to rush and tell Darrel everything, but one of the doctors here—a friend of his—says Brandon won't tell him, unless he's sure he'll beat it. I'm not sure if I believe that, exactly, but I feel so relieved and guilty at the same time."

"I know what you mean."

Silence fell between them, each content to be near the other.

A nurse entered the room with Dr. Shubacker. "Welcome back," the doctor boomed. "I came in the minute I heard. Anything so I won't have to help my wife in the yard." He smiled to show he didn't mean it, but Wayne figured there was a lot of truth in the words. The doctor didn't look like one to enjoy yard work. "I know the nurses here are taking good care of you, but I want to do a few tests myself."

"Only if you can beat me in an arm wrestle," Wayne joked.

Smiling, Mercedes glanced over her shoulder at the door. "Darrel should be back by now." Her hands slipped from his.

"I'll just go peek outside and be right back, okay? Maybe he's having trouble finding Austin."

He nodded, and as she bent to kiss his cheek, it came to him again how fortunate he was. On the day he had married Mercedes, he thought he'd never be happier, but that day paled in comparison to the love now in his heart. His hand went up around her neck and held her close, his lips to her cheek, wordlessly communicating his love.

Dr. Shubacker reached for his arm, and Wayne reluctantly let Mercedes go.

Mercedes found Darrel standing outside the intensive care unit with Brandon. Brandon was smiling at Darrel, but the smile faltered when he caught sight of her. Despite what Dustbottom had told her, Mercedes was worried. Now that Wayne was awake, he had no reason not to demand what she had promised. But surely he could see that telling Darrel would only cause the boy needless suffering. At least until the cancer was behind Brandon—if he could beat it again.

"Uncle Austin is calling Aunt Liana on his phone," Darrel told her. "She'll come and bring the boys to see Dad. Uncle Austin went outside to call because they don't like mobile phones in the hospital. Brandon tells me it's because it might interfere with the equipment. But he's never seen it happen, even though people are always sneaking around using their phones. I wonder how they'd feel if it was someone they loved who might get hurt because of it. Then I bet they wouldn't do it."

"You're probably right." Mercedes touched her son's shoulder, needing to feel him close.

Brandon's eyes followed the movement. "Darrel tells me Wayne's awake."

"Yes. Just a while ago. I need to get back in there."

"I'm happy for you. Really."

Her eyes locked on his. "I can't thank you enough."

"Yeah, you saved his life," Darrel said. "Are you going to check on him now? Because I was going to ask him what he thinks of mobile phones."

Brandon smiled. "The nurses told me Dr. Shubacker was headed there, so I'm sure your dad's okay. I can see him later." He started to turn.

"Brandon?" she said.

"Yes?"

What to say? The seconds ticked by until there was so much tension she wanted to scream. "I talked to Dustbottom," she finally blurted out.

The green of his eyes deepened. "He's got a big mouth. Ignore him. It's not your concern."

His words stung, and Mercedes looked down so he wouldn't see the abrupt tears in her eyes. Of course it wasn't her business, but when all was said and done, he was the father of her child, and she did care about him.

Blindly, she veered away. "Come on, Darrel, let's go see your dad." She felt like a liar, though Wayne was the only father Darrel knew.

Brandon's arm shot out and grabbed her wrist, his skin cold and slightly moist. *Touch of death,* she thought, shivering.

"I'm sorry," he said. "I didn't mean it that way. I'm just having some issues. But everything will be fine. I beat it once. I'll do it again." The words held passion, but when she lifted her eyes to his, the emotion didn't reach his eyes. She had the distinct feeling he'd already given up.

"I'm sorry." She pulled her hand from his. "I'm really, really sorry. Thank you for everything you've done for Wayne. It—it means a lot."

He nodded, and she felt his eyes on them as they retreated. "Momma?" Darrel tugged her hand as he had when he was a little boy. "The ICU is the other way. Is everything okay?"

Mercedes blew out a breath, trying to calm herself. "I'm fine now, but it's been a hard couple of days." She started again in the right direction, relieved Brandon was no longer in sight.

Wayne's door was ajar, and she pushed it open with the palm of her hand. He was there, waiting for them, his eyes tracking them eagerly. His brow furrowed as he noticed her tears.

"Dad, the little boys are on their way!" Darrel ran to the bed, and for a blessed moment he was busy talking to Wayne about mobile phones. Wayne didn't look bored; in fact, the furrow on his forehead seemed to smooth out with every word.

"We'll be moving him from ICU soon," the nurse told her on the way out, averting her face from Mercedes' apparent emotion. "Dr. Shubacker says everything looks really good."

"Thank you," Mercedes whispered.

She struggled to regain her composure, but the conversation with Brandon had shaken her deeply. *Let it pass,* she told herself. Yet the moment still hovered. What if one day Darrel learned the truth and regretted the opportunity to know his birth father? It would be far too late then, if her intuition was correct. If Brandon really had given up.

"Mercedes?" Wayne held out the hand with the IV in it, beckoning.

Her tears came more forcefully, and Mercedes had no choice but to let them fall. She longed to crawl into the bed with Wayne and have him hold her. Longed for him to kiss away her tears.

Wayne's hand closed over hers. "What is it?"

Before Mercedes could answer, Darrel spoke. "It's that doctor, Brandon. He said something to her." When neither of them responded, the child continued. "What did he say, Momma? I thought he was nice. I thought he was making Dad better."

"Nothing. Everything's fine," she said. "I'm just emotional right now."

Darrel shook his head. "I'm not a little boy anymore, Momma. Tell me what happened." His somber, dark eyes, so much like her own, begged for an explanation.

The moment of truth was approaching. Mercedes felt it in every inch of her body. Darrel had noticed something was dreadfully wrong, or perhaps he'd sensed they were hiding something from him. At the same time, he trusted her and didn't want to hurt her or see her in pain. If she let this moment pass, Darrel might never know about Brandon. He might never have to face the confusion of an uncertain heritage or the pain of watching someone he was supposed to love wither away with cancer. She would have fulfilled her duty as a mother to protect her son. Brandon had told her he wasn't her concern, so she had only to deflect Darrel's interest.

Yet what if she was wrong? What if Darrel felt a connection to Brandon on some level and would forever regret missing the opportunity to know his birth father? What if telling Darrel would save Brandon's life?

She glanced at Wayne and saw him watching her. He made a slight shrugging motion, followed by a more decisive nod. His signal telling her to say something to Darrel, leaving exactly what up to her.

Swallowing was suddenly difficult. Her tongue felt thick in her mouth, unwilling to articulate. She managed a breath.

"Brandon had some awful news." She slipped an arm around Darrel. "He had cancer a while back, and he learned last night that it's back. He'll need a lot of treatments."

"Is he going to die?" Darrel's voice quavered, and he looked younger than he had a few minutes ago.

"We won't know for months."

"But you were acting weird before today, and he made you cry last week! You haven't seen him for years, and suddenly he's come back and making you upset. Is it because of me?" He paused before adding in a smaller voice, "Am I adopted or something?" He stepped back from her arm as he spoke, pressing up against the wall by Wayne's bed.

Wayne shifted in the bed, grimacing with pain from his incision. "Mercedes." She looked at him, and he nodded again, his intent clear. He thought it was time to tell Darrel everything. All of it. But only if she wanted. Wayne was still leaving it up to her.

The moment of truth.

After all Brandon had done for them. He had owed them, maybe, but that didn't mean they were even. There was no such thing as even in the world of parenthood and love.

She held out a hand to Darrel. "You've seen the pictures of me expecting you, so don't worry about that. But there is something more. Something it might be time to talk about. Come here, son. I promise you. Everything will be okay. Remember that more than anything, your father and I love you. We will always love you, and we will always be a family."

Darrel came into her arms, his face trusting. "I love you too, Momma."

CHAPTER 25

Diary of Mercedes Walker Johnson
December 16, 2007

Darrel is twelve today. Such a wonderful son and a good example to his brothers. I couldn't ask for more. Yet sometimes I worry about the past, and I start to feel afraid. Afraid for Darrel, and for Wayne, and for myself. I have a feeling something is going to happen that will change our lives. Please let me be wrong! Still, I must trust in our family and that somehow together we'll make it through.

Brandon was sitting in the doctors' lounge when his phone vibrated in his pocket. He felt guilty as he thought about Darrel and his talk about mobile phones and was glad it hadn't rung in his son's presence. The call was from his parents.

"We should be landing shortly," his mother said. "Are you all right?"

"I'm fine. You don't need to be here."

"Of course we do, though I still don't understand why you won't come home to Boston."

"Mom, please."

"Oh, honey, I'm so sorry. I know it's a bad time for you." She began sobbing, and Brandon felt horrible.

Why had he allowed Dustbottom to call them? He might have spared his mother the pain if he'd simply flown to California and started treatments. Then again, he was their only child, and they deserved to know what was happening. They might not have much time left together.

He tried to shake the thoughts away, but they refused to leave. The cancer was multiplying as he talked. Every minute he was closer to death.

Yet he still didn't want to leave Wyoming. Or Darrel.

"I told Hannah." His mother had regained control. "She wants to talk with you."

"I wish you hadn't done that, Mom."

"Why not? She still loves you. If you'd only tell her how you feel about her, she'd be there to help you through this."

I don't know that I'm going to make it through this. He couldn't say it aloud, not to his mother. Instead, he said, "I'm thinking about moving to Wyoming. It's peaceful, and I could work at the hospital here."

"You won't consider coming home?"

She didn't know about Darrel, so she'd never understand what was in Wyoming, but even a short, sideline view of his son's life would be better than an almost nonexistent relationship through email and phone calls. Darrel wouldn't know who he was, but they could be friends. A sliver of bitterness cut through the numbness that had fallen over him since last night.

If only he could tell his parents about Darrel. Then they would have something to hold onto after he was gone.

After he was gone?

Brandon wouldn't be half the doctor he was if he didn't recognize the defeat within himself. He wasn't giving in; he was giving up. In his patients, this defeat usually signaled impending death. But what did it matter, really? He'd chosen the right thing for Darrel . . . and for Mercedes. Not that he'd had any choice with her.

He closed his eyes and tried to refocus on the conversation with his mother. "Should I pick you up?"

"No, your father wants to rent a car. We have the address of the bed and breakfast. We'll meet you there."

"I'm at the hospital."

"What?"

"Not for me. I operated on a patient a few days ago. He awoke from a coma this morning, and I need to order some follow-up tests."

"Can't anyone else do that? Honey, you should be resting."

"I am. I'm sitting down right now. Don't worry. Someone has taken over the patient. I just wanted to check a few last things myself. Look, I have to go now. Call me when you leave the airport. Love you, Mom. Goodbye."

He turned off his phone and stared at the wall. Hannah knew about his illness. What did she think? Probably nothing. Well, he hoped she'd be happy married to this teacher.

Wait a minute. Who was he kidding? He *hated* the idea of her being married to someone else. But neither would he resign her to a potentially impossible battle against cancer, even if she was, as his mother indicated, willing to try again. He let his head drop to his hands, feeling the sting of tears. He didn't want to die, but there didn't seem to be much point in living either.

"Excuse me, doctor."

He looked up to see a nurse in the doorway. She had frizzled gray hair that didn't match her round, soft face.

"Are you Dr. Rhodes?"

"Yes."

"A woman and a boy are looking for you. We paged you, but no one answered. One of the other nurses thought you might be here sleeping. I wouldn't have disturbed you, but they said it's important."

"That's okay." The woman and child had to be Mercedes and Darrel. He'd left them only two or three hours ago—had something happened to Wayne? Maybe he shouldn't have left things to Dr. Shubacker. "Where are they?"

"Just down the hall by the nurses' station."

"Thanks." Brandon's exhaustion vanished as he hurried from the lounge. He saw Mercedes and Darrel before they saw him.

Mercedes' beauty was marred by swollen eyes and lines of exhaustion. She stood with a resoluteness he had never noticed before, one arm protectively draped around Darrel's shoulder, the other clutching a ridiculously large bundle in a black plastic garbage bag. The boy's eyes were open and eager as he watched the activity around him. Brandon imagined him cataloguing each action in that marvelous brain of his. Would this past week inspire him to be a doctor? Brandon imagined he'd be a good one—with those small, strong hands and keen intellect. Brandon would love to teach him, if the cancer didn't take him first.

Mercedes looked in his direction. The stiffening of her

body signaled his presence to Darrel. The child's eyes turned to him, staring, searching. *What did I do?* Brandon wondered.

"Thanks for coming," Mercedes said as he approached.

"Is Wayne all right?"

"It's not that." She glanced at the three nurses who were busy at the desk but obviously within hearing range. "Is there somewhere private we could go?"

"There's a room down there. Not in use." He tried to read in her face what she might want from him, but the black eyes were fathomless. By contrast, Darrel's stare was full of eager curiosity.

When they reached the room, Mercedes faced him, looking vulnerable and uncomfortable in the light streaming in through the curtain. She'd have looked much more at home in her garden or riding her horse, but this backdrop didn't flatter her in the least.

She was right, he thought. *She no longer belongs in my world.*

"We told Darrel," she said simply.

Brandon's breath stopped in his throat. He tried to speak, but not a sound emerged. So many questions tumbled through his mind, but none he could vocalize.

Mercedes shifted uneasily. "I was wrong. If things don't go well . . ." She faltered and then began again. "What I mean is, you two should get to know one another."

Darrel dropped his gaze to the ground, suddenly shy. That's when the reality sank in for Brandon. His son knew!

Brandon put a hand on Darrel's shoulder, a place that felt so right it made him want to weep. The boy looked up into his eyes. There was uncertainty there beneath the curiosity—and more than a little fear.

"Darrel," Brandon said, "two months ago, I didn't even

know you existed"—somehow it was important to him that Darrel hear it from him—"but when I did learn about you, it was the best day of my life. More than anything, I want to be a part of your life in any way that's comfortable for you." He thought of how Darrel had run to his uncle for support in the waiting room. Perhaps one day, Darrel would feel a similar trust in Brandon.

"You won't try to take me away from my parents?" Darrel glanced at Mercedes quickly and then back again. "Or the farm? Because I don't want to leave."

"Never. I give you my solemn promise." Brandon managed a grin. "I think you have it pretty good where you are. But you know, you'll have to go away to college when you're older." It was the right thing to say; he could see it in Darrel's eyes, in his shy smile.

"Well, of course, I have to go to college. Momma would kill me if I didn't."

"So let's try to be friends first, okay?"

"I can handle that." Darrel nodded with more of his usual confidence.

Brandon felt a rush of love that exceeded every vision he'd had of this moment. His eyes found Mercedes, who was staring at them, tears in her eyes. "Do you want to go out to lunch?" he asked. "I know it's a bit early, but I bet you haven't eaten, and boys always have an appetite."

She shook her head. "I need to get back to Wayne. You two go ahead. Bring him back here when you're finished." They stared at each other for a moment over Darrel's head, two parents joined for the welfare of their son, and then, with a whisper of encouragement and a kiss to Darrel's forehead, she walked to the door.

"About Hannah," she said, hesitating in the hall. "I think you should try again. But do me a favor and don't write it in a letter. Okay?"

He stared. Why would she bring up Hannah? Why was everyone always bringing up Hannah? Unless he'd done it again—realizing too late what he had right before him. Hadn't he only moments before been filled with regrets about his ex-wife? Maybe everyone was right. Maybe it wasn't too late.

"I won't write a letter," he promised.

"Momma, the quilt," Darrel said.

"I almost forgot." Mercedes opened the garbage bag and pulled a smaller white bag from it before handing the black one to him. "I started this for you all those years ago. I finally finished it."

He pulled out a quilt that seemed vaguely familiar. Had he seen her working on this at the river? Or had it been stretched out in the living room at her house?

His throat felt tight at the hours of work it represented. "Thank you, Mercedes. It's very nice." Whenever he needed to, he'd curl up in that blanket and feel her encouragement—and her faith in his ability to be good for Darrel.

With a nod and a smile, Mercedes was gone. Back to where she belonged.

Brandon stood awkwardly, feeling uncertain. For so long he'd waited for the miracle of this moment, and now he was at a loss. Darrel gazed at him, waiting for a cue. How did they begin their new relationship?

Then he remembered his parents, and his heart choked with the reality of their love and the good news he would finally have for them. Right now he could use the buffer of their company as he and Darrel became accustomed to their new relationship.

"What do you say to meeting your grandparents?" he asked

Darrel. "Believe me, it's going to be a little weird, surprising them like this, but I think we're up to it. What do you say?"

"Okay." Darrel's grin was wide. "Good thing you're a doctor—in case they go into shock."

Brandon ushered Darrel out into the hall, his step buoyant now. In an instant his world had changed.

There was hope.

On her way back to the room where they had moved Wayne, Mercedes took a quick detour, the white plastic bag clutched in her hand. There was only one place large enough to put it that she'd noticed here in the hospital—in the waiting room.

There it was, the garbage can near the door. She held out the white bag, hesitating only briefly. It was ripped at the bottom, and she could see the black hearts and tear drops that should never have been on a quilt for a baby. Deliberately she pushed the bag through the opening, and it disappeared from view.

Gone. It was that easy.

Light filled her entire body as she went to see her husband.

Book Club Discussion

1. Mercedes was twenty-six when she fell in love with Brandon, but why was she emotionally a lot younger?

2. When Wayne caught young Mercedes kissing Brandon by the river, why do you feel she was embarrassed and decided never to be there alone with Brandon again?

3. How did both Mercedes and Brandon's parents get in the way of their children's happiness? Were their actions solely selfish?

4. Do you think Wayne should have told Mercedes about Brandon's letters when he first heard about them? Why or why not? Why do you feel he didn't? Was he more afraid of losing her or seeing her hurt again?

5. How did losing his first wife prepare Wayne to be a husband to Mercedes?

6. How did losing Lucy bring Mercedes and Wayne closer?

7. Do you feel it would have been best for Darrel not to know his birth father?

8. Who would be a better father, Wayne or Brandon? What advantages could each give Darrel?

9. Did Mercedes love Brandon? What shows this?

10. Did Brandon love Mercedes? What shows this?

11. Do you believe Mercedes would ever leave her husband and children for Brandon, even if she loved him?

12. Why did Mercedes feel she would never turn to Brandon even if her husband died? Do you feel she was right?

13. How does Mercedes view of self-discovery differ from characters in other books you've read who have cheated on their spouses? Do you feel she's right?

14. What changes or sacrifices did each of the characters make because they love Darrel?

13. Do you think Mercedes and Brandon would have made it if he'd learned she was pregnant with Darrel in the very beginning?

16. Do you think Brandon will make up with Hannah? Do you think Hannah would give their relationship another try?

17. What is your favorite part of the book?

RACHEL BRANTON has worked in publishing for over twenty years. She loves writing women's fiction and traveling, and she hopes to write and travel a lot more. As a mother of seven, it's not easy to find time to write, but the semi-ordered chaos gives her a constant source of writing material. She's been known to wear pajamas all day when working on a deadline, and is often distracted enough to burn dinner. (Okay, pretty much 90% of the time.) A sign on her office door reads: Danger. Enter at Your Own Risk. Writer at Work.

Under the name Rachel Branton, she writes romance, romantic suspense, and women's fiction. Rachel also writes urban fantasy, paranormal romance, and science fiction under the name Teyla Branton. For more information or to sign up to hear about new releases, please visit www.RachelBranton.com.

www.ingramcontent.com/pod-product-compliance
Lightning Source LLC
Chambersburg PA
CBHW051238260626
47162CB00002B/494